THE
Deception
Artist

Fayette Fox

ROARING FORTIES
P R E S S

Roaring Forties Press
1053 Santa Fe Avenue
Berkeley, CA 94706

Printed in the United States of America
Copyright © Fayette Fox 2013, 2015

Originally published in the United Kingdom in 2013 by Myriad
Editions; published in North America by Roaring Forties Press

Library of Congress Cataloging-in-Publication Data

Fox, Fayette
  The deception artist / Fayette Fox
    pages cm
    ISBN 978-1-938901-36-2 (paperback) -- ISBN 978-1-938901-
40-9 (pdf) -- ISBN 978-1-938901-41-6 (kindle)
1. Families--California--Fiction. 2. California, Northern--
Fiction. 3. Domestic fiction. I. Title.
  PS3606.O94D43 2015
  813'.6--dc23
                        2015000431

This is a work of fiction.

With much love to my parents,
Annie and David

Acknowledgments

To my brother Ezra, fellow writer and improviser *extraordinaire*, for your playful spirit, insatiable wackiness, wisdom, and unflagging emotional support. Your editing insights were always spot on and you single-handedly did so much to help me bring this narrative forward in the right direction.

My parents, Annie and David, I need to thank twice. First for providing me with a wonderful, emotionally stable childhood and lots of art supplies and for always encouraging my creativity. Second, for your editorial assistance with this novel. Mom, the original Fox writer, thank you for being a wonderful editor throughout this project. Dad, thank you for your enthusiasm and perspective as a reader and your moving trombone arias.

To my wonderful readers—my Mint Sister Sarah Jebrock and Griselda Murray Brown, Kimberly Goodell, Liz Co, Serene Arena, and Noah Falstein—thank you for reading my manuscript in its earlier incarnations and for taking the time to offer invaluable suggestions, edits, and encouragement. The book is what it is today thanks to your help.

To Vicky Blunden, my editor at Myriad Editions—thank you for your astounding insight, passion, and sense of humor. You helped me bring this story into its own. Working with you has been an absolute pleasure.

Thank you also to Linda McQueen, Candida Lacey, Corinne Pearlman, Holly Ainley, Adrian Weston, Anna Morrison, and Dawn Sackett at Myriad Editions. Your enthusiasm and talent are an inspiration. It's been an honor to work with you as well.

To Deirdre Greene and Nigel Quinney at Roaring Forties Press, thank you so much for bringing this novel to a whole new market in the US.

To Samantha Faccio for being Ivy's first fan during our long walks through the English countryside.

To Lauren Brydon Duchene and the girls at the Stapleton School of Dance for your insight on ballet. Ben Mitchell for our time in India and introducing me to Myriad.

Thank you to Danni Dawson and Rick Weaver, who talked about art and taught me about writing. I hope Ivy is lucky enough to have such amazing art teachers one day.

To National Novel Writing Month for giving me just the push I needed to tackle writing a novel. To my writing professors Lynne Hanley and Michael Lesy at Hampshire College for your wisdom about writing and plot. You were right about the icing. Here is the cake.

Lastly, thank you to Ivy. It's been such a treat getting to know you these past many years. Thank you for letting me tell your story.

About the Author

Fayette Fox lives in Oakland, California, and works as a freelance writer. *The Deception Artist* is her first novel.

Part I
The End of Normal

Scar

Rain slides down the car window, making blurry paths where the street lights shine through. Mom and I baked chocolate chip cookies, but I'm not allowed any, even though I want, I want. I can have one afterwards if I'm good. I hope I will be good.

"Poor kid," Dad says at the wheel. "Do you know if they were friends?"

"Well, they shared a room for a few days," Mom says.

"How old was he?" Dad asks.

"Twelve," Mom says quietly. "Same as Brice."

"God, it's awful. He had leukemia or something, right?"

"Yeah." Mom nods.

I peer through the wet as we pass the new house at the end of our street. Brice and I played there, back when it was just planks of wood. Now it has walls and a roof. The house is all done, but no one lives there yet. My finger follows a raindrop sliding down the window. My chest feels tight and I've had math-test belly for days.

"Poor kid," Dad says.

"So, let's keep this to ourselves," Mom says. "The staff haven't told him and Brenda said it's our call."

Dad honks the horn, swerving. "Goddamn lousy driver!"

Mom puts her hand on his leg. "Do you agree?" she asks after a moment.

"Sure—I said it was awful."

"No," Mom says. "That we shouldn't tell Brice."

"Tell Brice what?" I ask.

We pass a smear of shops and restaurants. It's raining harder now. There's a drought and the ground is thirsty. I usually love the sound of rain hitting the car, but today it makes me feel alone in the back seat.

"That the kid died," Dad says. "Oh, learn to fucking drive!"

"Neil!" Mom shouts.

"What kid?" I ask.

"What's-his-name … Oliver," Dad says. I gasp. Oliver was the bald boy with freckles, in the bed next to Brice's. When we came to visit yesterday, he told us that he missed his dog and couldn't wait to go home. People go to the hospital to get all better. Plus, you're not supposed to die until you're old.

"Jesus, Neil," Mom says. "Now she's just going to tell Brice."

"No, she won't," Dad says. He looks at me in the rear-view mirror. "Hey, Ivy, you can keep a secret, can't you?"

In the hospital parking lot, I open my Rainbow Brite umbrella. Like the cookies, rain is a special treat that I can't enjoy right now. Hopping over puddles in my ladybug boots, I pass a woman helping an old man with a walker. I follow my parents through the automatic doors and blink hard in the fluorescent lights. It smells like lemons and bleach. People in white coats drift across the shiny floor like moths. In the elevator, I tug the sleeves of my magic red sweater.

"Well, hello there, Ivy," says Brenda, the nurse at the counter. She has brown skin and a woolly helmet of hair.

"Hi," I say. Mom nudges me. "Do you want a cookie?"

Brenda thanks me and takes a bite. "Mmm! Did you help your momma bake these?"

"Uh-huh," I say. Mom let me hold the electric mixer, mashing sugar and butter. Afterwards I got to lick the beaters.

4

"When did you find the time?" Brenda asks Mom. "Didn't you just leave here five minutes ago?"

Mom smiles. "You're sweet, but really they were super-easy." When she turns to me, her face is flat. "Ivy, go say hello to your brother, but remember what we talked about in the car. We'll be there in a few minutes."

"So, how's Brice doing?" Dad asks Brenda. He puts his hand on Mom's shoulder and she pushes me on.

Heading down the hall with my basket of goodies, I pass kids lying in beds, wearing hospital gowns. Some look pale and have tubes up their noses. I wonder how sick they really are. I offer cookies to doctors and nurses, but not the kids because Dad said we don't know what's wrong with them and cookies might make them worse.

I take a deep breath and burst into my brother's room.

"Aloha, Brice!" I say. He's pale too, and his mouth is tight, eyes small. The other bed is neatly made.

"Aloha." Brice squeezes out the word. This is practice for when we go on vacation to Hawaii. The other day the Big News was our trip, but now the news is Brice. My best friend Jenny went a hundred years ago, back when we were in kindergarten. My family's going over Easter, but now it's only November. We have to wait so long the island might melt first from burning lava. I want to talk about Oliver but that would be bad.

"I drew you a picture," I say, pulling it out of my backpack. I look back at the other bed and shiver.

"Is that me surfing?"

I nod. "And that's a sea monster. Want a cookie?"

He shakes his head and my eyes go wide. This is the first time in the history of forever that Brice has turned down a treat. It is scarier than the tube in his arm, which is called an Ivy Drip, which is what I'd be if I melted. I ask if his stomach still hurts a lot.

"Super a lot."

"How much on a scale of one to ten?" I ask.

"Eight. But now my ten is way worse than your ten."

"Can I see again?"

Brice smiles and carefully pulls the blankets away, showing dark train tracks across his stomach. This is where they opened him up and took out his appendix. I imagine what happened when Mom and Dad rushed Brice to the hospital and Grandma stayed with me. I picture doctors in white coats racing around, with Brice screaming on the operating table until they gave him a shot to make him go to sleep.

"Doctor, this is the worst case of appendicitis I've ever seen."

"Me too, Nurse. Stethoscope, please."

"Stethoscope. Can we save him?"

"We've got to do our best. He's so young. Knee-hammer. He has so much to live for."

"Doctor, why can't we save all the kids?"

Mom and Dad come in, all smiles and kisses. Mom tucks Brice in and hands him his homework. Mrs. Stanton's sixth-grade class is doing a unit on castles, which are actual real buildings in England and not just in fairytales.

"Do you know what happened to Oliver?" Brice asks them. I open my mouth and quickly close it again.

"Who?" Dad asks.

"Oliver." Brice points to the empty bed.

"Oh," Mom says. "He got to go home, honey."

"That's good." Brice settles back. "He really missed his dog."

I swallow and Dad starts talking about castles. He tells us about dungeons and crenels, which are stone slits for shooting arrows.

"Like in *Robin Hood* with the foxes," he says.

"I don't like that movie anymore," Brice says, pushing his floppy hair off his forehead.

"Sure you do. Everyone likes Disney."

"When they're, like, Ivy's age."

"Hey!" I cross my arms.

"What?" Brice says. "It's okay to like cartoons when you're eight."

Dad continues, talking about moats. Later tonight I'll be back home and Brice will still be here. My brother is beside me saying something about drawbridges, but I feel like he's already far away.

"So long, Ivy," Brenda says as we're leaving. "You be extra-good and do as you're told."

I nod.

"Your folks have a lot on their minds and need you to be mature right now."

I look down at my rain boots.

Outside it's dark and raining harder. In the big, empty back seat, I take off my magic red sweater and breathe deeply. I nibble my cookie, trying to make it last the whole way home.

Everything Is Tropical

If I had a candy store, I'd organize everything by color, with Hot Tamales, cherry-flavored Runts, Tootsie Pops, and just the red M&Ms all in one big jar. *I'll have one scoop from the red jar, and two from the blue, please.* Jenny is fiddling with the friendship bracelet I made her, while we watch the Sweet Stuff lady weigh our treats. Jenny's a little taller than me, even though I'm two months older. If I call her hair dirty blonde she yells, "It's not dirty!" Today she's wearing a baggy Care Bear T-shirt and a cloth headband. She never takes off her friendship bracelet, not even in the shower. Months and months from now, that band of knotted string will fall off naturally like a snake losing its skin. Then she'll make a wish and I'll make her a new one.

Jenny and I are by ourselves at Red Hill Shopping Center. It's okay because we can walk here without crossing any big streets. Mom's with Brice at the hospital and Dad probably has to work late again. He said we can all go visit Brice tomorrow. Maybe tomorrow Brice will be all better and we can just visit him at home.

Jenny makes me dig the emergency quarter out of my shoe, but we still don't have enough. We put back the jawbreakers, like explorers throwing the heaviest things overboard from a hot air balloon.

Jenny hands me a tiny lollipop as we leave Sweet Stuff. "Bring more money next time, Dum-Dum," she says. Outside, we sit by the fountain, munching our candy. I get everything with peanuts because Jenny doesn't like them.

There's a sailor boy statue in the fountain, riding a half-barrel boat. He points into the distance, his collar blowing in the sea breeze. A real little boy jumps up and down, begging his mom for a penny. He squeals, throwing it into the fountain. If he tells her what he wished for then it won't come true.

I ask Jenny what she thinks the statue's looking at.

Jenny shrugs. "The parking lot?"

"Or maybe a tropical island," I say. She looks at me blankly. "You know, like Hawaii."

"Hawaii's way too far away. You couldn't even see it with a telescope."

We walk past the shoe repair store and Muffin Mania.

"Wanna come over some time and watch *Duck Tales*?" I ask. It's a new cartoon and we like it even though there aren't enough girl characters. Maybe afterwards we can play dress-up as princesses or fairies or fairy princesses, or else pretend to be cat sisters.

"Okay, but let's watch it at my house," Jenny says. "Your TV's kinda dumb."

"What's wrong with our TV?"

"No cable, no remote." Jenny counts the problems on her fingers. "And since it's the *only* one you've got, it's pretty small." Jenny's house has a TV in every room except the bathrooms. She decorated her very own set with butterfly stickers. If I think about it, I want what she has. But I hadn't really thought about it before now. "If we're lucky," she continues, "there'll be an after-school special on and we can watch that instead."

I nod, but I'd rather watch *Duck Tales*.

We wander through the make-up section of the drug store, down to our last few gummy worms. Jenny shows me which lip glosses her big sister Natasha likes.

"Which one do you think Brice would like?" Jenny asks.

I laugh. "Brice doesn't wear make-up!"

9

"Nooo, on a *girl*."

"How would I know?"

Jenny rolls her eyes and plays with the blush brushes. After a minute I ask, "Is it really true the people wear flowers around their necks?"

"What people?"

"In Hawaii."

"Yeah, and coconuts on their boobies."

"No way!"

Jenny nods. "But anyways, is your family even going anymore?"

"Sure, why not?"

"You know, because Brice is sick, sick, sickity-sick."

"Oh." I go quiet, touching the eyeshadow. It's hard to imagine not going after Mom and Dad promised we would. I suddenly picture Brice in his hospital bed on the beach, with Oliver's empty bed getting covered by the rising tide. I try to shake it off. "Well, Brice will be all better by the time we go." I hope this is the truth. We don't buy anything because the lip glosses are too expensive and besides, we're out of money.

"Hey, I've got an idea!" Jenny says once we're outside. I let her blindfold me with her cloth headband and spin me around. She leads me by the arm. I trust her, but it's scary not being able to see. The sun glows red through my eyelids and when we walk in the shade it flickers dark. Red black red black. Red.

A bell jingles. The air changes and I smell sawdust. A bird squawks. Jenny takes off my blindfold and I gasp, blinking hard. A fish with yellow and black stripes swims by. It's an underwater party for neon-blue fish, with a shy orange fish hiding in a sea anemone.

"It's beautiful!" I say.

"Snorkeling is just like this," she says, pressing her nose against the glass. We're in the Red Hill Pet Store, but I bet it would look the same if we'd been magically teleported to Hawaii. The fish tank is a tropical ocean and I imagine I'm shrinking to become a tiny sea fairy, riding the seahorse's back. *I hold on tight as we explore the seaweed jungle. Giddy-up! And off we go through the bubbles. I find a giant shell and lean in for a closer look. There's a crab inside! Ahhhhhh! I scream to my seahorse. Let's get out of here! We start to zip away when I feel something jabbing me.*

"Hellooo!" Jenny is poking my arm. "Hey, E.T., where'd you go?"

"Ow. Cut it out."

"You weirdo. I kept repeating your name and you just stared at the fish like I didn't exist. Even Mortimer knows his own name." Mortimer is Jenny's amazing circus cat. I grin and tell Jenny about my make-believe. Maybe we can act it out together some time with costumes from my dress-up chest.

"A sea fairy?" She folds her arms. The hamsters and parrots are all staring at me too. "That's kind of babyish."

Lesson in Lying

"Clean-up on aisle three," repeats the voice on the loud-speaker.

It's the next day after school and after Brice-Visiting. I'm back at Red Hill Shopping Center, but with Mom this time. Mom usually doesn't want to take me to Sweet Stuff, and Jenny and I never go grocery shopping. I pick through a display of Red Delicious apples and think about Snow White. I wonder why the doctors couldn't make her all better. Maybe because the apple wasn't just poison but *magic* poison, which is twice as strong. But if Prince Charming hadn't kissed her, would she really have slept forever? I think maybe one day, hundreds of years later when the light was just right, she would have woken up on her own. I see Snow White sitting up suddenly, banging her head on the glass case the dwarves made to keep the leaves off her face. "Ow!" she'd say, looking around at the mini-golf course that used to be the Enchanted Forest.

"Ivy?" Mom's best friend Maxine Ludlow pushes her shopping cart toward me. Everything about Maxine is nice and rounded.

"Hiya." I swing my bag of apples, like a dog wagging its tail.

"Where's your mom?"

We round the corner and find Mom reaching for a carton of milk. I do the family whistle, our version of Marco Polo. Mom repeats it without looking up.

"Hellooo, Karen!" Maxine sings.

Mom spins around and her face lights up. "Mmm, beautiful sweater," she tells Maxine, giving her a hug. The sweater's long with a leaf pattern.

"Thanks." Maxine smiles. "It's really comfy. And you look stunning as always. Ivy, make sure you get your fashion tips from this one."

"You're so sweet." Mom touches Maxine's shoulder.

Maxine lowers her voice. "How's Brice?"

Mom flutters her hand and says, "He's okay. Still sleeping a lot. We were just there. You know, it kills me to leave him alone every night."

"Marin General's a good hospital."

"I know. But poor Neil's working so hard he hasn't made it over there for a few days." Then she smiles and asks, "Where are your boys?"

"I told them to pick out a box of cereal."

"Whichever one has the best toy, I guess," Mom says.

Maxine laughs. They talk about our neighbor Alice Miller's roses ("flawless") and her new stone wall ("attractive"). They discuss the books they're reading ("compelling") and Black Monday ("troubling"). Maxine says she's getting her piano tuned this week.

"Pianos don't play the right notes forever," Maxine explains to me. "So you need to have them retuned so they sound good again." Then they're talking about Grandma's eyes ("strained") and the new house at the end of our road ("vacant").

"It's driving Neil nuts, if you can believe it." Mom puts on a deep voice. "All that planning commission stuff, two years of construction and still empty. And it's so well designed! It's a waste of a good house."

Maxine chuckles. "Always the architect."

"Mom! Mom!" Caleb runs over, sliding on the tiles. His little brother Tommy trots after him, gripping a box of Ice

Cream Cones cereal to his chest like it's a teddy bear. Caleb's a year below me and likes knocking things over on purpose. If he was a bug he'd probably be a moth because they like to bump into lights. "Tommy made a mess!" he shouts. Maxine wrinkles her nose and touches Tommy's bottom. "Nuh-uh," Caleb says. "Eggs on the floor!"

"Tommy," Maxine groans. If Tommy was a bug, he'd be a stink beetle. She leans over to me. "Aren't boys yucky?"

As they leave, Mom whispers, "See how one's a little bigger than the other?" *Obviously*, I think. *They're different ages.* But then she explains that Maxine's missing a shoulder pad. "Not a good look. Moral of the story: if that ever happens to you, replace it, or at the very least take out the other one."

"What's a moral?"

"It's a lesson. Like in a fable or a fairytale. Also, that leaf pattern is too old for her."

"But you said it was a beautiful sweater."

Mom takes the apples. "A little white lie. *She* thinks it's a beautiful sweater. No harm done, and did you see how it made her smile?"

When we get home, I kick my shoes off in the hall and Mom makes me help put the groceries away. It takes longer without Brice.

"Does every story have a moral?" I ask, putting the lettuce in the fridge.

"No, some stories are just stories."

"But does every fairytale have one?"

"I don't know, honey. Most do."

I try to figure out the moral of *Snow White*. Don't be too beautiful? Don't eat apples?

Finally I'm free and run up to my room. I pull the scarves out of my dress-up chest and turn on my boombox. The music makes me spin and twirl. I leap and wave my scarves, gliding through the air. Then a radio commercial comes on and I stop. The man talks quickly, saying we should hurry on down to somewhere to snatch up something before the sale ends! You can't dance to talking, so I turn it off and flop into my beanbag. I take off my socks and wiggle my toes. Make-believe is babyish so I'll just think instead. It's not wrong to think.

I think about Hawaii. *Mom and I are walking down the beach in matching bathing suits with shoulder pads sticking out from the straps. Dad and I build a huge enormous sandcastle that My Little Ponies can live in. Then the tide comes in and I rescue them, bringing them to their sand stable up the beach. Brice and I hunt for shells and climb palm trees for coconuts, throwing them down below for Mom and Dad to catch.* I want it so much, I wish we were there already, with Brice all happy-healthy-good.

I remember last year when I was only seven, and six and five before that. This was a long time ago. One time when I was three, I got lost in the supermarket and, when I found Mom, it wasn't her but some other lady. I don't remember much before then. Next year I'll be a fourth-grader and I'll get to go on the California Gold Rush Field Trip. I can even imagine being ten, when I'm a fifth-grader and go everywhere fast on my bike. But after that, I'm not sure.

Normally, this is how it goes: Brice lives here, not at the hospital. We go to school, and when we come home, Mom is here to make us snack plates. Dad comes home and goes to work and comes home and goes to work. And in between he likes to run, just because, and doesn't even mind when he gets sweaty. And then it's the weekend and we all go places together.

In my mind, I fly over Marin's golden hills and across the Pacific Ocean. Down below are peaceful whales. I fly low, touching the water. They sing to me and I sing back. Then huge fish with sharp teeth leap up to bite me, so I fly higher so they can't get me. I realize I'm make-believing again but I don't want to stop.

Suddenly, I picture myself at twenty-eight. That's twenty years from now ... from today, a Wednesday. My body tingles because I've never imagined so far in the future before. The grown-up me has chin-length hair and long legs. Also boobs. I stay back, watching myself like you watch a movie, except I'm right in front of me. I'm living far away in a place where the air is hot and wet. It's morning and I follow several steps behind myself along the street. I am my own ghost or an invisible shadow. I smell incense as we pass what looks like a sort of shiny gingerbread house with a steep roof. Through the opened doors I see a giant gold statue with droopy earlobes, sitting Indian-style. He looks calm, like Brice when he's sleeping. I follow the grown-up me around an outdoor market, where she buys a pineapple and unusual fruits I don't recognize. She swings a cloth bag and has paint on her hands. We walk beside a slow river, and she smiles at people who pass on motorbikes. They smile back at her, but no one seems to see me, so it's like I'm a friendly monster or maybe dead. I stand hidden to one side while the grown-up me sits on a short plastic stool by the side of the road and eats noodle soup for breakfast. It seems weird, but there are lots of other people doing it, so maybe it's okay.

Then I'm in my very own grown-up apartment. She puts the pineapple on a little table with a bowl of pond flowers and a miniature Calm Man statue. A big orange cat sleeps in the sunny patch on the floor. My grown-up self stands at an easel, painting the statue surrounded by flowers and pineapples. She ... *I* am an artist! While she paints, she keeps looking up at the table like she's checking everything's still there. She steps back and stares at the painting. Then she picks a different brush and keeps going.

The sound of the garage door breaks me out of my daydream. I find my shoes and run outside.

"Hi, Dad!" I say while he's getting out of his car. He gives me a hug. His fat striped tie is loose around his neck. He works in the City, so every day he gets to drive across the Golden Gate Bridge, there and back again.

"Hey, kiddo." He sounds tired.

"Guess what? Mom and I went to see Brice in the hospital today. He said he misses you."

Dad's face tightens. "I miss him too."

"He fell asleep even though it was the afternoon."

"That's because his body is focusing on getting better." Dad hands me his briefcase to carry. I hug it to my chest like Stink Beetle Tommy and the box of cereal. Except there's no prize inside, only papers. Bor-ring.

"Can you come with us to see Brice tomorrow after school?"

"I don't know, baby," Dad says. "It's pretty hard for me to take the time off work. Brice will understand."

Ditch

Blood rushes to my head, humming, tingling. I'm hanging upside-down on the jungle gym, looking at the rough tanbark shapes. Up-ended trees scrape the edge of the blue valley. Suddenly good dizzy turns to bad dizzy. I pull myself up and blood drains from my head like sand in a board game timer. Here it's recess, but what time is it for Brice back at the hospital? Maybe lie-in-bed time, or too-bored-to-read time. I wonder if they gave him a new roommate. The older kids have recess at a different time, but it still makes me sad knowing Brice isn't here.

Christa, the best foursquare player in the third grade, swings past on the monkey bars. She has a pointed nose and blonde hair that falls to the middle of her back. Her best friend Melanie comes after her, dressed in lavender, with a flash of gold at her neck. Once I asked Melanie why she always wears purple and she moaned, "It's not purple! It's lavender." I checked my crayons and it turns out she's right. I think about what kinds of bugs they'd be if we were all insects instead of people. Christa acts like a butterfly but she'd only be a caterpillar. I picture Melanie as a ladybug. Jenny, who is my best friend, would be a honeybee.

"Ivy, Ivy, Ivy, Ivy, Ivy." Caterpillar Christa joins me on the jungle gym.

"Um, hi," I say.

"Hellooo!" Christa pokes me. "Can you hear me?"

"Cut it out." I rub my arm. "Of course I can hear you."

"Where's your pet *seahorse*?" she asks.

Ladybug Melanie giggles. I feel a chill. "I don't know what you're talking about," I say, jaw tight, and lower myself to the tanbark.

"I think you do!" Christa sings after me.

I fly across the blacktop, past two lines of kids facing each other.

"Red rover, red rover, send Tiffany over!" one side chants in unison. A small girl leaves her side, running toward the wall of linked hands, like solid paper dolls. If she breaks through, she'll be allowed to return to her own side. If she doesn't, she'll become part of the enemy. I want her to make it, but she's so small and they're holding on real tight. She hits them like a brave mouse smacking into a snake ... but it's not hard enough and the line swallows her up. With Red Rover, you always know who's on your side and who isn't.

I find Jenny playing tetherball with a girl from her class. I stand back watching her hit the ball, rope wrapping tightly around the pole.

"Jenny, I've got to ask you something," I say.

"Hey, Ivy," she says, sweet as a jellybean. "Wanna play?"

She has no idea I'm even angry at her. Jenny's one of those honeybees that you think is friendly until it stings you.

"No."

"Is your brother all better yet?"

My skin prickles. "Not yet. Can you come here a minute?"

"Okay. Be right back," she tells the girl, who shrugs and keeps playing on her own. She doesn't need Jenny in order to have fun, and neither do I.

I walk Jenny to the fence above the ditch where the run-off flows when it rains. Part of me wants to push her in. She'd fall and might get hurt. Part of me wants her to hurt. I imagine her reaching up, hands and knees skinned and bleeding, begging for my help.

"Why'd you tell?" I yell.

19

"Tell what?" Jenny asks, startled.

"You *know* what."

"I haven't told anyone you like Matt."

"*What?*" I shout, then lower my voice. "I don't even like him anymore." The second-grade girls still giggle about Matt's dimple and big brown eyes, but now that I'm eight I know he's boring. If he was a bug, he'd probably be an ant.

"Well, I still didn't tell anyone."

"I'm talking about the pet store," I say through my teeth.

"I didn't say anything."

"Then how exactly do Christa and Melanie know?"

"Well … " Jenny plays with her friendship bracelet, "I might have said *something* to them."

"Why?" My voice cracks.

"I thought it was funny. Jeez."

"Real funny." I cross my arms and turn away.

"Look, I'm sorry, okay?" She touches my arm. I try to stay angry. I want to hang on to this feeling because I'm right and she's wrong and it's not fair. But then I picture walking past her house and not ever going inside again. I imagine never drinking another lemonade through a curly straw or seeing Mortimer's latest tricks. Jenny and I have been friends for half our lives. With Brice in the hospital, I really need a friend right now.

"Okay, here's the deal," I tell her. "I'll forgive you. But only if you tell the girls that I was actually drawing a picture of a sea fairy riding a seahorse."

"Drawing?"

"Yeah. I wasn't pretending at all. I just didn't hear you because I'm an artist and was busy drawing."

"But for real you were doing make-believe in your head, right?"

I narrow my eyes. "This is the truth now."

After school I'm upstairs by myself. Grandma's supposed

to be watching me but actually she's in the family room watching TV. Mom's at the hospital with Brice and I'm on Brice's floor, building a Lego house. I touch his airplanes and trace the back bumps of his dinosaur skeletons. If Brice saw, he'd yell me out of his room. But I'm careful. And anyway who cares, because he won't be back for days or weeks or maybe forever. He has to stay longer at the hospital, but how long is "longer"? No one will say.

My family moved here just before I was born. They let Brice choose between our rooms. How does a four-year-old decide? Lions or tigers, cookies or ice cream? He picked the larger, L-shaped room on the left. The closet goes deeper and you can see the tire swing from one window and the front path from the other, which makes it good for spying. I didn't get to choose. By the time I arrived, mine was the only room left. It's like when you get to the movies late and you have to sit too close to the screen so your neck hurts, sneakers stuck to the floor with someone else's spilled soda. I have a beanbag, boombox, dress-up chest, books, and art supplies. But there is nothing special about the room itself. The thing is, Brice isn't here right now, so, like Dad says about the new house, it's a waste of a good room.

I go get my crayons and paper and draw my furniture as simple shapes like they'd look from above. Here is my rectangle bed. There is my square desk and beanbag circle. On a separate piece of paper I draw a big, hollow "L" with the symbol that means "door" and stripes that mean window. I move the paper furniture around inside Brice's paper room. I know about blueprints because Dad taught me and he knows because it's his job to know. When I find the best place for everything, I glue down the pieces. I write "Brice's Room" at the top, cross out his name and write my own. Grandma says possession is nine-tenths of the law. That's a fraction.

The Opposite of Love

There's a good breeze on my skin. I'm on the swings a few days later during recess. Holding the chains, I lean way back then forward, pumping my legs. The swing whines like air sucked in and out of a harmonica. I can see straight across the blacktop to the boys playing kickball near the school gate. The edge of our world. Earlier today we learned about Sir Francis Drake, who has the same name as the street near my house and also Drakes Beach, which is my favorite. He lived in the olden days and sailed to California with boys he kidnapped off the street in London. I didn't know they had kidnapping back then too. On Sir Francis Drake's ship, if you got caught stealing an apple, you got whipped. Who'd want to steal an apple? Maybe this was before they invented candy.

"Hi, Ivy," says Caterpillar Christa, Foursquare Queen, tossing her long blonde ponytail as she hops on the swing. Ladybug Melanie, in a lavender dress and lavender sweater, gets on the swing next to her. Mom likes me wearing all different colors (except for yellow because it makes me look sickly). I imagine Melanie's closet with all her clothes the same pale Easter egg color. I look at Melanie's round cheeks and the delicate gold "✝" around her neck. The letter "✝" is for turtle, tiger, tango, tangerine. But this "✝" is for Jesus, who Grandma says is the The-Lord-Our-Savior-Who-Died-for-Our-Sins.

I want to get away before they make fun of me like the other day on the monkey bars. But then they'd call me a scaredy-cat, so instead I grip the chains tighter and say hi.

"Hey, is it true your brother's in the hospital?" Christa asks. She's wearing a pleated skirt and Sleepy Hollow Swim Club sweatshirt.

It might be a trick, but I say, "Yes."

"Is he going to die?"

"No!" Part of me wants to slam into Melanie so she smashes into Christa, sending her flying, like the grown-up toy on Dad's desk with the row of balls on wires. Instead I pump my legs harder.

"Okay." Christa rolls her eyes. After a moment she asks, "Did you hear about Sara?"

"No, what?" I ask. Sara sits behind me in Ms. Kelley's class. She has straight bangs and a flat chin and likes horses. If Sara was a bug I think she'd be a cricket, with a saddle on her back for a microfairy.

Melanie gasps. "You haven't heard?"

Sara is at school today, so I know she doesn't have appendicitis and the Killer Bees didn't get her.

"It's pretty big news," Christa agrees.

I relax, matching their rhythm. They want to tell me something.

"It's about her parents," Melanie hints.

I watch Caleb Ludlow run through the giant sandpit to a group of other second-grade boys. He pauses, watching them dig, and then jumps on their volcano. The boys roar and one shoves him. Moth Caleb shoves back and the boy falls, crushing his own sand hill. He howls and flings a handful of sand at Caleb. Caleb covers his eyes and wails. A Yard Duty blows her whistle and stomps over.

"Are Sara's parents having a baby?" I ask. Babies get their own special kind of food in little glass jars. This is interesting because there's no special food for eight-year-olds or some sort of snack that's just for twelve-year-olds.

"Oh," Melanie says, "I wish."

"Are they going to be on a game show?"

"No," Christa says.

"*Wheel of Fortune*?"

"I said no."

"Are they buying her a pony?" I ask.

"No," Melanie says. "It's nothing like that."

"Is Sara … adopted?" I ask.

"Nope," Christa says. "Sara's parents are getting divorced!"

I sigh. I can't believe I guessed pony before divorce.

"Isn't that super-sad?" Melanie asks. "Poor thing."

When your parents are divorced, you mostly live with your mom and only visit your dad on weekends. Your mom picks you up and your parents get angry just being in the same room together. Their not-love makes them growl like dogs.

"Yeah," I agree. "That's mega-super-sad." I look up at the sky, thinking how glad I am that that will never happen to my parents. Sometimes I even see Mom and Dad kiss on the lips, which is proof.

We pump our legs hard, swinging as high as we can. We are birds on chains. We kick off our right shoes, sending them sailing through the air. Christa's lands the farthest away in the sand. "Yes!" she shouts. The bell rings. Across the playground, kids stop playing and flow toward the classrooms like a dandelion puff in reverse. On the swings we feel the pull too. We kick off our left shoes. This time I win. One by one, we jump, sailing through the air in slow motion.

"Take one and pass it on." Tony the Earwig at the desk in front of me twists in his seat, handing me photocopies. Ms. Kelley's classroom has posters of different kinds of weather and the multiplication table. There's a reading corner with books and *National Geographic* magazines. The bulletin board has our drawings of California birds. I like the red-wing-blackbird, the acorn woodpecker, and best of all the scrub jay, but not seagulls because they're mean. Brice likes crows because they're smart. Above the board is a pull-down map of the whole entire world. On Ms. Kelley's desk is a jar of marbles.

"Take one and pass it on," I repeat to Sara behind me. She does look kind of sad under those straight bangs of hers. I imagine her making lonely music with her cricket legs. I wonder if the divorce is her fault.

We turn in our seats to pass, then take, pass, take, down the rows like dominoes. Ms. Kelley collects the extras and I notice an owl pinned to her shirt. She is young, I think, but wears glasses because her eyes are bad. If you have a bad sense of smell you can't wear something to make it better. Not everything can be fixed.

The tops of our photocopies say, "Meet the Food Groups." Meat, beans, and nuts are in the Protein group. Pasta, bread, and rice are in the Grain group. Ms. Kelley teaches us that we need all four groups to grow big and strong and stay healthy. But it's different for animals. Deer just eat grass and cats only eat kibble.

I raise my hand. "What if you just eat one at a time?"

"What do you mean, Ivy?" Ms. Kelley asks.

"One day you just eat Protein, then the next day only Dairy. You'd rotate so you'd still eat them all, just not at the same time."

"That's stupid." Matt the Ant looks at me with his big brown eyes, dimple appearing. "Why would you only want to eat peanut butter all day?"

I can't believe I had a crush on him last year.

"On Grain Day, you could just eat waffles," I point out.

"What do people think?" Ms. Kelley asks.

Math Genius Julie says, "You couldn't have fruit on your waffles or you'd get two food groups."

If she was a bug she'd be a centipede, counting the world with her legs.

"Just eating one thing would be boring." Matt the Ant sticks out his tongue when Ms. Kelley's back is turned.

"You're boring," I say.

"Ivy," Ms. Kelley says. "No putdowns." She writes my name on the board and takes a marble from the jar. The class groans. When we do something good, a new marble goes in the jar, and we lose one when anyone is bad. When the jar is full, the whole class gets a prize, like an ice cream party, or a video even when it's not raining.

"Good one," Caterpillar Christa whispers.

We get out our crayons to draw healthy food. I draw a pancake skyscraper, an evil carrot, a ballerina pig, and a glass of milk with the world's craziest curly straw, which is also a rollercoaster.

"Great drawing, Ivy," Ms. Kelley says when she comes around. I give her a big smile to show I'm sorry, but good art doesn't bring back marbles.

Ladybug Melanie has covered her paper in orange shapes. You'd think it'd be lavender but maybe that's just for wearing, not eating.

"What's that?" I point to a square.

"Cheese," she snaps at me, pulling on her "t."

"What's that one?" I point to a circle.

She won't look at me. "Chicken nugget."

After school, I'm in the kitchen of my empty house, talking with Mom on the phone.

"Can I talk to Dad?" I ask. They're at the hospital with Grandma, visiting Brice, and are probably having lots of fun without me. I take a tangerine from the fruit bowl and roll it around the counter. Its skin is cool and bumpy. Fruit and Vegetable group.

"Your dad's at work."

I hear a scratchy voice in the background.

"Stop defending him," Mom snaps. "He should be with his son."

No one wanted to play with me at recess because of the stupid marble. And now I have to spend the whole afternoon alone too. The house feels wrong without Brice here. I wish I had a big orange cat named Marmalade to keep me company. I think about the Artist's sleeping cat in the future and sigh heavily.

"Come on, Ivy," Mom says, "be a big girl." The muffled voice speaks again. "Grandma says you should make yourself a snack."

"I want you to do it," I whine.

"I'll cook dinner when I get home. If you're hungry now you've got to help yourself." Mom reminds me about the sheet of emergency numbers. I try to decide if being hungry counts as an emergency. I don't think it does. Mom says Maxine will swing by to check on me in a little bit and I should make some more artwork for Brice. I tell her I can't find my red glitter. She says, "Just do the best you can."

I kick off my shoes, hoping someone will trip on them. Then I fix myself a rice cake with peanut butter (Grain and Protein) and stomp upstairs. I haven't swapped rooms with Brice yet because most of the furniture is too heavy. I'll ask Dad for help some time when he's not too busy. I turn on the radio and chew loudly. *Now* I get it. Brice's appendix decides to go bad and I get punished. I open my deluxe box of sixty-four crayons with the built-in sharpener. If *I* was sick in the hospital, I bet Mom would want to stay home with Brice.

I start drawing and the rest of the world fades away. I bring pictures out of the white, rubbing my crayons across the page. Maybe they were always there and I just needed to uncover them, like pirates digging for buried treasure.

I draw a girl taking a bubble bath, then I imagine myself inside my drawing, sculpting my hair into a shampoo mountain. *I close my eyes, rinsing the soap away. I hear something slapping the water and open my eyes just in time to see a scaly green tail slithering under the water. I scream and scramble out of the tub. I turn around to see if the horrible creature is following me when I realize it's my tail! I stare at my hands as they go green and scaly too. I scurry into the living room, not bothering with a towel.*

"Help!" I scream. "I'm turning into an alligator!"

My parents look up from their books. I hope Dad will swear "Shit damn Jesus!" and pull on his running shoes to go get help. I want Mom to sob, holding her poor daughter monster in her arms, stroking the scaly bumps along my back. But they just look tired and irritated.

"Snap out of it," Dad says.

Mom says, "Go put on some clothes."

I shake my head as I finish coloring my half-girl-half-alligator.

Suddenly I get a creepy feeling like someone is watching me. I look up from my drawing and turn around fast. There's no one there, so I go to the window but don't see anything unusual outside. I put on my red sweater and explore the house, opening closets and cupboards, looking inside. The medicine cabinet is crammed full of little bottles that I'm not supposed to touch. I run around, looking for clues and trip over something. "Aarggh!" I yell, falling over. I look down. It was one of my shoes. By the time I get to the kitchen, I feel like I just imagined the whole thing. I get myself a cookie and slink upstairs.

On a new sheet of paper, I draw an ostrich with a feather mohawk and leather jacket. He sticks out a wing hitchhiking—too tough to get kidnapped. Next, I draw a balloon-farmer and his daughter. The rubber fruits slowly fill with air as they grow. If you wait too long to pick them, they snap off and float away. The girl stands on a ladder to pluck a ripe, red balloon, just like I'd help my dad if he was a farmer. I keep drawing. Pressing hard. Using up wax.

Visiting Hours

Like dancers, we spread to the far corners of our house, searching, finding, bending, scooping things into opened bags.

"That closet's a mess," Dad says Saturday morning when we're getting ready to go. "I don't know how you can find anything in there."

I shrug and hand him the board games. We pack music and books and food. Mom wanted help with the food, but Dad joked he doesn't want to make anyone sicker. I haven't seen Brice for a few days and I'm hunting for my red sweater.

"We need to get going!" Dad calls from upstairs.

"So *now* you want to go!" Mom yells. I step into the kitchen and see her making turkey sandwiches on sourdough. "One visit to the goddamn hospital this whole week," Mom grumbles to the mayo. The mayo says nothing.

Dad and I pass on the stairs, I'm going up and he's coming down.

"Oh, that's real cute, Karen," he shouts. "I've got this pesky thing called work."

"Yeah? What about your job as a father?"

"Exactly. I'm providing for my family. My Asshole Boss doesn't let me just skip out whenever I feel like it. We're lucky I *have* a job to stay late at."

I spot a red sleeve reaching out from under my beanbag. I put it on and exhale deeply.

"Come on, Ivy, we're leaving now," Mom yells.

I thud down the stairs.

"Wait, I have to pee!"

Dad sighs. "I'll be in the car."

I run to the bathroom and Mom calls after me, "Did you remember your drawings?" I don't know how I'm supposed to remember everything. Mom tells me, "Just be quick," and goes up to grab them.

"Moving in?" Brenda the nurse asks, seeing our bags.

"Yep, let me just get out our welcome mat," Dad chuckles.

"Go on ahead," Mom tells me, as usual.

"How's our boy?" Dad asks.

I walk down the hall, past the kids with tubes up their noses. I pass a room with a coughing little girl. I hold my breath and rub my sweater for protection. I can hear her all the way to Brice's room.

"Howdy, Brice!" I burst into his room, gasping for air. The other bed is still empty.

"Howdy, Ivy!" He sits up in bed. He's got more pink in his cheeks. "How's your pony Windy?" Brice asks in his cowboy voice.

"Real good!" I say. "I fed her a carrot and she nuzzled me."

"Been out riding?"

"Yup! Out across the prairie and all the way here. But Mom and Dad drove."

"Drove what?"

"Um ... " What a silly question. " ... the car?"

"So they left the covered wagon at home?" Brice asks. My eyes squeeze shut. Everyone knows there were no cars in the Olden Days. Brice never messes up. I squeeze my hand, thinking how to make it better.

"Well," I say, "remember those nice people from the future who gave Ma and Pa that crazy *horseless carriage*?"

"Sure do." Brice laughs.

"Well, they came back in their time machine to yell at Ma and Pa."

"Uh-oh."

"Yeah! They've been watching and know we keep using our old covered wagon to go to the general store and ... uh, well, actually that's the only store we have. They say Ma and Pa are just plain rude because they gave us a miracle driving machine and how do we thank them? By still riding around in a wooden cart pulled by animals."

"You don't say?" Brice says.

"Yessiree!"

"Well, in that case, it's a mighty good thing they drove the au-to-mo-bile." Brice struggles over the word. "We don't want to make those folks from the future mad. They've got *Velcro*."

My eyes prick with tears. I wish Brice could just come home with us. He doesn't deserve to be stuck here, lying in bed. He must get so bored.

"Does it still hurt a lot?"

"You know," Brice says, still in character, "that rattlesnake bite hurts something awful. But the good news is, the claw marks from the grizzly bear are starting to heal."

Mom and Dad appear in the doorway and Brice's cowboy voice jumps away like a jackrabbit. "Hey, guys!"

"Hi, baby." Mom puts her bags down and covers him in kisses. "You remember your father?"

Dad turns away from her and puts a big hand on Brice's shoulder.

"Hey, kiddo, did you miss me? Rough week at work. I just couldn't get away."

Brice nods.

"How're you feeling?" Dad asks.

"Okay," Brice says. "Better."

"That's what we like to hear. We're going to have so much fun today. Just look at all this stuff we brought."

Mom pulls a chair over, telling Brice she hopes he's hungry because she made him a special turkey sandwich with monster cheese and olives, just the way he likes it. I give him some tapes to listen to after we've left. We all play crazy eights, then *Sorry!* where everyone just wants to get home. Next I'm Miss Scarlet (which is a kind of red), in *Clue*. My family are all expert detectives but I would rather play with the miniature weapons. Then Brice and I drink Squeezits while Dad reads out loud from *The Hobbit*. Mom peels tangerines, handing out sections like she's still dealing cards. Brice eats half his sandwich and pushes the rest away.

"Your sister made you some artwork," Mom tells Brice after lunch. She hands me one drawing at a time which I pass to Brice, like buckets of water to put out a fire.

"Are the balloons growing on the tree or stuck in the branches?" Brice asks, studying the first picture.

"Growing. See? That's the farmer."

"I like it," he says.

"I wouldn't feed *this* guy any birdseed!" Mom passes me the hitchhiker bird, which I give to Brice.

"Is it a punk ostrich?" he asks.

I nod.

"The meanest bird in all of Africa," he says.

"Even the lions are scared of them," I say.

"This next one's a collage."

Mom hands me a sheet of paper and I scrunch up my face.

"Oh, that's not for Brice." I pass it back to Mom. She must have scooped it off my desk.

"Lemme see," Brice says. Dad says it looks like a blueprint and Mom passes it over my head to Brice. I try to snatch it, and Mom tells me not to be rude. "Hey, why's my name crossed out?" Brice asks as I desperately try to grab it back. "That's my room, isn't it?" He studies the paper, two little lines appearing between his eyebrows. "But that's all *your* stuff! Are you taking over my room?"

"Noooo." I force a laugh, but it comes out like a cough.

I search for the words to make it okay. "It's just that you might not need it."

"What do you mean?"

"You might never come home," I whisper.

Brice yelps, letting the blueprint drift to the floor.

"Don't be horrible!" Mom hugs him and pets his hair like he's a cat. "Of course your brother will be home soon."

"As good as new." Dad folds his arms.

"You can't just steal my room!" Brice pulls away from Mom.

"I'm not," I moan. "I was just thinking about the empty house at the end of the road. Dad says it's waste of a good house."

"That's ridiculous." Dad sighs. "Brice still lives in his room. You'd be pretty mad if we took away a toy you hadn't played with for a few days."

"How'd you like it if *you* were stuck here and someone stole your My Little Ponies?" Brice pushes his floppy hair off his forehead. "And then they left them in the road to get run over by a garbage truck!"

"But I wasn't going to hurt your room." I start to cry.

"Right," Brice says. "You were just going to steal it."

"Ivy, that blueprint was insensitive and mean-spirited." Mom stands over me. "Imagine how your brother must feel."

"I hate it here," Brice says. "Oliver is so lucky."

Mom opens her eyes wide in shock. "My God, what an awful thing to say!"

"What? Why?" Brice says. "I just mean I want to go home."

"Oh, honey." Mom's voice cracks. "We all want that too."

"You're in big trouble, missy." Dad turns to me with angry eyes. "Out. Wait in the hall."

Pudding Time

Walking back and forth outside Brice's hospital room, I decide this is all Mom's fault. She should have listened to me when I said the blueprint wasn't for Brice. I wipe my eyes on my sleeve and sniff hard, sucking the snot back into my nose. I kick the wall. I didn't even mention Oliver and I'm still in huge trouble. I should have thrown out the stupid blueprint. I am a Bad Person. I kick again. Brice just needs to get better and then everything will go back to normal.

Suddenly I wonder if Brice's "appendicitis" is just a made-up story. I'd never even heard of an appendix until his supposedly started hurting. They said it's a body part that doesn't do anything, but everything does something. Even toenails grow, and earlobes can hold earrings. What if there's no such thing and the real truth is that my brother is dying?

I sit on the floor in the hallway, hugging my knees. If Brice died, he'd stop getting older and would stay the same age forever. One day I'll be twelve and he'd still be twelve. Then I'd be thirteen and older than my big brother. When I'm a grown-up artist I might move somewhere far away where the air is hot and wet, but the pain would hide in my suitcase and come with me. I'd paint myself as a woman with boobs and chin-length hair, holding hands with Brice as he is now, floppy hair and hopeful eyes.

I tiptoe to the nurses' station where Brenda is sorting files.

"Ivy! I didn't see you there. Everything okay?"

I force a big smile and hope she can't tell I've been crying,

"Oh, yeah. My parents just wanted some alone time with Brice."

"Don't worry, your brother will be back home and getting into trouble again before you know it. Bet you miss him."

I nod. "Yeah, but when … "

"There you go, Dr. Bushnell." She hands a folder to a bearded man in a white coat.

"If you see my parents, can you tell them I went to the cafeteria?"

She looks at me closely. "Did your folks say it was okay to go on your own?"

I think through my options.

"They didn't say they minded."

It's afternoon, and the hospital cafeteria is mostly empty. I'm by myself at a big long table, eating chocolate pudding I paid for with my emergency quarters. I've got a good view of the hospital parking lot, where the sun is bouncing off the cars. It looks like a huge board game with white lines marking the spaces. Roll the dice, pick a card. Make Sick Brother a drawing—move ahead three squares. Try and take over Sick Brother's room—go back to Start. Our station wagon is down there on the board, but I can't find it. Is it winning or losing? The parking lots at Red Hill Shopping Center and the Fairfax movie theatre would probably look the same if I ever saw them from above. Except here people aren't getting their shoes fixed or munching popcorn in the dark. Their bodies have fallen apart and are being put back together again. All the king's horses know when something is wrong, but cars are machines and don't know the difference. Windy would neigh, shaking her mane. *Trouble! Brice is sick! Trouble!*

"You look about the same age as my granddaughter," says a sad old man in a green sweater with yellow squares.

"Mind if I join you?" He could have a whole long table all to himself, but maybe he wants to look at the parking lot too. I shrug and continue eating my pudding. The old man has coffee and a bowl of white lumps.

"What's that?" I point. It looks like paste.

"Tapioca," he says. I look at him blankly. He smiles. "Doesn't your mother ever make tapioca pudding?"

"*This* is pudding."

"Well, this is just a different kind." The skin sags under his eyes, but he looks friendly. There are deep lines all over his face and as I look closer, I see eggshell-thin cracks, like his wrinkles have wrinkles. He asks if someone I know is in the hospital. *My whole family's here and they're all mad at me.* But he's asking if someone is sick. When I think about Brice I get a sour twist in my stomach.

"My mom," I say, surprising myself.

New wrinkles appear around his eyes. "Sorry to hear that. What's wrong with her?"

"She's ... going deaf."

"Oh, dear. I guess they're running some tests on her?"

"Yes and," I say because Brice says this is a good place to start, "it might take all afternoon for them to figure out what's wrong."

"She must be so young."

"She's thirty-nine," I say, which is true, and I wonder if that's young or not. My breath stops. When you're pretending, everything needs to be made up or else it's cheating. I look outside at the parking lot, searching for my next move. "But the worst thing is, she's a professional piano-tuner."

"You don't say."

"Yeah, the other day we were watching TV and she said, 'Who turned off the volume?' But the volume was fine." I lean forward. "The problem was her ears."

37

The old man frowns and shakes his head.

I can't stop myself. "Another time, we heard banging coming from the kitchen. Know what it was?"

"What?"

I pause, running my spoon through my pudding. "My mom was smashing pots together, saying, "Nothing, nothing."' I look down for dramatic effect. I would like to draw Mom freaking out in the kitchen, the rest of us covering our ears in pain and Mom hearing only silence. I swing my legs. If she really were deaf, maybe she would be home more instead of always being here with Brice. Or if she was actually a piano tuner, maybe Dad wouldn't have to work so much for his Asshole Boss.

I picture Dad packing up his briefcase, getting ready to leave the office. *On his desk, there's a photo of all of us, the toy with the metal balls, and a book about Frank Lloyd Wright who made the Civic Center with its blue roof like the pancake place. Dad's bulletin board has some of my drawings. His fat, bald boss stomps over with a mean smile.*

"And just where do you think you're going? I've got more work for you."

He hands Dad a two-foot stack of papers.

"Sorry," Dad tells him. "I can't stay late. I've got to go home and take care of the kids. Karen's tuning tonight."

"I'm here because of my wife," the old man says, stirring his tapioca.

"Is she sick?" I ask.

"'Fraid so."

"Is it super-serious?"

I wait for him to chuckle and say it's nothing really and she'll be home any day now. Instead he nods and says, "It's cancer." I look at my pudding. Cancer killed my grandpa. That's why Grandma lives near us now, so she wouldn't be all alone Back East. She used to live near my Aunt Bea, but then my aunt moved to Chicago with stupid Uncle Ronald who smells like cigarettes. The old man continues, "We're all praying and hoping for the best."

My throat tightens. I'd forgotten all about praying. Grandma says God loves the little children, but we can get hurt and bleed ... and die. Maybe Brice is still sick because I haven't asked God to make him better. I don't know how God decides who lives or dies. Is it based on who gets the most prayers, like voting for class president? Or is it more like cheerleaders, with whoever prays the loudest? With a shock I realize that maybe everyone forgot to pray for Brice's old roommate too.

I slip off my chair. "Gotta go."

"Take care now," he says. "I'll say a prayer for your mother."

"Jesus." Mom lets out a deep breath when she sees me.

Brice narrows his eyes and says, "You are so dead."

Good. My parents didn't leave without me. I bet the hospital is scary at night, and if Brice is still mad, he wouldn't protect me. I think of this time at Drakes Beach when I was all alone and a seagull ate my lunch. Dad joins me in the hallway, shutting the door behind him.

"I only went to the bathroom."

"You weren't there when Mom looked."

"It was on a different floor. And I got lost."

"Do you have any idea how long you were gone?"

"Probably about five minutes."

"Ha." But he's not smiling. "Try again."

I look at my shoes for answers. "Ten?"

"You were gone for over forty minutes. You can't just wander off like that. We even paged you. Didn't you hear your name?"

I shake my head. *Hey, E.T., where'd you go?* I shudder.

"It was number two," I say lamely. I can't wait until I'm older and they finally stop worrying about me.

"I think you're lying and went playing around the hospital."

"I am not lying," I whine.

"Careful, Ivy. That was a Time Out before. You shouldn't have left the hall without asking permission … "

"I didn't want to bother you. I told Brenda."

"What did you tell her?"

My stomach drops.

"I just said I was going somewhere and to tell you I'd be back."

Dad says, *nurse blah blah very busy lady* and *blahdy-blah responsibility.* I shut my eyes. If Mom really was deaf and Dad was blind, then they wouldn't know when I was gone. I could just slip away and do whatever I like.

"You were in trouble before," Dad says. "Look at me. You'd better believe you're in trouble now."

I stare at Dad's eyebrows and imagine how he'll look when they've turned gray.

Grounded

Do not pass Go. Do not collect $200. Busted and grounded.
For a whole week I have to come straight home after school.
No TV, treats, or telephone and I can't go to Jenny's. Every
afternoon, Mom calls from the hospital to check up on me.
She reminds me that Maxine Ludlow is just down the road
if I run into any trouble and that I've got the emergency
numbers if anything bad happens. Mom has no idea I'm
sneaking cookies from the kitchen. They taste even sweeter
now. She doesn't know I jump off the couch, turning off the
TV the moment I hear her car in the driveway. But I can't
play with Honeybee Jenny, which means I'm practically in
jail. She's in the other third-grade class, so now we only see
each other at recess.

I sit in my beanbag and close my eyes. Breathing deeply,
I imagine myself in the faraway place where the air is hot
and wet. I picture myself in my grown-up apartment with
the unusual fruit. There's music playing. I see my grown-up
self, the Artist, with her chin-length hair, her back to me at
the easel. She's wearing a long skirt and is standing in front of
a mirror, drawing a picture of herself with charcoal. I stand
in the corner, watching as she sings quietly, rubbing gray
shadows around the eyes. Part of me wishes she could see
me. Another part is glad I'm invisible so I can watch without
being seen. The big orange cat walks by. I stay still and silent.
He turns his head, and for a moment he's looking right at me.
Can he see me? The thought gives me a chill, and I quickly
open my eyes back into my room.

I'm breathing heavily. Mom's still not home yet. I go downstairs and fix myself a snack of apple with peanut butter (Fruit and Protein). Did the cat really see me? The whole thing makes me anxious until I decide it doesn't matter anyway. Who cares if an imaginary cat in a pretend future can see me or not? It's all in my mind.

Back in my beanbag, I start reading a book about a girl in Kenya, Africa. She has a pet lion cub with big paws. He's cute now, but you know down the road he'll grow up and cause lots of problems. When that happens I just hope he doesn't eat the girl. Grandma says you shouldn't bite the hand that feeds you, but lions might not know that rule. I want to ask Brice if people can really have baby lions as pets or if it's just pretend. There are a lot of things I want to ask, but when I visit him in the hospital, the white walls and funny smells make me forget. Brenda says he's getting better, which makes my heart race in my chest, I want it so bad.

The phone rings and I run into my parents' room.

"Hi, Ivy, it's me."

"Me who?"

"It's Jenny! Jeez, how come you never recognize my voice?"

"I dunno." I loop the cord around my finger.

"Guess what? I just taught Mortimer some new tricks."

"Really?" I wonder if the girl in the book will train her lion to not eat people. Or maybe just to eat certain people she doesn't like.

"Yeah, they're super-impressive. Come see."

"I can't, I'm still grounded, remember?" I look at Brice's baby shoe on the windowsill next to a cat I made out of clay. I make the little shoe hop over the plants and framed photos.

"Oh, yeah, I forgot," Jenny says. "Is your Mom home?"

"Nope, hospital. If she *was* home I wouldn't even be talking to you right now."

"Poor Bricey-wicey," Jenny sighs. "Then just come over super-quick. It'll only take five minutes."

"Nah, I'd better not. Just tell me."

"I can't tell you. You have to see."

I groan. "Who says?"

"I do. Well, are you coming or not?"

"Okay, but I can't stay long."

Jenny's big sister Natasha answers the door with bumpy waves running down half her hair. She yells up to Jenny and joins a girl with long legs on the living room floor. They're both teenagers and very mature. Natasha flips through a magazine as her friend grabs her straight hair with electric clamps.

"Ooh!" Natasha squeals, making me jump. She points to a picture. "Isn't that a cute top, Heather?"

"I like the Day-Glo belt." Heather moves the clamps. Jenny bounces down the stairs and waves me up. This feels even better than usual because I'm not supposed to be here. Secret, sneaky fun.

Heart and bear stickers have spread around the side of Jenny's little TV. Her room is filled with Natasha's old things: dozens of *Sweet Valley High* and *Babysitter Club* books and a box of half-dressed Barbies. It's like they started getting ready to go out and suddenly changed their minds. Natasha said all the books and Barbies are a total waste of time. Sisterless, my things are always new. When I outgrow them, they go to Goodwill for the Less Fortunate. Brice's clothes become hand-me-downs for Moth Caleb Ludlow and then his Stink Beetle brother Tommy. I don't know what happens after Tommy. Maybe they're sent to the poor little children in Ethiopia that Grandma talks about. They have pot bellies but are still starving.

I stroke Mortimer. He has a tuft of white fur on his chest and dark stripes along his back.

"Ready for the biggest breakthrough in cat-training history?" Jenny asks. She removes a toy from the pocket of her denim skirt. "Here, kitty, kitty. Wanna be a circus cat?" Mortimer's ears twitch.

"Did you tell him to do that?"

"No, and that's not the trick." Holding up a finger, she says, "Mortimer, sing." He meows. Jenny clicks the toy and gives him a treat. My mouth drops open. Jenny picks up a hula hoop. "Mortimer, hoop." He steps through, she clicks and gives him another treat.

"What're you feeding him?" *And does it work on people?*

"Cheese."

Before, Mortimer's best trick was standing on his hind legs to get scratched on the head. Jenny swore to God he could fetch a catnip mouse, just not when I was watching.

"Can he *jump* through the hoop?" I ask.

"Not yet." Jenny twists her friendship bracelet. "But hopefully soon." She says she watched a dog training TV show and bought the clicker from the Red Hill Pet Store. My heart beats faster and I squeeze my eyes shut, waiting to be teased. But she doesn't mention seahorses. I bet even Natasha is impressed, but Jenny says she won't show her sister until Mortimer's really good. So far I'm the only one who's seen. That makes me pretty special.

"When he can do a whole bunch of tricks," Jenny says, "do you think people would come to a circus in my backyard?"

"You bet!" I say. Mortimer jumps on the bed. I rub him behind the ears and he curls up on my lap.

"Would you help me make posters?"

"I can draw you as a lion tamer with Mortimer jumping over the moon."

Jenny grins. She looks up at the ceiling and asks, "So when's your brother going to be all better?"

"They say soon," I tell her. "He's lots healthier now, so maybe he can come home in a few days." This is what Mom said, but I hope I haven't just jinxed it by saying it out loud. I wonder if Oliver's family thought he'd be all better soon and then it never happened. Maybe his dog is still waiting for him to come home.

"Are you excited for Brice to come home?" Jenny asks.

"Mmmmmm!" I say, so I don't risk saying the words. When Brice comes home, we'll spin each other on the tire swing and play make-believe games and I'll draw him a new picture every day. I pet Mortimer, loving the soft fur between my fingers. "So what's that girl doing to Natasha's hair?"

Jenny wrinkles her forehead. "You serious?"

I swallow. If I say, "Just kidding," she'll say, "Prove it." Mortimer stretches and lies down at the foot of the bed.

"Um, yeah."

"It's called crimping. It's pretty, isn't it?"

I nod.

"You do it with a crimping iron. How could you not know about this stuff?"

I shrug.

"Come on! Let's see if they'll do it to you," Jenny says. I'm afraid it'll hurt a lot, but I follow her downstairs because I'm too scared to be a coward.

Now Natasha's hair is covered in mermaid zigzags. Laughing, Heather reads the magazine's advice column while Natasha works on her friend's ponytail. They've got a snack plate of Oreos and two glasses of chocolate milk.

"Hey, what are you drinking?" Jenny asks.

"Nothing." Natasha takes a sip.

"What do you mean, 'nothing'?"

"Nothing you can have." They giggle. Maybe it's coffee.

Heather says they'll crimp my hair if I read them the next "Dear Mimi" letter. Jenny agrees for me and my throat tightens. I get sweaty hands when Ms. Kelley makes me read out loud. I'm afraid the kids in my class will think I'm a retard if I go too slow, but when I read fast, my tongue catches between the words.

Natasha has me sit on the carpet and hands me the magazine. My skin prickles and I take a deep breath. I read to them about a fifteen-year-old girl who's worried there's something wrong with her because she hasn't gotten her period yet. Period means blood and also the dot at the end of a sentence. It seems like a weird thing to want, like getting slapped in the face. Also—also it means, "And that's it." Period, the end, so good luck.

I read, the dirty words making me blush. Natasha and Heather giggle, and I lose my place. Speaking these grown-up-teenage secrets makes me feel car sick. Natasha gently tugs my hair, but it doesn't hurt.

"Fifteen!" Heather shouts when I finally reach the end.

"That's *über*-late," Natasha agrees. She mists my head with hairspray and pats my back, "Okay, Vine Girl. All done, go and look."

"Rad," Jenny says, and we dance to the bathroom like rock stars. Tomorrow at school, everyone will stare, wishing they knew me, wishing they *were* me.

I look at myself in the mirror. There's a playful wiggle in a strand of my hair. I'm still me, but my hair is fancier.

"It's pretty," I tell Jenny's reflection. Suddenly I gasp, hand over mouth. *Stupid, stupid girl.*

I run along the sidewalk. It's been a lot longer than five minutes, and if Mom is home she'll be mad … and worried. Leaving without permission is against the rules, and having fun when you're grounded is even worse. I run fast, swinging my arms like Dad does. If I'm lucky, Mom won't be back yet. If I'm super-lucky, she'll be dead. Wait, I don't mean that. I take it back, I take it back. No one gets their hair

46

crimped at school, so as soon as Mom sees me I'm doomed. I rub spit into the waves, trying to disappear them like chalk. Running hard, I pray to Santa and baby Jesus that Mom is okay and still at the hospital.

I tiptoe into my house like a burglar and lock myself in the downstairs bathroom. (Like a burglar who has to pee.) My lungs ache, my reflection is pink and panting. My hair is damp and messy, but the waves are still there. The sink drips. I try to raise one eyebrow but both go up.

I throw open the medicine cabinet, but it's crammed so full, I quickly close it again. If Inspector Gadget was here, he'd make a de-crimping iron with Q-tips and dental floss. Under the sink I find bleach, bubble bath, and scissors. One time, Sara got a bad haircut that lost us a marble. She got bubblegum stuck in her hair, and her dad cut it free, so she had a funny short patch above one ear. The next day, Matt called her "Baldy" and she threw a book at him. Ms. Kelley went straight for the marble jar and they *both* had to stay after school. If she'd had a lollipop instead of gum, then none of it would have happened, so sometimes you don't even know what's going to get you in trouble until it's too late.

I put my ear to the door, but only hear the dripping tap. I wish I knew if Mom was home. I don't want to cut my hair off, but I have to do something. I find cotton balls, little hotel soaps, rubber bands, and Ajax. Go-Go-Gadget rubber band! I braid the wavy hair and rubber band the end.

Mom's still not home, so I go back to my room to finish my snack. But the apple has turned brown and I don't feel like reading anymore.

Home at Last

I color stripes and polka dots inside the fat letters. My sign is made from ten sheets of still-stuck-together printer paper. I carefully tear the skinny strips with the holes off the sides. Then I hang the sign on the living room wall so my brother will see it the same exact moment he comes in. It says, "Welcome home Brice!"

Brice is coming home. Saying the words gives me a fluttery feeling in my stomach. I'm even more excited than when we get to go to Marine World Africa USA. There won't be any dolphins or giraffes here, but it's still even more special than all the wild animals and Butterfly World put together.

I hear Mom's car pull into the driveway and I run outside.

"Hey, Ivy!" Brice says, getting out of the station wagon. We hug tight. He did it. He got all better and escaped the hospital. Oliver didn't make it, but my brother got healthy again and now he's home. Inside, Brice says my sign is rad and he likes the balloons we've put all over the house. They're all for him.

That evening, we're all four of us around the kitchen table again. It's the first Normal in a long time. It feels warm, like Drakes Beach only with no evil seagulls. We're having fried chicken as a special treat and there's ice cream cake for dessert.

"Can we go to the movies some time soon?" he asks, digging into his mashed potatoes.

"Sure, kiddo," Dad says. "Anything you like."

"Would you take me and Trevor bowling?" Trevor has stinky feet like a wet shed and braces.

"You bet," Mom says.

It's a kind of magic. Brice was sick and then the doctors made him better.

Then the gifts start. Mom buys Brice a pair of Air Jordans and I get a Lite-Brite. Mom keeps taking us shopping for new books, tapes, and toys and we get to pick out whatever we want. And it's not even Christmas yet.

"You're spoiling them," Grandma says one Sunday over brunch. I smile at her sweetly and try to make my feet touch the floor under the table for luck, but it's too far to reach.

Mom looks over at Brice's plate, a pancake buried under a cloud of whipped cream and chocolate syrup spirals.

The Beast

One morning several weeks later, in January, we're all at the kitchen table and Dad is buttering his toast.

"We have a surprise for you," he says. A Surprise means Fun News. Brice and I look at each other across our bowls of Fruity Yummy Mummy cereal with Monster Mallows.

"Can we have a clue?" Brice asks. Mom laughs as Dad slowly chews his toast, leaving us to wriggle in suspense. They whisper to each other.

Dad nods and says, "It's ... big."

Our big Easter vacation to Hawaii is still forever away, and what could be a bigger surprise than that? I gasp, realizing we must be *moving* there! I'll be Tropical Island Ivy with my own pet dolphin to ride every day after school. And I'll have special beach accessories: orange sunglasses, a bucket, and a flower necklace. Jet ski sold separately, batteries not included.

"Finish your breakfast and we'll show you," Mom says. Brice and I gobble our cereal. Maybe it's a photo of our *Swiss Family Robinson* treehouse that Dad designed himself. I imagine our new home, deep in the jungle, surrounded by bird-eating flowers. I'll shower in a waterfall and Mom will grow pineapples in her garden. Brice and I will swing to school on vines. Of course I'll miss Honeybee Jenny a lot, but she can visit and maybe stay all summer long.

Mom and Dad lead us down the hall to the family room.

Brice and I gasp. The TV we've had my whole life is on the floor and in its place on the stand is a giant. This new set is easily twice the size, a huge screen inside a polished wooden box like a puppet theatre.

"That's a Sylvania console. Twenty-five inches," Dad says, and Mom puts an arm around his waist.

"Cool!" Brice grins. "It's a beast!"

"Just in time for the Winter Olympics and the Battle of the Brians," Dad says. "See how the base swivels? And there's more." He hands Brice a remote control. Before, any time we wanted to change the channel, I had to jump off the couch to twist the knob.

My brother zips through the stations. "We've got cable!"

I stroke the Beast's smooth wooden side. With this huge screen, Dad will have the best seats in the stadium for every 49ers game. We'll smell the cashew chicken on *Yan Can Cook*. Watching the news, we'll actually feel the heat from forest fires. And the Care Bears will climb out of the TV to cuddle us on the couch. Jenny will die when she sees it.

I look down at our old TV, small and unplugged on the floor. It taught me about police chases and the fried egg, which is your brain on drugs. It proved there really are ghosts and UFOs and kidnappers. But now it's like I'm looking at someone else's TV. The old TV is like a dusty record player next to a new boombox. I can only imagine what Jenny must have thought of us with this piece of junk in our house. It's embarrassing, like a glamorous movie star's country cousin.

"Well shucks, ain't you going to introduce me to all yer nice friends?" The country cousin puts down her potato sack, wiping her hands on her muddy overalls. Just then, a chicken wiggles out of the sack and runs around the fancy restaurant. The important movie people lower their sunglasses and stare, mouths open while the country cousin chases the bird between tables. The glamorous movie star straightens her pearls and hides her face in her hands.

Keeping Score

Grandma hits her mini-golf ball through the spinning-wheel and into the hole.

"Bogey," she says. Her red lips move into a smile, but her eyes look serious behind her thick glasses. I notice how the skin on her face hangs creased and heavy. She knocks her knuckles against a gold haystack. It's hollow. She squints at the scorecard and says, "I don't know why they've made the lines on this thing so small. Neil, put me down for four."

Brice swings his golf club and his ball bounces off a statue of the Poor Miller's Daughter. She's poor because her family doesn't have much money and also because her dad wants her to be something she's not. The moral of the story is, don't brag or you could get your kid in big trouble. I hit my ball and it smacks into a wall. Then it's Mom's turn.

"Karen scores an eagle and the crowd goes wild!" Dad says in his announcer's voice. Mom laughs as he whirls her around. Now it's just me and Brice left playing the third hole. I bet Honeybee Jenny's a good mini-golfer, because cat trainers are very patient people. I miss. Again.

"This is too hard," I moan, throwing down my kiddy golf club. "I'll never beat you guys."

"Don't be so dramatic, Ivy," Mom says. "It's just a game."

"I'll never be the fastest runner in the world." Dad picks up my club. "So why do I bother?"

I shrug. "Because you *like* running?"

"Right. And when I try to beat my own time I'm not

competing against anyone else. I'm just trying to do my best."

We move on to the fourth hole—Jack and the Beanstalk with the goose that lays golden eggs. The moral of *that* story is that it's okay to steal (from a giant). Five is Rapunzel in her tower with her longer-than-Barbie-hair (don't steal from a witch). Six is Pinocchio (don't lie if you've got a trick nose). At each hole, the grown-ups cheer each other's tiny scores and then Brice and I miss for hours.

"He's not doing himself any favors," Dad is saying, half-watching Brice knock his ball against the side of the whale statue at the sixth hole. "If he'd figure out when to lie, he'd at least look like he knows what's going on. Instead he seems totally incompetent."

"You make it sound like it's good to lie to your boss." Grandma narrows her eyes.

"Well, my boss is a complete … jerk. But *lying's* probably a little strong. Let's say stretch the truth," Dad says. "Here's an example for you. A project slips Randall's mind, and when our boss asks how it's coming along his mouth drops open and he says, 'Oh, I'd forgotten all about that.' He looks like an idiot."

"What would you say?" Mom takes Dad's hand.

"I'd say, 'I'm making steady progress and I'll have it on your desk by end of business Thursday,'" Dad says.

Mom laughs. "Even if you haven't started?"

"Sure. If I've forgotten, I'd be grateful for the reminder. My coworker is basically telling everyone he's a disorganized idiot."

I grip my club and pray the ball will go where I want. I swing hard and it thuds against Pinocchio's shoe.

"Careful, Ivy, you don't want to hurt anyone," Grandma says. "And stand up straight."

The teenage couple behind us are done with Rapunzel now and are hanging around, waiting for us to finish. The girl is wearing hot pink leggings and plays with an earring while her boyfriend takes practice swings in slow motion. They glare at us and sigh loudly. I give up playing, but Brice keeps knocking his ball around the fake grass, determined to finish. Suddenly he notices the couple. He stares like a dog with its ears up, listening to a sound I can't hear.

Cinderella is the tenth hole, with a pumpkin coach and a glass slipper on the lower level. What's the moral? Clean the house and be good? Actually, that's pretty much the lesson in *Snow White* too.

"I just move my chair closer to the screen," Grandma is saying. "It's such a little television set; I need to be right on top of it anyway."

"Maybe you need a new prescription," Mom says.

"I know how to take care of my own eyes, Karen."

Brice's ball bounces off a mouse statue and rolls near the pumpkin. Mom tells him good job and turns back to Grandma. "I only meant that you might see better with new glasses."

If the inside of Cinderella's coach was still an ordinary pumpkin, she'd arrive at the ball covered in goo. But the prince would fall in love with her anyway, gently removing seeds from her hair as they danced. True love should be forever and no matter what, even if the person is dirty and smells bad. Even if you get angry at them sometimes or they disappoint you. So, really, Cinderella could have just worn her rags and wouldn't have even needed a magic ballgown. The prince loves *her*, not her dress. Grandma says beauty is only skin deep, but she always wears make-up and Mom has her clothes. So, I'm not sure.

Brice and I rush to the edge of the upper level to watch, as Mom's ball pops out below and stops halfway to the glass slipper. "You've got to put a little more power into it," Dad says. "Watch and learn." He strikes and the ball rolls right past the hole. "Goddamn it!" Mom gives him a look.

"See, Karen?" Grandma says after she gets a hole-in-one. "Would I be able to do that if my eyes were failing? The problem is my TV, not my glasses."

"What's wrong with your TV?" Dad asks.

"Nothing," Grandma says. "It's not fancy like yours or Bea's but I've always had a black-and-white set. You won't catch me complaining."

Brice's ball bounces off two mice and a wall before it rests at my feet. I tap mine a little closer.

"Why don't you take our old TV?" Dad asks.

"I couldn't do that."

"Really. We've just upgraded, but the old one's still fine."

"You should keep it for another room," Grandma says.

"One's plenty for us," Mom says. "You should take it."

"It's just sitting unplugged on the floor," Dad says.

"And it's color," Mom says.

"Well, obviously," Grandma says. Mom's face tightens.

"Honestly, Helen," Dad says. "We'd love you to have it."

"It *would* be nice to watch *Wheel of Fortune* in color," Grandma agrees. But she looks annoyed.

As we pass through the main building on our way out, I notice a small boy inspecting the kiddy golf clubs.

"Come on, Andy," says an old man with drooping skin under his eyes. "Just pick one."

"But I want a *good* one," Andy whines.

"They're all the same," says an older girl with braids.

"Nuh-uh."

"Yuh-huh."

"Nuh-uh."

"Well, hello there." The old man spots me. He's wearing a blue sweater with yellow diamonds and red squares. "You're the little girl from the hospital, aren't you?" It's Tapioca Man. "Is that your mom?"

"Yeah," I say.

Mom comes over after she's returned our clubs and stubby pencils.

"HELLO!" he yells. "I'M ALAN COOPER! I MET YOUR DAUGHTER AT MARIN GENERAL."

Mom winces and holds out her hand. "I'M KAREN," she yells, carefully pronouncing her name. "NICE TO MEET YOU."

"YOUR DAUGHTER AND I BOTH LIKE PUDDING."

"HOW NICE." Mom takes a step back. "ARE THESE YOUR GRANDCHILDREN?"

"MEET WHITNEY AND ANDY."

"WELL, HAVE FUN OUT THERE," Mom shouts. "WE LIKED THE PINOCCHIO HOLE, DIDN'T WE, IVY?"

"Yeah," I say.

"Speak up," Mom whispers.

"YEAH!" I yell.

Champagne

"Movie stars have more accessories," Honeybee Jenny tells me the next day. I'm wearing my curly blonde wig and Mom's layered skirt. Jenny ties a scarf under her chin like young Grandma in the black-and-white photo by the stairs. I find a pearl necklace, and she puts on long white gloves. Plastic bracelets rattling, I dig through my dress-up chest. It's the same one that Mom and Aunt Bea had when they were kids. I think it used to be an old travel chest from when people went places on big ships. Since Brice got out of the hospital A-OK, Mom has started treating herself to new outfits again. Her "tired" clothes go to Goodwill or else I get them for dress-up. She has to go shopping a lot because fashion is always changing and she won't be left behind.

"Ta-da!" I fit a tiara on to a floppy straw hat.

"Oh, that's good." Jenny looks at herself in the mirror and whispers, "Do you think Brice will think I look pretty?"

I look at her in Mom's ruffle-sleeved dress and shrug. It's not like Brice is any sort of fashion expert.

"Do you ever imagine what it'll be like when we grow up?" I ask.

Jenny looks at herself in the mirror. "I dunno. I'm going to be a famous cat trainer."

"Yeah but, do you think about the Future?"

"I don't know. Who cares?"

I smooth my skirt and look out the window. There are men carrying stones up the driveway. Then in my most

57

elegant voice I ask, "Excuse me, my dear, would you care for some champagne?"

"Um, okay."

I sigh. "I'm sorry, darling. Aren't you a movie star too?"

In a fancy voice, Jenny says, "I don't know what to say."

"Just think what a glamorous actress would talk about."

"How?"

"Guess and make it up." I smile at Jenny in the mirror. She makes a face at me. I make an uglier face. She laughs. I ask, "Would you care for some champagne?"

"Yes, please," Jenny says stiffly. "That would be divine?"

"Good!" I whisper. "Do follow me to the champagne room." We head downstairs, gliding our hands along the scratched banister.

"Champagne room?"

"Oh, yes. It's a special room in my mansion that's just for drinking champagne. Have you gone swimming yet in your new heart-shaped pool?"

"Have I?" she whispers.

"Say yes," I whisper back. "Yes is always a good place to start."

"Yes," she says in her princess voice.

"I heard you're going to dye the water pink for special occasions."

"Yes."

"And how is your adorable poodle Penelope?"

"Yes!" Jenny giggles.

"That doesn't even make sense," I say in my normal voice.

"But you said to say yes."

"I didn't mean to *only* say yes." This never happens with Brice. I try to explain, "You could say that your poodle did seventeen backflips in a row or that her fleas are actually robot spies. It doesn't really matter, you just need to play along."

Jenny nods and climbs on to a stool at the kitchen counter. Mom is in the garden telling the men what to do, so she won't bother us. I make Jenny cover her eyes while I fill two wine glasses from a hissing bottle.

"*Voilà!*" I say. Jenny opens her eyes and gasps. "I propose a toast," I say.

Biting her lip, Jenny carefully picks up her drink. I continue, "Champagne, in honor of your new starring role. I know you will be mahvelous."

Jenny laughs and we clink glasses. She watches the bubbles, then squeezes her eyes shut and takes a gulp. "Mmm, delicious," she says, surprised, like she was expecting broccoli juice. I fix my hat and we take dainty sips, making it last.

"Jenny," I say in my normal voice once we're done, "come here, I want to show you something."

She struggles off the stool, nearly tripping over her dress, and follows me to the family room.

"Whoa!" she shouts, eyes darting between the Beast and the TV on the floor. "Way bigger than the old one!"

We hear elephants on the stairs and Brice and his friend Trevor with the stinky-shed-feet burst into the room. They collapse on the couch and Brice flips through channels so fast that the different shows are just flickering light.

"There! There! There!" Trevor yells. Brice stops on a loud show with a big truck driving over a row of cars.

"Hey!" I say, bracelets jangling. "We were here first." The boys look at us for the first time and laugh.

"What are you supposed to be?" Brice asks over the blaring music.

"Hiya, Brice." Jenny gives a little wave. Wobbling slightly, she faces the TV and says, "Vroom."

"Movie stars," I mumble.

"Oh, yeah?" Brice asks. "Anyone I might have heard of?"

"No."

"Wait, don't tell me ... is that really Ivy?" Trevor flashes his braces. "Wow, I hardly recognized you. Is that a wig?"

I shift from one foot to another, wishing I was back in my regular clothes. On the TV, a spinning truck draws circles in the dirt.

"Vroom vroom!" Jenny says, eyes fixed on the screen.

"What's up with her?" Trevor asks. I stare at Jenny spinning around.

"Looks like Jenny's pretending to be a truck." Brice laughs.

"What are you doing?" I whisper. "What's wrong with you?"

"I think ... " Jenny sways. "I think I might be drunk!"

Brice and Trevor look at each other, bug-eyed. "Drunk?" Brice chokes. "What have you been drinking?"

"Champagne!" Jenny sings.

"Champagne?! Ivy, you are going to be in such big trouble."

"Yeah, you guys are like thirteen years under the legal drinking age," Trevor says.

"But she *can't* be drunk," I explain.

Jenny taps me on the chest, "And why not? Because I only had one drink? Ooh!" A motorcycle flies through a burning hoop.

"No, it's not that," I tell her. I whisper to the boys, "She can't be drunk because it wasn't really champagne."

"What?" Trevor asks loudly. "Sparkling wine? White wine spritzer? Vodka and soda?"

"No," I whisper. "7Up."

"7Up!" Trevor shouts.

"Really?" Jenny asks, in her normal voice. I nod.

"What a weirdo," Trevor says. He turns to Jenny and says, "Maybe you're a sodaholic!"

Brice tries to walk across the room like someone on a rocking boat. They explode with laughter and Jenny runs upstairs. I glare at the boys.

"I'm not a weirdo," Jenny says from inside the bathroom. "And I didn't want to do your stupid make-believe anyway."

"I'm sorry, Jenny." I pull off my wig and hat. "Movie stars and champagne seemed like fun."

"7Up!"

"My parents are saving the real champagne for a special occasion."

"I never should have believed you."

"I thought you'd know it was just pretend."

"You *said* it was champagne."

"I didn't know you'd think you were drunk!"

"Yeah, you didn't think at all." The lock turns and Jenny shoves her bundle of dress-up clothes at me. "Your make-believe games are always so dumb. You're a total waste of time."

Alone Forever

Aunt Bea says, "Don't wish the time away." That means try and be happy with now. She says whatever I'm waiting for will come soon enough. But that's a big fat lie, because I'm always waiting for something. Halloween, Hawaii, my birthday, the Marin County Fair, being old enough to sit in the front seat of the car. When she and stinky Uncle Ronald come to visit from Chicago, she twirls me around and says I'm "growing up so fast." She says before we know it, Brice and I will be teenagers, then off to college and then all grown-up. Maybe it's a white lie to make me smile. Grown-ups say it won't be this way forever. But they're wrong.

I run my fingers along the new stone wall in the garden and hop over the little bridge the men built. The bridge goes over the run-off ditch where the water goes when it rains. I like touching the smooth stones and am excited to show Dad.

"Come on, Karen, was this really necessary?" Dad says as I practice balancing along the wall.

"Don't you like it?" Mom asks.

"It looks fine, but it looked fine before."

"That old retaining wall was rotting. It was becoming an eyesore."

"I think it had another few years left in it," Dad says, tapping the new wall with his shoe. "But regardless—what's with the bridge?"

"It's just fun, Neil. I think that's reason enough, don't you?"

"This all looks expensive."

"You worry too much."

Dad sighs. He looks at me and then says to Mom, "I would have liked for us to have talked about this first."

"I wanted to surprise you," Mom says. "I think the bridge is really cute. Ivy, what do you think of the bridge?"

"I like it," I say.

"Well, of course she likes it," Dad snaps. He takes a deep breath and when he continues his voice is tight. "I just don't know if we should be spending so much."

"Relax." Mom touches Dad's arm. "We can afford it." She points to the wall and says, "I'd like to put some new plants around this area and make it more of a feature."

"Fine. Just don't go overboard."

"And don't patronize me."

I'm kneeling on the sidewalk outside my house, with my hands dusted in color. I'm surrounded by my chalk drawings of flying horses and cactuses. Looking up, I notice a scrub jay perched in a tree in our front yard. I draw a blue bird outline on the cement with chalk. The jay hops to another branch and I take my time coloring the belly and listening. He sounds happy even though he's alone. When I'm drawing I don't mind being on my own, but I don't want to stay alone forever. Hopefully Jenny will forgive me soon for that whole stupid champagne thing from a few days ago and we can go back to normal. I want us to dress up like rock stars and lip-sync to Brice's tapes. I want to help teach Mortimer to walk a tightrope. I want to invent a secret code that only we know.

Suddenly my arms feel tingly and cold. I'm breathing hard and the chalk falls out of my hand. Someone is *watching* me. I freeze, imagining a hairy man in a trench coat with his giant drooling dog. I turn around.

"Jenny!" I yell when I see her. She's standing under a pine tree across the street, watching me, arms folded. "Come here."

She shakes her head.

I wave a piece of chalk. "Wanna play tic-tac-toe?"

Jenny sighs and comes over. She squints at my drawings on the sidewalk.

"That's not very good," she says, pointing. My skin prickles again. "Is that supposed to be a bird or a monster?"

I don't know if I should stand up for my lumpy scrub jay or just make excuses. *My chalk is too dusty. The sidewalk is too rough.* Jenny tightens her mouth and hands me something. It feels like dirty string. It's the friendship bracelet.

"Can you guard the door?" I ask Mom in the department store changing room. It's just a curtain and curtains don't have locks. The stack of clothes in my arms is getting heavy. I hope Mom will decide quickly which skirts and shirts she wants for me so we can go get frozen yogurt.

"No one's going to come in." Mom nudges me inside.

"I know, but just in case." In the changing room stall, I give my reflection a mean stare. Caterpillar Christa says some stores have a secret room behind the mirrors where people watch for shoplifters. Only a pervert would want a job like that. A pervert is someone who likes gross things like watching people take off their clothes or kiss. Sometimes kidnappers are also perverts. I change quickly and pull back the curtain.

"Cute shirt!" Mom puts her book down and tugs at the jeans. "Do these feel too tight?"

I shrug. Mom says she'll get the next size up. I study myself in the mirror. I see a bored girl with skinny arms. I should be home reading or cardboarding down the hill. Mom likes the shirt and says she's getting it for me. She has me try on so many clothes that my hair goes frizzy. Eventually I'm too tired to care about the Mirror People. But it's not over yet, and the tricky buttons and scratchy price tags keep pouring into the stall. I put on a baby-blue dress with white stirrup leggings, which Mom says look like something Jenny would wear. I scrunch up my nose.

"What's the matter?" Mom asks. "You guys having a fight or something?"

Once, when Jenny and I were five, we sat on her deck, swinging our legs over the edge. She pushed me—not being mean, just playing—but I fell and hurt my arm. I cried and she yelled and that was our first fight. Natasha has called me Vine Girl since before she became a teenager with her crimping iron and mysterious chocolate milk. The nickname's not mean, so it's okay. One time Natasha painted whiskers on our cheeks and Jenny and I pretended we were sister kittens. In some ways I believed we were. I never imagined it could be over so suddenly. Just the other day Jenny was practically begging me to come see Mortimer's hoop trick. I wish it was just a fight. I would even give up make-believe if it meant I could have her back.

I shake my head. "We're not friends anymore."

I've nibbled off the toppings and a cold, sticky drip slides down my fingers. Mom and I finally finished our shopping trip and this is my reward for being good. Strawberry and mocha frozen yogurt mixed together sounded like a good idea at the time. I don't lick off the drip and Mom hands me a paper napkin.

"You don't understand," I say. "We're really not friends anymore."

"Well, how's this time different?" Mom asks.

Maybe I should have gotten strawberry and vanilla or mocha and vanilla. Vanilla goes with everything, but it's also the World's Most Boring Flavor. Blueberry Surprise could be tasty, unless the surprise is tuna fish. Mocha is like coffee, and grown-ups don't put strawberries in their coffee, so I probably should have known better. Mom says it's healthier, but the problem with frozen yogurt is that it's just not ice cream. After all that shopping I deserve a triple scoop ice cream sundae.

"Jenny won't even talk to me," I say. Mom listens, working her spoon around her low-fat chocolate. I don't mention the friendship bracelet. There are mirror splinters in my heart like in *The Snow Queen*. Mom wouldn't understand.

Mom's face lights up. "Why don't you have a Movie Party?"

"What's that?"

"You can invite a bunch of girls from school over to watch a video."

"On the Beast?" I ask.

"Exactly." She starts writing on a napkin. "An old classic film would be fun. Maybe *The Little Rascals*. We can get that fancy popcorn from Strawberry Shopping Center. Remember their green apple flavor? We can send each girl home with her own little bag tied with a ribbon. And we can order pizzas."

"If I made movie tickets maybe you could hole-punch them at the door."

"Sure, honey, like an usher."

"Wait, isn't that for funerals?"

"They have them at movie theatres too."

Creepy. "Can we make ice cream sundaes?"

"Sprinkles and whipped cream." She smiles. "Ooh, I saw these vintage parfait glasses in an antique store at the Hub."

I imagine a crowd of girls laughing and throwing popcorn in front of our incredible big new TV.

"This is gross," I say after a minute. "Want to trade?"

"Don't like what you picked?"

I shake my head.

"Well, I don't want it," Mom says. I look up at the counter. "You want me to just buy you another one, huh? If Grandma were here she'd talk about starving children in Ethiopia."

"They wouldn't want strawberry and mocha either," I say. "Plus it'd be all melted."

Mom smiles, her eyes squinting, and gets out her wallet. "Okay, baby, just this once."

Invited

I settle into my beanbag and push my new loose tooth back and forth with my finger. Sometimes I imagine my beanbag is full of ideas. I sit here, thoughts soaking through my skin and up to my brain. I can think of a few girls to invite, but there's only one person I really want at my party. I passed all the Friendship Tests with Jenny years ago and I might not be able to with anyone else. You might *think* you're friends, but if you can't pass the tests then you're not. Here's how you can tell:

1) The Like Test—friends like each other. (This one's easy.)

2) The House Test—real friends invite you over to their house. If you only play together at school, then you're probably not really real friends.

3) The Sleepover Test—once you're really good friends you get to stay over at each other's house. This involves pillow fights and ice cream.

4) The Do Test—friends do things together like play dress-up and make-believe. Even if you don't want to do something, if you're a real friend then you will anyway. I don't really like after-school specials, but when Jenny and her sister Natasha wanted to watch them I'd go along with it. We'd eat Cracker Jacks and Jenny would give me her peanuts.

5) The Don't Do Test—if your friend tells you not to do something, you shouldn't do it. Like, if your friend says

make-believing is babyish, then you should stop. Maybe I'm not a very good friend …

I wonder if it's possible for my beanbag to run out of ideas. When Brice puts an almost empty carton of milk back in the fridge, I accidentally pour the last three drops over my cereal. If my beanbag ever runs dry, maybe I'll have to move far away to get more ideas. Ms. Kelley says this is called *inspiration* and we can get it from books and music and art and going new places. Looking at the pull-down world map in my classroom, I wondered if you get better ideas the further you go. Now, I wiggle like a bird in a nest, like a scrub jay.

Earlier today, I dragged my shoes across the sidewalk, smearing chalk. Get lost, scrub jay. Go away, cactuses and flying horses. When you make a mistake on paper, you can crumple it up and throw it away. When you draw on the ground, it's there for everyone to see until the chalk finally rubs away or it rains. (Except there's a drought so it hardly ever rains.) When artists paint a mural it has to be perfect because it will be on the wall forever. Ms. Kelley gave me a "++" for Art on my last report card. Mom is always home and hears my Fun News first, Dad second. She got me a new set of colored pencils and special drawing paper, to encourage me, she said. I want to be Artist Ivy, one day selling my paintings for millions of dollars. My accessories would be a beret and a round palette with a hole for my thumb. Except, after what Jenny said about my chalk bird, I'm not so sure.

I settle deeper into my beanbag and picture myself traveling in time and space. It's twenty years in the future, from today, a Sunday. I imagine myself appearing in the apartment with tropical plants and jars of paintbrushes lining the windowsill. I run my hand over the brushes, which feel soft like the ends of my braids. I smell incense burning. I poke through a box of toothpaste tubes with strange flavors like cadmium yellow, burnt umber, and cobalt blue. At home, ours is just minty. I decide not to taste them.

On the easel is the painting of the Calm Man's face. He has big drooping ears, peaceful eyes, and a pointed head. He's surrounded by roses and a kind of fruit I don't recognize. The paint is thick like frosting. The floor underneath is protected by newspapers with a mix of English and a funny writing I don't know how to read. Yet. Maybe I will when I'm older. Hanging from a nail on the wall is a flattened black rubber Cheerio on a loop of string. *Is it a necklace?*

I think outside there must be flying cars and chore robots taking out the trash. I open a window and look at the busy street below. The air is hot and wet. There are people on motorbikes and women selling fruit. Everyone is Asian. I feel something warm brush against my leg. Startled, I look down and see the big orange cat. I crouch to pet him. His nametag says "Marmalade." I shiver.

I hear loud scraping and look up. The grown-up me is back, with her boobs and chin-length hair. She stands at the easel, moving her hand over the canvas. I step a little closer to get a better look. She's scratching the thick paint off the Calm Man painting with a special knife. She's undoing all her hard work. Maybe someone told her the ears were too big. She stops scraping suddenly and turns around. She looks straight at me.

Suddenly I'm back home in my beanbag, breathing hard and shivering. Could she see me? I know it's not real, but I still don't like the idea of her seeing me. I pull my afghan off my bed and grab my notebook. I settle back in my beanbag and try to make myself breathe slower. No more make-believing, period. I wrap myself in the blanket and try to think about my Movie Party. I turn to a blank page, forcing myself to think of people to invite.

At the top of everyone's lists are Caterpillar Christa the Foursquare Queen who likes Ladybug Melanie and Ladybug Melanie who likes lavender and Jesus. I add them to my list. I remember Sad Cricket Sara whose parents don't love each other anymore. I think of other third-grade girls, like chubby Nicole who would be a roly-poly bug, Math Genius Julie Centipede, and then there's Erin. Funny, loud Erin who people say isn't afraid of anything. Maybe she would be a spider. When I wiggle my tooth, it hurts a good hurt. There are five girls on my list, which means I'm allowed to invite one more, but I can only think of Jenny.

Family Meeting

Our backyard swirls green and brown around me. There is nothing but the pull on my body. I close my eyes, feeling like I'm falling. The spinning ends and I stay on the tire swing for several moments of tingling calm. Footprints erased by waves. The sweet empty feeling of waking up and not knowing exactly where or even who I am.

Then the worry returns, dry in my throat. Maybe I'm in trouble. Maybe Brice and I haven't done our chores or homework. Staying good is like trying to stay full. It's just a matter of time before you get hungry again. We're having a Family Meeting this evening, which is why my hands are sweaty like before I read out loud.

When it's something good, they call it a Surprise or Fun News. Sometimes we try to guess and sometimes they just tell us. Last time it was the Beast, and we've got our Hawaii vacation to look forward to over Easter. Surprises can be small things like a banana chocolate chip muffin from Muffin Mania, or Puffy Paint for decorating my shoes. Fun News is my Movie Party on Saturday. The invitations said, "Biggest TV Ever!" I'm afraid the girls might complain that the videos are babyish or boring. Still, I'm excited to have them all over for the first time.

But when it's Bad News we have a Family Meeting. I twist the ropes, raising the tire swing high off the ground. Then I leap on, the world blurring again. I squeal. There is nothing but spinning and my own high-pitched yell. The swing winds itself up and spins the other way. Then the tire

71

slows to a stop and my heart finds its old rhythm. I can't think what the meeting's about, but my hands are wet so it can't be good. I twist the swing again, because if you have to wait for something bad, you might as well be dizzy.

"No, it wasn't my fault," Dad tells me and Brice. His big hands lie still on the kitchen table like sleeping animals. "Nothing personal. These are difficult times. A lot of families are going through the same thing."

"It was a shock for me too." Mom smoothes her hair. Her face is softly powdered with make-up but her eyes are red. There are two lines of worry between her eyebrows. "We were doing so well … "

"But we'll get through this," Dad says. "We're a team, right, kids?"

We are both silent.

"They were such fools to let you go." Mom touches Dad's arm. He looks away.

Finally Brice asks, "So now what?" I wonder if we will move into a smelly apartment in the City, walls crawling with bugs, rats nibbling our toes … until we *have no toes.* Mom and Dad look at each other. Dad says we have to cut back and spend less. This means no more shopping trips, Air Jordans or new toys, little stone bridges, art supplies or going out for dinner. Mom says hopefully it won't last long, and Dad says if we're lucky he'll get a new job really soon and everything will go back to normal.

"But just in case you don't, we've got to stop having fun."

"Brice, that's really not helpful," Dad says. "I didn't say no more fun, we've just got to tighten our belts." I think of the Day-Glo belt Mom bought me the other day and buckling it too small so it's hard to breathe.

"Dad *will* get a new job," Mom says. "A better position with a better firm."

I look out the window at the backyard. Is it better to be outside before the meeting, nervous and dizzy, anxious to learn the news? Or inside, knowing and scared? I picture myself stepping away from the table, walking backwards out the front door until I am on the tire swing again, rewinding time like twisted rope. I am spinning and have no idea what they will tell us. The air blows around me. I am surrounded by a cool fog of not knowing. Maybe this time, when I come inside, the news will be different. Maybe they will just be angry because they discovered I watched TV and ate cookies when I was grounded. I will cry, apologizing for being a greedy, sneaky girl. *Please.* I look at my family's worried faces, trying to convince myself that Dad still has his job and we're here because I'm in trouble. *Ground me again. I'll be good this time.*

"Okay, so we've all got to stop buying stuff." Brice brings me back to reality. "But what about everything we've already got? Do we have to sell our things?"

I picture the empty spaces my beanbag and boombox would leave in my room if they were gone. Dotted white lines marking where they used to be.

"We won't sell anything," Dad says. "But we may have to return a few things."

"Like what?" Brice narrows his eyes.

"Well, the new TV, for example."

"You're kidding!"

"Luckily we're just within the thirty-day return policy," Mom says.

This is not lucky.

Brice says, "No. Way."

"Do you have any idea how much that thing cost?" Dad barks.

"How much?" I ask, wiggling my tooth with my finger.

"Ivy, it's a rhetorical question," Dad says.

"Well, how much is that?" I ask.

"No." Dad smirks. "It means it's a special kind of question that you're not supposed to answer."

That's dumb. Asking a question that you don't want answered is like baking a cake that you don't want anyone to eat.

"Believe me, we feel bad about this too," Mom says. "I know this isn't what you kids wanted to hear. But once things pick up we'll buy another Beast, or whatever you call it."

Dad's hands rub the table like they're trying to burrow inside. He says, "It just doesn't make sense for us to keep it in our current situation."

We are all quiet. I think about the new stone wall and little bridge in the backyard. But I guess you can't return stones once they're all stuck together with cement.

"Ivy, honey," Mom turns to me, "I'm afraid we also need to return the clothes we bought last week." She threw away the receipt but thinks the store will still take them back. All except the denim skirt, which I've already worn. If I'd known, I would have worn them all immediately, like Sad Cricket Sara licks cookies she doesn't want to share.

"Do you want the frozen yogurt back too?" I stick out my tongue and make a gagging sound.

"Ivy, that's disgusting," Mom snaps.

"That's also rhetorical," Dad says, strangely pleased.

After the meeting, I sit in my beanbag, knees pulled under my chin. I watch my walls change from white to blue as it gets dark outside. I am a bird in my nest. I eat worms. I like to fly and sing. I don't buy things. I feel a chill, suddenly remembering my Movie Party. If the girls come over and we don't have the Beast, they'll laugh at me big time. They'll tell other kids at school and everyone will make fun of me forever.

I stand in front of my closet, lightly touching all my new clothes, the stonewashed jeans, pastel shirts, and dresses with puffed sleeves. I pull off the price tags, watching them flutter to the carpet like leaves. Next, I make a cut in the fabric with my scissors until there's a small rip in every one. I am hurting them because I love them. No one will want these clothes now except for me. It's hard to stay good and I am hungry for dinner.

Part II
Make-believe

Steam Rising

At recess the next day, I pass the stone to Caterpillar Christa, her long hair pulled into a tight blonde braid. She hops between the numbered squares as Ladybug Melanie plays with her "†," waiting for her turn. They're both coming to my party on Saturday, so we're friends now. Sort of almost friends at least, but it still makes me feel special. I'm glad hopscotch doesn't have any songs like jump rope or those mysterious clapping games. The playground is full of songs all the other girls know.

"I heard you're having a party," someone says. The voice makes me flush. I turn around. She's wearing white leggings and a light blue sweater. Her hair is crimped.

"Hi, Jenny," I say.

"I heard it's a Movie Party."

"That's right, we're going to watch movies." It's not exactly a secret, but still I wish she didn't know.

"On your big new TV?"

I swallow. "That's right."

"So how come I wasn't invited?"

Christa and Melanie play in slow motion and I can tell they're listening. Did I hurt Jenny's feelings? I wiggle my tooth with my tongue. It's just hanging by a thread now. Is Jenny jealous that Roly-Poly Nicole and Spider Erin from her class will be there? Is it possible she wants to come too?

"Well, how come?" Jenny puts a hand on her hip. I think she's testing me. I'm not sure if it's still part of the Friendship Test if you're not friends, and then I realize that's the answer.

"Because we're not friends anymore?"

"That's right. We're not."

Nose in the air, Jenny stomps off like a spoiled movie star. She can make-believe just fine when it's real. Christa hands me the stone. In my imagination, I throw it hard, hitting Jenny in the back of the head. She would cry out and fall bleeding to the ground. Christa and Melanie would cheer and give me high fives. But only in my mind.

That evening, I'm standing on a chair at the stove while Mom gives me ingredients to stir. First onions in the saucepan and now ground beef. I hear the front door and Dad comes into the kitchen, red-faced and wet in his short shorts and running shoes.

"Hey, beautiful," he says, kissing Mom on the cheek.

"Ugh, Neil." She pushes him away. "You're all sweaty."

"And you love it! Hi, Ivy."

"Hi, Dad. Look I'm helping."

"That's great. Hey, I'm going to jump in the shower— dinner ready soon?"

He leaves and I stir quietly for a minute.

"So, what about the TV?" I ask. I watched three hours of cartoons after school, saying goodbye to the characters and the Beast both.

"What about it?" Mom asks.

"My party's this weekend and ... " I nudge my tooth with my tongue and suddenly taste blood. I spit into my palm. "Mom, look!" I hold up the tooth.

"Ooh, smile, honey." I grin and she smiles back. "I think the tooth fairy's coming tonight."

I feel for the right moment like bare feet reaching for the bottom step in the dark.

"So will we still have the Beast for my party?"

Mom drops spaghetti in boiling water, slowly mixing the

yellow lines into a tangle. "I'm really sorry," she says, "but the store needs the TV back by Friday at the latest."

"But what are we going to do without the Beast?" She has me put away the spaghetti jar and I slam the cupboard shut. "Well?" I ask.

"Well … You girls can still have ice cream. It can be a Make-Your-Own-Sundae Party."

"But it said 'Movie Party' on the invitations. Everyone knows." *Even Jenny.*

Mom runs the electric can opener, which chews the labels as it spins the cans. There's something wrong about a machine that hurts the thing it's trying to help. She dumps in the tomatoes.

"I've got it!" I clap my hands. "We can *go* to the movies."

"No," Mom says. "The popcorn alone would be too expensive."

"We can promise not to get popcorn."

"Ivy, I said no." The spaghetti water is smoking but really it's just steam. "Are you and Jenny still having a fight?" she asks. I say nothing. Mom says, "I'll see what I can do." But that's just a nice way of saying no. We fling limp spaghetti on the tiled wall where it sticks like worms. She dumps the pasta into a plastic basket and a steam cloud floats up. "Time for dinner. Go get the boys."

"Wanna play a game?" I ask Brice after dinner.

He shakes his head.

"We could pretend we're a brother and sister, prince and princess who have to pretend to be peasants," I suggest.

"I want to finish my book," he says. I groan. If he's just going to lie around reading, he may as well have stayed sick. It's a waste of being healthy.

I try again. "We can pretend to be royal librarians."

"I don't want to play those games anymore," Brice says.

Dear Tooth Fairy, I write like I always do, asking if I can keep the tooth. There's probably no such thing, but maybe she's real, so I write just in case. And anyway, the dollar under my pillow is real. I imagine fairies using millions of kids' teeth like little bricks to build their cities. I'm not sure why I keep them, except that, tiny and useless as they are, they're still a part of me. I have a little matchbox for my baby teeth, just like I've got a shell collection in a shoebox. I found the shells at Drakes Beach, Stinson, Limantour, and Heart's Desire. But I don't remember anymore which shells came from which beach.

In my beanbag, I close my eyes and breathe. Brice thinks he's too grown-up for make-believe, but maybe he'll change his mind. Maybe we can still pretend together. My tooth fell out today and I am eight-years-old. But one day, I'll have all my grown-up teeth and maybe I won't want to make-believe either.

I picture myself back in the apartment where the air is hot and wet. The painting of the Calm Man has changed. Now his face looks more real and he's sitting off to the side under a tree. In the middle of the painting, a little girl on a tire swing throws her head back, laughing. Candies are painted around the edges like a sugar frame.

I crouch under the little table, quietly calling for Marmalade. I look behind the tropical plants, calling his name louder and clapping my hands. He trots into the room, stretching and yawning. We sit next to each other on the cool floor and I pet his orange fur. He purrs and I start to cry. The Beast is going back to the store on Friday and the girls will laugh at me. Then I'll have no friends at all.

I look up and see the Artist standing in the doorway. She's wearing a shirt that wraps around her body like a burrito. I stay very still and hope she won't see me. But two lines appear between her eyebrows, which reminds me of Mom.

She's looking right at me. My heart beats hard in my chest, but I look right back at her. Then her expression changes and she gasps, looking at me with a softness I can't name.

"What's wrong?" she asks me. I shake my head, drying my eyes. I'm not crying because of the TV, but I'm not sure she'd understand. "How'd you get here?" she asks. I shrug. She gets out paper and markers and sits near me on the cool floor. Dad doesn't have a job, my ex-best friend hates me, and even Brice doesn't want to make-believe anymore. But the Artist can see me, and that makes me feel a little better somehow. Together we fill page after page with cats. She draws Marmalade curled up on the floor with shadows, and I draw him dancing on the rooftops. I'm not alone, even if it's only in my mind. I sign my name to my drawing and the Artist smiles, her eyes going wet.

I open my eyes and am back on my beanbag. I pull the scarves out of my dress-up chest and, flipping on the radio, leap and spin around my room.

What's Your Beef?

Number one rule of the night: don't tell Grandma that Dad lost his job. Mom says it's not really lying because he'll get a new job soon and there's no reason to upset her. The other day, Mom was on the phone with her sister, Aunt Bea, in Chicago. Mom said, "I don't know what they'll do without him. He put so much into that company." Then Mom made her promise not to tell Grandma.

It's Thursday, and we're at Grandma's for Parent Teacher Night. She lives in Greenbrae which is very near by. She used to live on the East Coast, same as Aunt Bea, but now they've both moved away. I don't remember what Grandma's old house looked like, but she says her new place "lacks memories," which is funny, because she's been here most of my life. Grandma's walls have yarn pictures of a sheep and shepherd and another of sunbeams behind clouds that I think is supposed to be God. She says they're to remind us of The-Lord-Our-Savior-Who-Loves-Us-and-Knows-All-Our-Secrets. *Lacks* means doesn't have, so maybe if you stay here too long, you forget things. Maybe that's why she needs reminding.

Grandma's house is full of dark wood furniture with little things Mom calls *doodads* on the coffee tables and shelves. Grandma has salt and pepper shakers that look like chickens, and a collection of antique dolls. But we're not allowed to touch them. It's like going to the Marin County Fair but not being allowed on any of the rides.

"Look, Ivy! There's the merry-go-round," Dad says.

"I wanna ride the horse with the purple flowers," I say.

"Nope, the line's too long. Hey, check it out, it's that spinny ride that you like."

"The Scrambler! Can we go? That line's not too long."

"Oh, sorry, no. Let's just stand here and look."

"But that's boring. It's not fair."

"Ha ha, the fair's not fair. Look, I see a Ferris wheel!"

Before dinner, I go into Grandma's den and stick my tongue out at the TV. Our small old set has been showing a lot of *Jeopardy!* lately and has glass birds on a doily on its head. (We're not allowed to touch those doodads either, even though I wouldn't want to.) Tomorrow, when they return the Beast and we get our old TV back, Grandma can keep the lacy stuff.

"Your parents were very nice to give me their old set," Grandma says when she pops in to check on me. I nod. "Of course, it's not impressive like your new set, not that I'm complaining. How do you like your new television?"

I tug at my sweater, wondering what Mom and Dad will tell Grandma when we return the Beast.

"It's good," I say.

"It's an excellent television!" Grandma agrees. "And how useful that it has a remote control device. Your parents know it's a little hard for me to get up sometimes to change the channel."

"Why?"

"I'm not as limber as I used to be." Limber is another word for wood, which is confusing.

"Oh," I say, imagining young Grandma dressed up as a tree with glass birds perched on her arms.

"Now, I don't want you think I'm ungrateful. I'm just saying it would be nice to change the channel without getting out of my armchair."

I don't know why she's telling me all this and talking about the Beast makes me uncomfortable, so I smile and walk away.

"Doesn't your mother make veal parmesan?" Grandma asks a little while later when Brice and I are sitting at her kitchen table.

I almost shout, *Dad lost his job!* but instead say, "No."

"Funny, she always loved veal when she was a girl."

"I don't want any," Brice says.

"Are you feeling alright?" Grandma asks. "Does your stomach hurt?"

Right now, Dad is probably squeezed behind my desk while Ms. Kelley tells the parents about the food groups, fractions, and Sir Francis Drake. Mom is in Brice's classroom, but I don't know what he's learning because he doesn't talk about school anymore.

"I'm fine," Brice says. "I just don't want any veal."

"Come on, taste a little. You'll like it." Grandma lifts the meat toward Brice's plate.

"No." He holds up his hand. "I'll just have the bread and vegetables."

At this stage, I start to suspect there might be something wrong with the meat. Could it be poisoned like Snow White's apple? Mom and Dad will say how peaceful we look as they carry us to the car. Brice and I will sleep for days, and they'll start to wonder what's going on. When they ask Grandma, she'll hum and dust her dolls. Unless a prince kisses me, I might never wake up.

"Go on, Ivy, eat your food." Rule number two: be good.

"Ivy." Brice leans closer. "Do you know what veal is?"

I shake my head.

"It's baby cow."

"Really?" I nibble a soft carrot circle.

"Yup. They make them live in boxes with no natural light"—Brice looks at Grandma—"that are so small they can't even turn around."

Grandma rolls her eyes and cuts into her meat. "That's what makes it so tender."

"It's cruel," Brice says, thickly buttering a roll.

"It's all they've known. Besides, dairy cows need to keep having calves or their milk dries up."

"So? It's not right for them to be killed when they're still babies," Brice says. "I'm not eating any."

"Fine." Grandma shrugs. "Ivy, stop slouching and eat your supper."

I sit up straight. Now I don't want any veal either, but my party's two days away and will be canceled if I'm grounded. Brice helps himself to more potatoes, watching me out of the corner of his eye. It's the Don't Do Test and he's waiting to see if I'm a bad person. In my mind I ask the soul of the baby cow to forgive me. I lower my eyes and take a bite.

In my room the next day, I'm drawing while Brice is at a Family Meeting that I can't go to because it's none of my business. This makes me even *more* curious, but all I can hear is a lot of yelling, which I don't like. Mom said I need to stay out of the family room, too, because I've been watching too much TV and need to give my eyes a rest. I wouldn't want to go in there anyway. Today's the day they had to take the Beast back to the store, and seeing our old set would make me feel even worse. I turn up my boombox, trying to cover the angry sounds coming from the kitchen. Mom, Dad, and Brice all yell and the radio sings.

I pick another crayon out of the box and make the baby cow's eyes large and sad. "Can you hear them shouting?" I whisper to my drawing. "He's in trouble because of you. I didn't want to do it, but he's braver than me."

Outside, I dig a hole in the soft ground near the tire swing. Carefully, I lower my drawing into the earth.

"I'm sorry you had to die," I tell the baby cow. "And I'm so sorry I had to eat you." My drawing looks up at me, seeing sky for the first time. Sometimes I think of myself as a baby animal. Soft around the edges with big eyes. I am part of the pack, a member of the club of small creatures. I have eaten one of my own because I was scared of getting in trouble. I sprinkle rose petals in the hole and cover it all up with dirt. I am a coward.

Movie Party

Everything is ready and I'm in my party dress waiting, waiting like in mini-golf. Only this time I don't have a golf club and I don't think it would help if I did. Mom didn't buy the antique sundae dishes and we're not having pizza or fancy popcorn party favors. They're all too expensive, and Mom said we don't need them to have fun anyway. My handmade sign on the door to the family room says, "The Ivy Cinema." Mom set everything up in there and said I'm still not allowed in yet. I don't know how she's made the stupid old TV special and, like Grandma says, it's too little, too late. That's because the TV is too little and it's too late because the girls are coming soon and they're going to laugh at me.

Arranging bowls of sprinkles and maraschino cherries on the kitchen counter, I suddenly imagine no one showing up. I'd be here all alone with a video and too much ice cream. "It's okay, honey," Mom would say. "*I'll* come to your Movie Party." But it's not okay because I need the other girls or else it's not a party! I picture myself at school on Monday, asking Caterpillar Christa and Lavender Ladybug Melanie where they were. Christa will laugh and say, "Did you really think we'd come to your dumb party? We've got much better things to do." It's just pretend but it still gives me a twist in my stomach.

I'm tying balloons to the mailbox when I look up and see *her* watching me from behind a pine tree. Cat-training, peanut-hating, dumb dirty blonde, terrible-at-make-believing Jenny. Seeing her makes my chest hurt. I'm crossing the street and halfway there before I realize what my feet are doing.

"Hi, Jenny."

"Hello, Ivy." She puts a hand on her hip. Maybe it's not too late. I picture her running to change into a party dress and the two of us decorating a sundae together.

"What're you doing today?" I ask.

"Going shopping in the City. My sister's going to help me pick out some really cool clothes."

"Oh." I look at my patent leather shoes which seem too fancy for standing on dirt. "Well, I guess I'll see you at school."

"I guess."

Finally, the girls start to arrive. Ladybug Melanie is wearing a lavender party dress with a little ruffle along the edge. Sad Cricket Sara's dad drops her off and leaves, but Math Genius Julie Centipede's mom stays a while, chatting with Mom about private middle schools. It feels strange having so many almost-strangers in my house. None of the girls has been here before so I give them the tour, showing off my art supplies and letting them take turns on my beanbag. Sara says she's got two bedrooms now, one at each parent's house. I show everyone the trick to locking the bathroom door and the scratches on the banister from the ghost. Julie Centipede says there's no such thing, and I say it could have been a monster but whatever clawed up the wood must be pretty mean.

"Is that where you've got the biggest TV ever?" Caterpillar Christa asks as we pass "The Ivy Cinema."

I swallow hard. But before I can answer, Spider Erin looks out the window and asks, "Hey, is that your tire swing?"

"Yeah."

"Cool. I've got a trampoline."

"Next customer," Brice says in a deep voice, twirling the ice cream scoop, once we're all in the kitchen. "Step right up to make your own sundae. What'll it be? Vanilla, chocolate toffee, or both?" It turns out he's grounded because of bad grades, not veal. I'm not sure if ice cream duty is part of his punishment or if he's just being nice, and I don't ask.

Caterpillar Christa and Ladybug Melanie decorate matching sundaes, identical right down to the scattered peanuts. Roly-Poly Nicole pours on so much hot fudge that it melts her ice cream and she has to slurp up the sloppy mess with a straw. Julie Centipede presses M&Ms into her whipped cream in neat rows so she gets one in each bite. I dribble caramel with chocolate syrup zigzags, a thick fog of whipped cream with every single topping and two cherries.

"Wow," the Roly-Poly says. "Are you really going to eat all that?"

I look at my incredible edible masterpiece. "Absolutely!"

I look around, remembering that everyone is here because of me. I invited them and they came. The thought gives me a warm feeling in my belly. Spider Erin is making a frozen monster with gummy worm hair, sugar cone horns, and marshmallow teeth.

"That's rad," I tell her.

"Thanks." She brushes her dark hair behind an ear. "I like playing with my food. Yours is really good too. I like the stripes."

In the hall outside "The Ivy Cinema," Mom has everyone line up behind me. She hole-punches our tickets, letting us in one by one. The TV is covered with a velvet curtain that I think I recognize as one of Mom's old dresses. It's hard to tell, but somehow our old TV seems bigger than I remembered it. I bet Mom put extra things under there so it doesn't look so sad and little. Like TV shoulder pads.

We find places on the carpet and couch armrests. Mom stands by the velvet curtain, ready to pull it away. I shut my eyes, and imagine everyone laughing and pointing. "*That's your TV?!*" the girls will howl. They'll laugh so hard they'll fall off the couch.

I nod to Mom and hold my breath like she's about to pull off a Band-Aid. I watch the curtain fall to the ground.

"Oooh … " everyone says. I look up. It's the Beast! I almost knock over my sundae, leaping up to wrap my arms around Mom's waist in a big hug.

"Thank you," I whisper.

Mom rubs my back. "The store just gave us an extension for the weekend," she whispers to me. "We have to bring it back on Monday."

Dad pushes the VCR buttons, and the movie begins. They close the door behind them and we settle, digging into our sundaes. The movie starts with two girls meeting at summer camp. They look completely exactly alike, except one has short hair. But instead of being best friends like you'd expect, they play mean tricks on each other. One girl's cabin gets wrecked with mud and straw. At a dance, the other girl's dress gets cut-up so her undies show.

"Poor thing," Ladybug Melanie says. "So embarrassing!"

Spider Erin says, "This is better than going to the movies."

As punishment, the girls are forced to live together, in a cabin by themselves. On a rainy day over cookies, they discover they have the same mother *and* birthday which makes them twins, separated as babies. I squirm on the couch. Maybe *I* have a secret twin out there too. She could write stories and I'd draw pictures, making books together.

"Ivy, you should do this every Saturday," Caterpillar Christa says, and everyone agrees. Delighted, I think of other videos for future parties. Then I remember that the Beast has to go back to the store on Monday. Mom couldn't let us keep it forever. We're just pretending "The Ivy Cinema" is for keeps. Only I know that days like today can't ever happen again. Chilled hot fudge melts on my tongue. I still have so much sundae left. I don't think I can finish.

Take

"Let's go," I say. "It's boring in here." I'm in the drugstore with Spider Erin the day after my party. She runs her fingers over the display of lip glosses. Her dark hair is swept off her wide forehead. She has scabby knees because she runs fast and sometimes falls. She's in the other third-grade class, same as Jenny. I wonder if Jenny has told her bad things about me. *Don't be friends with her. She actually still does make-believe like a little kid. She'll embarrass you so bad, you'll wish you'd never met her.*

"We can't go without getting *something*." Erin points to the lip glosses. "You get that one and I'll get this one."

I only have the quarters in my shoe. I look at the price. "I don't have enough money."

"Big deal. Me either."

My shirt itches and I need to get out of here. A fat lady examines the mascara, make-up for pretending you've got longer eyelashes.

"So then how … ?" I start to ask Erin, but she shushes me. I want to visit the sailor boy statue or say hello to the parrots at the Red Hill Pet Store (who say hello back). I want to be anywhere except the drugstore make-up aisle. The fat lady moves on. Erin holds up a lip gloss like she's reading the ingredients. Suddenly it's in her pocket, a sort of magic trick. She flashes me a grin. My mouth drops open.

"Your turn," she says, like we're playing hopscotch. My skin is hot and my throat's too dry. My fingertips brush against the Very Berry lip gloss, not taking, just touching.

I need to get away. I want to hide in the dark corner of the shoe repair store where it smells like leather and glue. Only grown-ups need to get their shoes fixed, because we outgrow ours before they have a chance to break. I don't want the stupid lip gloss, but anyone who makes an ice cream sundae monster is worth being friends with.

I wipe my palms on my jeans. Erin tilts her head, watching me with a sly smile. My heart thumps in my chest as my hand closes around the lip gloss. *Mine!* Sweating, I pop it in my pocket.

"I did it!" I punch the air.

"Ivy?" asks a woman right behind me. Erin goes pale.

I blink fast, breathing hard. I've been caught and am going to jail. I think of bunnies and heart-shaped stickers so I won't look guilty. Then I slowly turn around. It's Maxine Ludlow, water balloon boobs jiggling in a fish sweater. Her boys tag along at her side. My eyes dart to her shoulders. They look even.

"I thought that was you," Maxine says. "Aren't you two a little young for make-up?"

"We're just looking," I say.

"Yeah, we're not *buying* anything." Erin nudges me.

"This is bor-ing," Moth Caleb whines. "Can we go look at the toys?" For once I wish I could go with them.

Maxine checks her watch, "Okay, five minutes."

"Come on Tommy, let's look at waterguns!"

"Don't go anywhere else and don't leave the store!" Maxine calls after them. She smiles at me, "Where's your mom?" *In the kitchen yelling at Dad.* When I left they were arguing about bills. I can't wait until our trip to Hawaii at Easter. It's impossible to fight when you're in tropical paradise. Maybe Mom and Dad would be just about to fight and then a parrot would fly overhead. Then they'd notice the sunset and with a loving sigh would hold hands and kiss instead.

"My Mom's at home," I say. "We're on our own."

"Well, aren't you grown-up?" Maxine looks at Erin and tells me, "And how nice you've finally got a new friend."

I blush and Erin takes my hand. "Yeah, well, us new friends gotta go," she says. "See ya!" We skip to the exit and, once we're outside, start running. We streak along the sidewalk, prancing to dodge shoppers. When we reach the sailor boy we collapse, panting on the bench. We are outlaws, criminals, bad girls together.

"Look what I've got," Erin sings. Pouting, she dabs the shiny goo on her lips. She looks very mature. I am not sure if I can do it without a mirror, but I do my best because she's watching.

"How do I look?"

Erin studies me, then says, "You look mahvelous, dahling."

Grinning, I sit up a little taller. I have passed the Like Test.

Bad Kids

The next morning, the wall of newspaper at the kitchen table makes little grunting noises. The paper droops and Dad's large hand appears, feeling for his cup of coffee. Mom is cutting coupons to save twenty-five cents off this and fifty cents off that. I reach for the sugar and knock over my juice.

"Jesus Christ, Ivy!" Mom jumps up, scooping her coupons out of the way. The orange tide spreads to the edge of the table and spills on to the floor. She's sopping it up with a sponge before Dad peeks around the paper. His pastel shirt is unbuttoned at the collar and the stubble on his square jaw has become an interesting texture. He lowers the newspaper to circle something.

"Be more careful, Ivy," he says.

"Sorry," I squeak. "Can I have the sugar?"

I'm trying to eat my bowl of Tastios which *look* like Cheerios but are cheaper and taste like potatoes. Mom tells me to bring down my new clothes when I've finished my breakfast. She and Dad are going to the Mall to return them along with the Beast. Brice, who's still grounded for bad grades, exhales loudly. My spoon captures one "O" at a time. I let out my own big sigh. I wish they could just keep getting extensions forever so we would never have to return the Beast.

"Sweetie," Mom says to the newspaper, "I'd love a hand cleaning the house today when we get back. Maybe you can vacuum the stairs and I'll mop the kitchen floor. And it'd be great if you have time to fix the sink." We're not supposed to talk to Dad while he's job-hunting. "Neil?"

"Hmm?" says the paper.

"Downstairs bathroom? It's still leaking."

"Come on, Karen. It's not that bad."

"It's wasting water."

"I'll get to it when I get to it."

"Okay, and when will that be?"

"I don't know. Soon."

"You want me to just call a plumber?"

"I said I've got it."

At school, we learn about building materials and the seven times table. Bricks are strong but not good in earthquakes. Palm leaves make good roofs in hot countries but in cold places would let in the snow. Seven times one is seven. Seven times two is fourteen. Mud houses wouldn't work in rainy parts of the world. Seven times three is twenty-one. Dad was an architect back when he had a job, so I think he'd like this lesson. Good is only good if you live in the right place. Math stays the same no matter where you are. Even on some other planet where the aliens live in houses made out of edible, glow-in-the-dark plastic, seven times seven would still be forty-nine.

Next, we write our own version of *The Three Little Pigs*. In my story, the second pig makes an igloo that the wolf melts with his terrible hot breath. I draw a row of squares like a comic strip: Pig in igloo, Wolf melting igloo, and finally a surprised pig in a puddle. Ms. Kelley holds it up so the whole class can see, for *inspiration*. Sad Cricket Sara says I'm a good draw-er and we play ponies together at recess.

I race home as soon as school lets out. Maybe the store decided they didn't want the Beast back after all. I imagine Mom saying, *"Well we tried to return it, but it looks like we'll just have to keep it after all.*" I picture Brice giving me a high five and Mom and Dad ungrounding him for the night so we can all watch a video to celebrate. Instead, I push open the family room door and gasp. The Beast is gone and I choke seeing the hideous thing it its place. I pull the knob and the little TV crackles to life, showing a dark shadow world. I frantically turn the dials but it's the same on every channel. All the color is gone.

"This sucks!" Brice says at the Family Meeting. "We've gone from having the best TV to the worst." I cross my arms in agreement. At this rate, we'll have to move into a straw hut and fetch water from a well. "Plus you're getting rid of our cable?!"

"Look, I know you kids are upset," Dad says. "We get that. But this is just the way it is for now. We need you both to be mature about this. We're a team, right?"

Brice says, "I figured we'd at least get our old one back." I nod. If we are a team, I think we might be on the losing side. Maybe Brice and I should try to join some other team.

"We gave that TV to Grandma," Mom says. "It's not appropriate to ask for a gift back."

"This is ridiculous," Brice says. I agree, but think he's making a pretty big fuss for someone who's so grounded he can't even watch PBS.

"Grandma needs it more than we do," Mom says. "Her eyesight's not so good anymore, and she doesn't have many friends around here."

"Yeah, no kidding," Brice mumbles. "Who'd want to be friends with a baby-animal-killer?"

My mouth drops open. I look at Brice then Mom and Dad. I think I catch something like a smile flicker across Dad's face, but Mom is stunned, and when I look back, he's dead serious.

"Are we still moaning about that damned veal parmesan?"

he asks. "Show some respect. That's your grandmother you're talking about."

"What can you do? I'm already grounded."

"We can make things a lot worse for you if we want," Dad says. "So don't push it." Everyone is silent. "I'm tired of being the bad guy around here." Dad holds out his big hands. "I'm doing the best I can. Let's have a little support and cooperation."

"Ivy," Mom says finally, "we tried to bring the clothes back to the store today, but they wouldn't take them. Why do you think that is?"

I shrug. I don't know how she can think about clothes at a time like this.

"Take a wild guess."

"Maybe the store got swallowed up in an earthquake."

Dad smirks and Mom rolls her eyes. "They wouldn't take them back," Mom says, "because *someone* had cut off all the price tags and made holes in the fabric."

Brice snorts. I look at my lap. She has me. I don't know how to make her believe I'm innocent, so I say nothing so I don't make it worse.

"Look, I know you wanted to keep those clothes. But with Dad laid off, we could have used that money. You're grounded for the next two weeks." I groan. Mom holds up her finger. "During that time I'm keeping the clothes." I groan again. I didn't even ask for new clothes, and trying them on took forever with sicko perverts probably staring at me the whole time. "Once you're not grounded, you can earn the clothes back one by one."

"How?"

"By proving to me and Dad that you're helping our family instead of causing more problems."

They let me keep the Beast for my party and now I've made them mad. My eyes sting. I hurt my family. I'm grounded same as Brice, and they don't even know I'm a thief.

Then I have an awful thought. What if they decide we can't afford to go to Hawaii? I'm pretty sure it's expensive because you have to fly there and airplane tickets cost hundreds of dollars. They promised we'd go, but that was way back before Dad lost his job. Also, they gave us the Beast and cable and my clothes and then they changed their mind, so maybe promises don't count anymore.

Laundry

I toss a pair of underpants on to the whites pile, and Brice throws a sock on the darks. We're on the floor at the bottom of the stairs, sorting dirty clothes. Since we can't watch TV or play with friends, we have a lot of free time, which Mom and Dad are filling with extra chores. Recycling is one of my regular chores but laundry isn't. When I was grounded before, I could pretty much do what I wanted as long as I didn't get caught. This time, Mom and Dad are both home and watching.

"What'll happen when Grandma finds out that Mom and Dad are actually watching her old TV?" I ask Brice. "Weren't they going to donate it or something?" It seems embarrassing somehow, like when you ask Roly-Poly Nicole to throw away a piece of trash for you and then you turn around and find her chewing on it.

I toss one of Mom's blouses on the lights pile. Brice picks it up, scans the label, and throws it on to a different heap. "Hand wash only," he explains. "Yeah, I think that's what they told her."

"Maybe they'll say someone broke into our house and stole the Beast."

"The Beast was practically too big to steal," Brice laughs. "I dunno, they'll probably make something up about us watching too much TV."

"Well, that's not a problem anymore."

"Yeah, we're fucking grounded."

I gasp, then cover my mouth to hide my surprise. I've

never heard my brother say the F-word before.

"Hey, check it out." I shake a striped sock, trying to change the subject. "I found a worm in the laundry."

Brice shakes his head and throws a pair of jeans on the darks. I throw the sock after it. We sort in silence.

Finally I ask, "Would it even matter if Grandma knew Dad lost his job?"

"Yeah, she'd freak out." So maybe parents never stop worrying, even when their kids are all grown-up with kids of their own. If you move far, far away, they can't bug you with their worry. Brice continues, "Remember that time at the Sleepy Hollow Pool when Grandma thought I was drowning?"

I smile, picturing how she threw her arms in the air, jumping and yelling at the lifeguard. I've never seen her move so fast.

"But Dad *will* find a new job, won't he?"

"Eventually," Brice says. I make a face. "I mean, of course, definitely. But until then it's better if Grandma thinks nothing's changed."

We told her when Brice had appendicitis, and she worried big-time, visiting him at the hospital with Mom when Dad was at work. If we had just waited, Brice still would have gotten better and we could have saved her all that worry.

"Will they tell her the truth once he gets a new job?"

"I guess they'll just say he's working for a different company then. She never has to know."

I wonder why some things are secrets and some aren't. I pull a pair of leggings from the mound. Dad's khakis and polo shirts join the lights.

"Brice, are we going to be poor?" I wonder if he knows anything about our Hawaii trip. I decide that if we're not going after all, I don't want to know right now. It would make me too sad, and having to do the laundry is bad enough. Plus I'm afraid I might jinx it if I ask. It's important that we go so Mom and Dad can be happy and stop arguing. I imagine me and Spider Erin stealing lots of lip glosses and other small things to sell at school. Stealing is wrong, but if I used the money to help my family, it might be worth it. I picture us slinking across the playground in trench coats stuffed with goodies. *"Psst,"* I'd whisper to a group of girls, *"wanna buy a jelly bracelet?"*

If we got caught, we'd have to go to jail. Mom and Dad would be too upset and disappointed to go to Hawaii, even if I'd made enough money for the plane tickets. The jailers would lock me and Erin up in different cells so we couldn't laugh and tell each other jokes. I'd be so lonely with nothing to do except paint my fingernails with stolen nail polish. I'd slowly pick off all the pink and then paint them again. I'd do this forever for the rest of my life. And if I didn't die in jail, by the time they'd let me out, I'd have white hair and everyone older than me would be dead, even Brice. Moth Caleb Ludlow and his Stink Beetle brother Tommy would still be alive, but I wouldn't be their friend even then.

"Nah, we're not going to be poor," Brice says. "Don't worry, Mom and Dad have some money saved up. They're just being real careful. Besides, I can always get a paper route or something if I have to."

"Maybe I could sell my drawings."

He smiles. "Hopefully you won't need to do that."

Betrayal

"So I guess you got busted for the lip gloss," Spider Erin says at lunch. Her dark hair is half up. She's eating a ham and cheese sandwich. I've got honey chicken with mustard and tomato. It's March now, and we're at a picnic table near the bamboo at the playground's edge. She swaps a few potato chips for some of my grapes. We both think we're getting the better deal, which makes it a good trade.

"Nope," I say. "They don't know."

"But you *are* grounded, aren't you?" Erin asks. "Your mom said you weren't allowed to talk on the phone."

"She didn't tell me you called."

"What's the difference, if you can't talk?"

"I guess."

"So how come you're grounded?"

"It's stupid," I say. "My mom bought me a whole bunch of new clothes and then wanted to return them all. So I cut off the price tags and … stuff so she couldn't."

"That's not fair!"

"I know!"

"Why'd your mom change her mind?"

I eat another of Erin's potato chips. Grandma's not supposed to know about Dad's job, but Aunt Bea does. On the phone the other day, Aunt Bea wanted to know if I have a crush on any boys and if Brice likes anyone. I told her, "No," and "I dunno." Then I told her about igloos and palm leaf roofs. She said in Chicago there are lots of brick buildings. Aunt Bea didn't mention Dad losing his job, even though I *know* she knows. So maybe I shouldn't tell Erin either. It might be easier if I never talk about it, because it's too much work keeping a secret only from some people.

I twirl my finger by my ear and whisper, "My mom's kind of crazy."

"She sure sounds like a weirdo," Erin agrees. I feel a lump of guilt at the back of my throat that I try to wash away with milk. She asks when I'll be ungrounded, and I tell her next Tuesday.

"Whew!" Erin says. "How long would it be if they knew about the lip gloss?"

I lick the salt off my fingers and shake my head.

Erin eats her sandwich, and I think about the Artist in her grown-up apartment where the air is hot and wet. I wonder what the Artist worries about and if she ever thinks about me here. Can she imagine herself here, the way I can pretend myself there?

After a minute, I ask Erin, "Do you ever imagine being all grown up?"

A slow smile comes over her face, "Sure, I'm going to live in San Francisco. I'll have a house with all my friends and we'll stay up late every night. You can live there too if you want."

"Really?"

"Yeah, it's going to be a great big Victorian house with lots of rooms and fancy trim on the outside. Also, you know those ball pits like they have at Chuck E. Cheese's?"

"With the plastic balls you dive into?"

"Uh-huh. I'm going to have a room like that in my house."

"Whoa," I say.

"Yeah, it's going to be super-fun." After a minute she says, "But first you should come over and play on my trampoline."

I swing my feet under the picnic table. I have passed the House Test.

Recycling

Recycling is my biggest chore, but it helps save Mother Earth. Making my bed doesn't help save anything. The sour smells stick to my fingers as I pull old bottles and cans from under the kitchen sink, sorting them into bags. My sneakers flatten beer cans like Moth Caleb Ludlow crushes sandcastles. Tomato sauce cans, made of stronger stuff, go in a separate bag. Things come into our house full and leave empty. We come home empty and leave full.

Every once in a while, we take the bags to the San Rafael Recycling Center. It's a loud place with machines and conveyor belts. They squash cans into a massive cube. I think the cans in the middle must feel very safe. I would like to be melted down into something new. Transformed into a shiny new Ivy who would giggle and play tetherball with the other girls, rope wrapping tightly around the pole. She wouldn't make blueprints or cut holes in her clothes or steal lip gloss. Everyone would like her no matter what and for always.

Brice comes into the kitchen, pulling me out of my daydream. He cuts up the six-pack rings, telling me that birds get stuck in them.

My hands continue their work while my mind travels to another place and time. Suddenly I have imagined myself back in the apartment in that faraway place. The painting of the Calm Man and the little girl on a tire swing is up on the wall. Next to it are the drawings of Marmalade that the Artist and I did last time. It makes me happy that she kept them.

I hear laughing and shouting in another language coming

from outside. I stick my head out the window and smell spices and coconut. I see women driving motorbikes, wearing long gloves like Miss Piggy. People buy snacks wrapped in newspaper from a cart. A circle of boys watch men squatting on the ground playing a game. I close the window and study the painting on the easel. It has a red shape in the middle, circled by blue patches. I squint, but it's too soon to tell what it's supposed to be. Quietly, then a little louder, I call for Marmalade.

"Ivy?" The Artist is wearing a flowing white top that reminds me of seagulls, but her voice is kind.

I nod.

"Oh, my God, this is incredible!" She grins at me, excited. We just stare at each other for a minute then she asks, "Did you see your drawings up there?"

I nod again. She gets out paper and colored pencils. "Okay, let's try something else this time," she says. She goes into the other room and comes back carrying a pineapple and a whole bunch of fruits I don't recognize. We sit on the cool floor, and she arranges the fruits between us. She hands me a stack of papers. "Now, I want you to only draw what you see."

I look at her, confused.

"Normally," she continues, "you draw from your imagination. And that's great. But right now, I want you to really look at this fruit, study it, and just draw exactly what's in front of you."

I watch her watching the fruit, making careful lines on her paper as her eyes move along the surface of a round purple or an orange oval fruit. Once I think I understand, I try to do it too, drawing in this slow, careful way. It's hard work, and it feels different in my head, but when I'm done, she takes my drawing and holds it up in front of me.

"Ivy, you are amazing," the Artist tells me. I open my mouth to speak, but then Brice opens the fridge, bringing me back to the present.

My brother pours himself a glass of orange juice. I smile and shake my head.

"You spacing out there?" Brice asks.

"Just thinking."

"That's cool. Thinking's good. I know doing the recycling's not much fun. But it looks like you're almost done." He leaves and I'm on my own again.

The Artist said I'm "amazing." I hope she's right. I think about the shiny new Ivy who giggles and plays tetherball. Suddenly she seems kind of boring.

I get back to work, stuffing newspapers into a bag. The old news rubs off on me, inking my hands. I look over the Sunday comics again. Garfield eats a pizza and Lucy is mean to Linus. In *Prince Valiant*, they stand on a hill waiting for battle. It's not funny, but maybe it's not supposed to be.

The classifieds section looks like a complicated game of tic-tac-toe, with some jobs circled and others crossed out. Classifieds are advertisements for jobs, but classified also means Top Secret. This is because grown-ups don't want anyone to know if they're not working. I don't see a single ad for chocolate-taster, flower-arranger, artist, or zookeeper. Where are all the good jobs? Then I see something.

Now hiring: Buyer for chic clothing boutique. Must have solid industry knowledge and an intuitive sense of what will sell. Impeccable dress sense a must.

I don't know a lot of the words, but it has to do with clothes and dresses, so I reach for the scissors.

Sloucher

"Why do I have to?" Brice asks over brunch at the dining room table. We're having blueberry pancakes and fruit salad. Brice is old enough to use a real knife, so he helped cut up the pears. I set the table with knives that are only sharp enough to slice through butter.

"It's excellent exercise, isn't it, Neil?" Grandma asks. I shut my eyes, praying she won't go into the family room and see her own TV.

Dad nods. "Sure, and all that running is great for the heart. More coffee, Helen?" He refills Grandma's mug.

"Easy on the syrup, Ivy," Mom says. "That stuff's not ch–' Dad stops her with his raised eyebrows.

"I get plenty of exercise already." Brice sips his hot chocolate. "They make us play sports in PE."

"Me too!" I say. "Dodgeball and kickball and tennis baseball."

"What's tennis baseball?" Dad asks.

"Baseball with a tennis racket instead of a bat," Brice explains. "It's easier to hit the ball."

Grandma laughs. "Sounds like cheating to me."

"That's just how the game works," Brice says.

"Soccer's an excellent team sport," Grandma tells Brice. "I read an article about how good it is for young people. Great physical fitness and there are even mental benefits. So I signed you up at the Rec Department. Let's hope it teaches you some discipline."

"Just stick me in a veal cage," Brice says under his breath.

"Brice!" Dad says. "Thank you, Helen. That's a really thoughtful gift. I'm sure he'll benefit from it."

"I'm sure he will." Grandma takes a little sip of orange juice. "Getting along with others," she adds. I try to catch Brice's eye, but he is busy cutting his pancake into little pieces. "Ivy, I've organized after-school lessons for you too," Grandma says. I try and touch the floor for luck but my feet don't reach. "Starting next week, you'll have ballet lessons at the Stapleton School every Tuesday."

"Ballet?"

Grandma nods. "It will improve your posture and give you poise. Your mother took ballet when she was a girl, right, Karen?"

"Seven years. Your Aunt Bea, too, for a while, until she switched to tap." Mom gets up from the table to show us different positions. I didn't know Mom was ever a dancer. I wonder what else they can do that they've kept secret. Maybe Dad is a secret cowboy with expert lasso skills. Mom says, "Ivy, you'll look adorable in the pretty costumes. Grandma will take you shopping later today."

I picture myself gracefully leaping across a stage to classical music, the audience applauding after a complicated spin. Maybe I'll turn out to be very talented. I imagine wearing a tutu while emptying the dishwasher, brushing my teeth, and sorting the recycling. Maybe ballet will be the thing that everyone likes about me, something to make me special.

Later that night, the shouting travels through my house, bumping over carpet and closed doors, slipping into my dark room. I pull my afghan close and hide under the covers, but the noise finds me. The sounds creep into my heart and pump through my blood. I am sick with them. I want so badly to sleep. The noises press down, crushing me like stacks of old newspapers. I wish they'd use their Inside Voices.

A car pauses at the stop sign, headlights shining through my shutters. Motor rumbling softly, the stripes of light roll across my wall. Maybe it's here to rescue me. I picture myself climbing into that stranger's quiet car.

"You poor baby, are they yelling again?" the nice lady at the wheel asks. She wears a big feathered hat and the car smells like honeysuckle flowers.

"Yeah," I say, slamming the door.

"Well, make yourself comfy and we'll go for a ride." I rest my head against the window. Street lights flicker through my eyelids and the engine hums me to sleep.

The shouting brings me back to my bed. There's a tight ball of twine in my belly. The yelling makes me ache, tunneling into my chest like a gopher. I get up and straighten my nightgown. Light underlines my brother's door.

"Come in." He's sitting up in bed with a book.

I sit at the end of his bed and sigh, wrapping my arms around myself.

"What're you reading?"

"*Lord of the Rings*. It's fantasy; you wouldn't like it."

"Maybe I would." Fantasy is make-believe, which I like very much.

"Naw, it's got lots of fighting in it."

I can't help but laugh. Brice laughs too, then we're both quiet. Through the floorboards we hear them—Mom's shrill shouts and Dad's muffled boom.

"Brice, I hate this."

"Me too."

"Are they going to get a divorce?"

Brice shuts his book and looks at me. "Nah," he says. "They're just really worried about money."

I nod, thinking about Hawaii.

"Dad's got more interviews coming up," Brice continues, "but it takes time."

"I guess." I slide off his bed. The yelling grows louder, fades, then grows again, like wind blowing down the chimney.

"Here, take these." He hands me two blue pills from under his pillow.

"What are they?" I trust Brice, but we're supposed to Just Say No.

He shows me how to roll them between my fingers. "Earplugs," he says.

I put them in and his mouth moves but no words come out. "What?" I ask.

Brice gives me a thumbs-up.

I switch on my desk light and find the classified ad for the dress job. Like planting a seed, I put the square of newspaper under Mom's pillow. Then I go downstairs. The yelling gets louder as I get closer to the kitchen, but I feel protected with the earplugs. It's like the worst of their anger and fear can't get inside of me. Mom and Dad are standing by the fridge, her hands on her hips, his arms raised in frustration. I feel very small in my nightgown. After a moment they see me and stop shouting.

"Wa-blah blah blah, Ivy?" Mom asks. Her voice is muffled.

"Blah blah-blah, blah-blah blah?" Dad asks.

"Um," I say. My voice is heavy and quiet, vibrating in my chest. "Are we still going to go to Hawaii?"

"No, we're not fucking going to Hawaii!" Mom yells.

My eyes go wide, stinging with tears. I run upstairs, my feet pounding silently on the steps. I hide under the covers, crying a wet patch on my pillow. My muffled cries sound so strange and sad they make me cry harder. After a few minutes, someone comes in and sits on the edge of my bed in the dark.

"Blah blah-blah," Dad says in a soothing voice, lifting the

blankets away from my face and handing me a tissue. "Blah blah blah, blah-blah." Like he's speaking another language or maybe is an alien. He rubs my back. I wanted the flower necklaces and coconuts and tropical fish and besides, they *promised*. But most of all I just want them to stop fighting. Dad gives me a kiss on the forehead and after a while I calm down. I fall asleep, dreaming of rain and twisting vines, reaching for the sky.

Part III

Nature

Hawaii Substitute

When Mom doesn't have all the ingredients for a recipe, she uses something else instead. Apples and sugar instead of pears and honey. When Ms. Kelley is sick, we have a substitute teacher and Christa and Melanie trade names for the day. Now, instead of swimming with dolphins and wearing flowers, we're going to swim with trout and wear bug spray.

Hearing the news about Hawaii through the earplugs, that night, felt like cold milk thrown in my face. Mom using the F-word at me was scary. Even though she said she was sorry the next day, it still makes me feel bad if I think about it. I was shocked, but I guess it makes sense. If our wonderful TV could just slip out of our living room, what were our chances for Hawaii? That day at Red Hill with Jenny and the tropical fish was probably the closest I'll ever get. Thinking about Hawaii now, I feel like the wrinkled balloons on our mailbox, days after my party. Having and losing is worse than not having. I wish I had a cat, but it'd be worse if I had one and it ran away. We were supposed to have Hawaii but they changed their minds. I know they didn't do it to be mean, but that doesn't keep it from hurting.

Dad loads all the things we've borrowed from the Ludlows into the trunk of the station wagon, rearranging and swearing to make it all fit. Finally we take off, rolling past Jenny's, Alice Miller's with the big roses and the stone wall, and the still-for-sale house at the end of the road. Dad pops a tape into the car stereo and Brice mutters, pulling out his Walkman. My brother stares out the window, body next to me, mind somewhere else. Maybe he's imagining an Easter vacation with some other family. The houses get farther apart and more trees appear. It's the beginning of April, and the rounded hills are green. We drive for a long time until there are no houses, just tall, skinny redwoods.

Finally we arrive and carry our supplies along the path through the forest. Tents grow between the trees like giant mushrooms. I see a couple lighting a camp stove and old people playing cards.

"Let's not be too close to the bathrooms," Mom says.

"Or the fire pits," Dad says. "We need a good buffer zone between our tent and 'Kumbaya.'"

While he and Brice put up the tent, Mom and I make trips back and forth to the car like ants, carrying everything we need into the wilderness.

"We'd better not be missing a tent pole," Dad says. "Jesus Christ, who designed this piece of shit?"

"Neil!" Mom says.

I would like to play Hansel and Gretel, but Brice hurries ahead on the steep trail. I wonder if he noticed the lizard sunning itself on a rock. We hike up up up. My legs are tired, and I can't make-believe they aren't. When my family reaches the top of the hill, we look beyond the forest below to a lake in the distance. This would make the perfect spot for a castle. If I were a princess, I'd fly my pet dragon down to the lake for a bath. Dad takes photos of me and Brice. They want to make a big print for Grandma. I imagine this moment framed on her photo wall, near her yarn picture of baby Jesus. My hair in two braids, I am squinting a little from the sun. Brice is impatient and distracted but smiling because he has been told to. Grandma will keep this photo after we're all grown up and don't look this way anymore. Maybe the picture will embarrass us somehow, the way I feel now seeing my naked baby photos. Maybe I'll be ashamed I was ever this young.

Dad puts a big hand on Brice's shoulder. "Want to come fishing with me later on?"

"That'll be fun for you guys." Mom looks out at the lake.

"Do I have to?" Brice asks. "I kind of want to explore on my own."

"No, that's fine." Dad turns away. "Just don't go too far."

I look at Dad looking at the water. "Can I come?"

That afternoon, I'm at the lake's edge, on a bench with Dad, watching the water quietly rub the muddy shore. Overhead, ducks quack quack quack. Black cormorants rest on a log, wings outstretched. It's all pretty different from the beach.

"Worm, please," Dad says.

I hand him a fat, wiggling earthworm. He throws the line and we wait. He asks about school and I draw him pictures of the Big Bad Wolf and three little pigs in the dirt with a stick. Mostly we just wait.

After a while, Dad asks how ballet's going. Miss Garville doesn't let me wear the tutu that Grandma got me. She said they're just for performances. That means I have to just wear a leotard, which is basically a bathing suit with sleeves. I figured I'd be the star of my class, graceful and dramatic even without my new tutu. But it's hard, and most of the other girls have been taking ballet since they were three. Miss Garville teaches dance steps with tricky names and you've got to keep your legs straight like you're drawn with a ruler. There's a lot to remember. A girl with pointy ears giggles when I get it wrong, which makes me want to trip her. I miss my own kind of dancing with scarves, spinning around my bedroom any way the music pulls me.

I leap along the lake's edge, showing Dad my best *sauté arabesques*. I hope he can't tell they're not perfect.

"Good job," Dad says. "Are you enjoying it?"

I sit back on the bench and shake my head.

"I don't think Brice is taking to soccer either." He sighs. "Maybe Mom and I should have said something."

"Can I stop going?"

"See it through to the end of the school year. You don't have to do another term if you don't want."

I nod. It's not Dad's fault. I wish Grandma had signed me up for art lessons or something else I'm already good at. Grandmas are supposed to bake cookies and take you to the zoo, not force you do things. She should know this.

Dad lets me hold the fishing rod just until I feel a tug. It reminds me of the time I got to sit on his lap, holding the steering wheel as we drove circles through an empty parking lot. Kind of driving, kind of not.

"You know," he says, "I'm sorry we couldn't take you kids to Hawaii like we'd hoped."

It's the first time Hawaii has been mentioned for ages.

"Yeah, it would've been fun."

"Camping will be fun too, you'll see. And we haven't forgotten about Hawaii. We'll go some day."

I nod.

"Hawaii's not going anywhere," Dad jokes.

I look across the water to the tall trees on the other side of the lake. I hear birds talking to each other.

"I wanna go to Hawaii," one bird says.

"Me too!" crows his friend from another tree.

"But it's too far to fly," the first bird says sadly.

"Too far! Too far! Too far!" peep the little birds.

"Oh, well," crows his friend. "Let's just stay here."

I hear the wind rubbing leaves together. There are no cars or roads here because campers like walking. In fact, the bathroom block is the only real building for miles.

"Are there architects in other countries too?" I ask after a while.

"Sure. Everywhere there are buildings, people have to design them."

"Do igloos have blueprints?"

"No, Eskimos just make them out of blocks of ice. There's no HVAC system or anything."

"But how do they know how to build them if there's no blueprint?"

Dad thinks about this for a moment. "I guess the design's in their heads."

"What do you mean?"

"Like when you draw a cat. You know it's got pointy ears and whiskers and a long tail. Even if you're not looking at a real cat, you can see it in your mind's eye."

True. But if I am looking, my drawing will look more real. Like with the tropical fruit. Maybe Dad doesn't know this trick.

"But how does the igloo design get in their heads in the first place?"

"They've perfected it over generations. I guess parents teach their kids how to make igloos so everyone has that knowledge."

"Can you teach me something?"

"I'm teaching you how to fish right now, aren't I?"

There's a pull on the line and I quickly hand over the rod. He takes it, then hands it back.

"It's okay," he says. "You can do it. Reel it in, nice and steady like you've seen me doing. I'm right here."

I grip the fishing pole and turn the crank like a jack-in-the-box. It's heavy, but I hold tight and keep bringing in the fish. I hope it's as big as a shark. I see a flash of green just below the surface. It breaks through the water and I groan.

"You're not a fish!" I tell the limp plant spinning on the line. Dad and I look at each other and laugh.

"Worm, please," Dad says.

Name Your Burger

"Do you want a regular burger or a veggie burger?" Dad pokes the burning charcoal in the campsite grill later that afternoon. There's a soft light pushing between the trees. Time moves slower, I think, when I'm outside. I ask Brice what he's having. He recently told me that every day more rainforest is destroyed to raise cows for hamburgers. I like hamburgers, but I like monkeys and tree frogs better. I wish I knew everything that Brice knows.

"Veggie," he says from the picnic table. Brice told me that when the good dirt washes away, the land becomes a desert and the ranchers go mess up somewhere else.

"Me too," I tell Dad. "Veggie burger." Brice told me about chickens packed into pens, their beaks cut off so they don't peck each other. He said dolphins drown in tuna nets. Now I try to copy what my brother eats, even if it might get me in trouble with Grandma.

"Your mom and I are going to the tent for a nap," Dad says. "Brice, when the coals turn gray, throw the burgers on the grill."

"Which ones?" he asks.

"Regular. They need longer. And don't disturb us, okay? We need some privacy."

Once Dad leaves, I ask Brice if I can help and he passes wooden skewers across the picnic table.

"Stick on whatever vegetables you want," Brice says.

I thread cherry tomatoes and pearl onions, like beads on a necklace. He asks if fishing was boring since we didn't catch anything. "It was fun," I say. "We saw birds and stuff." Zucchini, mushroom, zucchini. "What'd you do?"

"I walked around and met another family."

My eyes squeeze shut like I've been stung. *Another* family? I hope they're not better than us, with parents who never fight and a ballerina daughter who keeps her legs straight. Brice says they're from Oakland.

Brice points toward a tall girl crawling out of a tent with a book under her arm. When she sees my brother, her face lights up. "Hi, Brice!" she says in a mature, deep voice.

"Hey," Brice says. The girl sits next to him, laying her book next to the chopped vegetables. She has curly hair and nice freckles. "Lucy, this is my little sister Ivy."

"Hi, Ivy." She waves.

"What are you reading?" I ask.

"*The Jungle Book.*" She pops a piece of red pepper into her mouth. "It's way better than the Disney movie."

Brice looks at the cover. "Rudyard Kipling. Didn't he write the *Just So Stories*? You know, how the elephant got its trunk and all that?"

"Maybe. Can I help?" Lucy picks up a skewer and spears vegetables at random. "How old are you?" she asks me.

"Eight. What about you?" I think she's tall enough to be a teenager.

"Twelve."

"Same as Brice."

"Exactly," she says. "So you guys are having veggie kebabs for dinner?"

"Yeah," Brice says. "Also burgers and veggie burgers."

"Yum. We're having pasta. Hey, maybe my family can eat with your family. We could, you know, share."

The sun is low in the sky and there's a smelly candle on the picnic table to keep the bugs away. Mom passes the skewers, talking about our hike earlier and the view from the top of the hill. Lucy's parents say we should go on some canyon hike that sounds like it'd make my legs fall off. Maybe I would be allowed to stay behind with Lucy. Twelve is old enough to babysit during the day.

"You can't have made this on a little camping stove," Dad says.

Lucy's mom laughs, tucking her frizzy hair under her bandanna. "It's actually a really simple recipe."

"Well, it tastes great. I can't cook to save my life." Dad digs in the cooler. "Anyone want another beer?"

"So, what do the two of you do?" Lucy's dad asks, cracking open a can. His sweatpants are dusty and he has bushy eyebrows. Grown-ups complain about work, but love asking each other about their jobs. Dad says he's an architect but got laid off. For a while they talk about the Recession and all the good people who don't have jobs. I nibble the grilled vegetables, trying not to stab myself with the skewer.

"How about you, Karen?" Lucy's dad asks.

"I take care of the kids." Mom brushes away an insect. "And yourselves?"

"We're both professors at Cal," Lucy's Mom says. "I teach European history, and Carl teaches molecular biology."

"Wow," Dad says. "What different fields."

"They are," Lucy's mom says. "We find it fascinating having such different perspectives of time and space."

After dinner and before it gets dark, the grown-ups send us off hunting for sticks for the fire. It's like Hansel and Gretel only there are too many characters. Brice and Lucy walk fast, leaving me on my own. After I've found lots of good sticks, I discover a heart carved in a tree trunk. Inside it says "Annie + David." I trace the deep lines with my finger. These people loved each other so much that they hurt a tree. Maybe they got married and have kids my age. Or maybe they've forgotten their walk in the woods and that they ever met. Either way, their names are here forever.

It's getting dark and a little spooky in the forest. I'm ready to head back on my own when I spot Brice behind a tree. Peeking around a bush, I see Lucy's arm. I tiptoe closer. I'm about to yell *Boo!* when I get a much bigger surprise. They're kissing! Brice is *kissing* a girl. Their eyes are closed so they don't see me. I leap away like a startled deer.

"Did you see Brice and Lucy out there?" Mom asks when I drop my sticks. I shake my head.

"They'll be back soon," Lucy's mom says.

"Great kindling, Ivy," Carl says, arranging my sticks in the fire pit.

I'm sitting on a log watching the fire when Brice and Lucy come back. He grins at me, but I stare at the flames and pretend not to notice.

Longest Night Ever

That night, three bears are asleep beside me in our tent-cave. Their breathing fills the blue darkness. I imagine they're dreaming of jumping fish and honey raids. I wish I could join them but my sleeping bag is too cold. The ground is hard and the outside noises of wind and other wild creatures keep me awake. Also, I suspect I am too different.

"Why, you're not a bear at all," they growl, *suddenly noticing. "You're just a little girl. Get lost."* Momma Bear *swats at me with a big paw and I scurry off alone.*

They are my family, but sometimes I feel like I'm the odd one out. The smallest, youngest, always in the way. Goldilocks the Criminal. Bad girl in trouble again. Poison Ivy. Brice kissed a girl and I saw I saw I saw. I am a dirty spy, a Peeping Tom. I didn't know my brother was so grown-up. Kissing is for teenagers.

I try to force myself back to sleep but I have to pee and I'm scared to go out on my own. Finally I wiggle out of my sleeping bag and start unzipping the tent. Papa Bear sighs and rolls over. I hold my breath, then step outside as quietly as I can. It's even colder out here and I pull my sweatshirt sleeves around my hands. The yellow bathroom lights look far away. I chase the circle of light from my flashlight along the path. The fires are out, the tents are dark—it must be late. I wonder if Lucy has kissed a lot of boys.

I'm halfway to the bathroom block when I hear a crinkling sound. It's coming from a trashcan a few feet away. I step closer to investigate and, just then, a raccoon's wide head pops up. I freeze. The raccoon slides to the ground like liquid. Another appears, and both animals stare straight at me. Once, when I was sleeping over at Jenny's, we saw a raccoon stealing cat food. Safely on the other side of the sliding glass door, we watched him wash and eat Mortimer's kibble, dirtying the water bowl. I try to remember if raccoons are Dangerous Animals. I think they can have rabies, which is a terrible biting disease. Dogs with rabies have foamy spit like when you brush your teeth. If they bite you, you go crazy and want to bite things too. Then you probably die.

I wish I was back in the tent or at least safe in the bathroom. The raccoons stare at me from behind their dark masks. I stare back. I can't stand here forever because I'm cold and have to pee. I want to yell for Dad, but I'll get in trouble if I wake up strangers. If I was older I'd know what to do. I pray to my Guardian Angel and the Last Unicorn. I point my flashlight at the raccoons and their eyes glow like alien eyes. They don't come closer, but they don't go away either. I think of my sleeping family, together and safe. No one even knows I need help.

Finally, I show the raccoons my mean face and, growling, wave my arms above my head. Then I run fast and don't stop until I've closed the bathroom door behind me. Sitting on the cold toilet, I let out a little moan. *They can't get me here.* Afterwards, I spend a long time braiding and unbraiding my hair in the mirror, giving them time to leave.

On the way back to the tent, I'm jumpy from all the forest noises. I swing my flashlight like a night watchman but the raccoons are gone and I don't see anymore wild animals. I hum "Late Last Night When We Were All in Bed," which is about a cow who started a fire. She did it kicking over a lantern, not by playing with matches, which we shouldn't do either. When I reach the end of the song,

I've come to the last tent and beyond that are only trees. We have tent neighbors on both sides, so I've gone too far. I turn around and see the bathroom light twinkling far away. I try to remember if our tent is green or blue. I pray to God and Inspector Gadget for just five minutes of X-ray vision so I can see through the tents to my family. *Maybe it's gray.* I hurry back along the path, not humming anymore. I know it's a dome tent, but none of them look right. If I crawl into the wrong tent, it'd be like walking into a stranger's bedroom. I imagine unzipping a tent and squinting into the dark. There'd be sleeping people who might or might not be my family. I'd whisper, "Mom?" Then a strange couple would sit up screaming.

"Burglar!" The man hits me with his pillow, feathers flying.

"Get her!" the woman yells, dragging me inside and sitting on me.

"Ow!" I squeak. "Get off me."

"Call the police!" the man says, still whacking me with his pillow.

"How?" the woman asks.

"Damn. Good point." The man stops hitting me for a minute. "I think I saw a pay phone about ten miles back on the main road."

"Wait!" I shout, spitting out feathers. "I'm innocent. I'm just trying to find my family."

"Yeah, right," the woman says. "A likely story."

"Let's tie her up," says the man. "We can't take any chances with this sort of criminal. I'll call the cops. You stay here and make sure she doesn't get away."

I keep walking until I'm back at the bathroom again. Exhausted, I sit on the ground. I watch moths bounce into the lights and think of Caleb Ludlow.

"Ivy?"

I look up. Lucy's curly hair is messy like a rock star's. She's drying her hands on her jeans. "What are you doing? Are you okay?"

It's the middle of the night. I'm sitting outside the bathroom, staring at bugs.

"I'm okay," I say in a small voice. If I tell her I can't find the tent, she'll think I'm the kind of dumb little kid who gets lost at school. If I ask her to walk with me, she'll think I'm a scaredy-cat. Which is worse? Is it better to be lost or afraid? Is it better to be stupid or frightened? If she leaves, I'll be all alone again.

"Actually … " I stand. "I can't find my tent."

"You want me to help you look?"

I nod. She holds out her hand.

Momma Bear opens her eyes as I'm crawling into our tent. "Everything okay, baby?" she whispers. I want her to hold me tight while I tell her about the raccoons and getting lost in the woods. I needed help and there was only me in the dark. Me in the wilderness. Only Ivy, frightened during the longest night ever. But I'm not sure if telling will make my hurt better and it might make it worse. If Mom knows I got lost, she might not let me go to Red Hill Shopping Center without her anymore. So I keep quiet. Back in my sleeping bag, I try to pet my own hair like I'm a cat, until I fall asleep.

Secret World

"How do you know if something's alive?" Lucy's dad Carl asks, dipping a jar in the lake. Mom and Dad are hiking to the canyon and Lucy's mom is reading back at the campsite. I pick a flower and put it behind my ear, Hawaii-style.

It's been three days since the longest night ever and still no one's said anything about it. Lucy has a secret about me in the woods and I have one about her and Brice. She doesn't even realize that we're Even Steven, balanced on a classified see-saw.

"Living things move," I tell Carl.

"What about plants?" Brice asks me.

"The wind makes them move."

"What if it's not windy?" Brice throws a stone, skipping it twice before it sinks. "Are plants still alive when there's no wind?"

"Sure."

"What about that stone?" Carl asks me. "It moved just now."

I laugh. "That's because Brice threw it."

"So?" Carl raises a bushy eyebrow.

I shake my head. "Rocks aren't alive."

"True," Carl says. "But how can you tell?"

I think for a moment.

"They don't grow?"

'Good," says Carl.

"Living things breathe," Lucy says.

"Plants don't breathe!" I say.

"Yuh-huh," Lucy bounces her curls. "We breathe in oxygen and breathe out carbon dioxide. Plants do it the other way around."

This is news to me. "But ... they don't have noses."

Brice smiles but doesn't laugh.

"It's an exchange of gases through their leaves," Carl says. I don't ask what he means. I take the flower from behind my ear and roll it between my palms to make perfume. I sniff my hands. They smell damp. Carl screws the lid on the jar. "Good stuff, Lucy. What else?" We walk back along the path, passing a bald man with a fishing pole.

"Living things eat," Lucy says.

"Right," Carl says.

"And drink water," I say, even though I'm not sure if this is technically true of fish.

"Good job."

"They also—you know, reproduce," Brice says.

"Great," Carl says. We watch a bird with a red head, tapping on a tree. I recognize him from our California birds drawings from the beginning of the year.

"It's an acorn woodpecker!" I say.

"Ten points," Carl says. "We've got a smart one here." I blush and stand a little taller. We continue down the path. I look at my flower, crumpled like a wad of bubble gum, and wipe my hands on my jeans. Then I realize that's one too.

"All living things die," I say.

The oval is moving. A see-through body with dark shapes inside a living shape. With one eye closed I watch the creature bumping into jungle. Blinking, I pull away from the eyepiece. The jungle is actually only green dots; the oval creature a tiny speck. A whole world, sandwiched between two pieces of glass. I sigh, gazing back into the microscope. The oval finds its way around the plants and breaks free into an empty stretch of water. Carl says it's a *paramecium*. Brice makes another slide with a drop of water from the jar. We see wheel animals and circle plants. I'm allowed to touch the microscope only with my eye, but Brice and Lucy are old enough to turn the knobs on their own.

I squint up at the bright sky, wondering if there are giants peering down at us. Maybe they're watching us stumble through our lives of school and play, food and sleep. The things under the microscope don't know we're here, so how do we know there isn't someone watching us? Maybe our problems would seem silly to them, as if *we* were simple see-through creatures.

We have fish for dinner, both families together. Mom and Dad keep laughing and smiling at each other. Afterwards, Lucy's mom gets out a guitar and we relax around the fire, toasting marshmallows. We sing "Yellow Submarine" and other songs we all know. Usually Mom only sings in the shower. Lucy has a pretty voice. The marshmallows are hot and gooey and I have six before Mom takes the bag away. I am cozy in my sweatshirt, vibrating with sugar and the excitement of being up late. I don't want this to end. Mom leans her head on Dad's shoulder. A burning log rolls over and embers fly into the night.

Later, when it's time for bed, I look up at the sky, now thick with stars.

"Can you see me?" I whisper.

Part IV

Work

Saved

There are lines of concentration between Dad's eyebrows, and he's wearing a bathrobe even though it's afternoon. Sometimes it feels good just sitting near him even if we don't say anything. Right now I'm pretending he's a large, silent dog. I hear a car in the driveway, but Dad's eyes stay fixed on his notes. I munch my jammy rice cake while he drinks beer. Now that we're back home, I hear Mom and Dad arguing again sometimes. Things seemed better when we were camping, but you can't stay on vacation forever. Besides, I missed my beanbag. And also Erin.

In school today, we learned about Mozart, who at my age was traveling all over Europe playing music for royalty. When I was a really little kid I probably should have been practicing ballet, learning to keep my legs straight, but instead I spent all my time playing with Jenny and drawing pictures. I hope it's not too late to become a child prodigy.

"Hi, there, honeys!" Mom bursts into the kitchen wearing a boxy navy suit with a chunky necklace.

"Hi, Mom."

"Hey," Dad says to his pad of paper.

"I got it!" Mom sings. "I start Monday."

"Got what?" I ask.

"Neil. I *got* it."

Dad exhales and puts his pen down. His eyebrows rise and lines appear on his forehead. "Why are you dressed like that? Got what?"

Mom puts a hand on her hip. "I got the job."

"Whoa—what job?" Dad asks. "What are you talking about?"

Mom narrows her eyes and Dad moves his mouth to one side.

Mom gives me a look. "Ivy, why don't you go finish your snack upstairs?"

I turn the corner and wait quietly in the hall. I imagine Dad turned into a secret cowboy and Mom transformed into a famous ballerina.

"The clothing boutique buyer position, remember?" Mom asks, possibly doing a *pirouette*. "Why are you looking at me like that? How much have you been drinking? You wanted me to go for it, right?"

"This is my first one, Karen, and I'm not playing games." I imagine him taking out a gun and shooting a tin can. "I have no idea what you're talking about." *Bang!*

"Remember that ad you put under my pillow a while back?" She does an impressive leap before stopping suddenly and smoothing her tutu.

"What? I didn't put anything under your pillow." Dad sounds tired, like he's been lassoing cows all day.

"It wasn't you?"

"It wasn't me. Must have been one of the kids trying to be helpful. So what's the job exactly?"

I sneak upstairs, grinning wildly. I found Mom a job and we're not going to be poor. They'll stop fighting about money and won't get divorced.

I settle into my beanbag and squeeze my eyes shut. I think about the Artist and Marmalade. But I'm only remembering last time when I drew fruit with her, which feels different from being there in my mind. I squeeze my eyes harder. Go go go! But it doesn't work. So I let my mind wander to Mozart, who lived when boys wore tights. When Mozart was eight, he composed his first symphony. I am eight and have saved my family. My breathing slows, my eyes relax, and then I'm back in the apartment where the air is warm and wet.

It's raining hard outside and I hear rhythmic tapping sounds. I gasp and race to the window. The rain is pounding, beautiful, sliding down wavy metal roofs into the street. The water is so deep in the street it's practically a river and the people have to step high so their flip-flops don't fall off. Back in California, any rain is special. *This* rain is incredible.

At the easel, I see sketches of girls playing, alongside photographs and pictures torn from magazines. Marmalade steps through the doorway, tail waving behind him like wild grasses. He meows when he sees me. I meow back. I reach down to pet him, but he trots away, meowing loudly, so I follow him back through the doorway into the small kitchen.

The Artist is at the counter, wearing an old-fashioned apron with frills and big flowers. Her head is bent so her short hair falls in front of her face. She's chopping big leafy vegetables, tap tap tap. The kitchen has paper lanterns on the ceiling and a few plants on the windowsill. Marmalade meows again and the Artist looks up, seeing me. I grin at her and she smiles back.

"I found Mom a job," I tell her.

"Jesus, you can talk?" She lets the knife drop to the chopping board.

"Of course I can talk," I say. "I'm not a baby."

"That's not what I mean. When you came here before you never said anything," she says. "Man, this just keeps getting more incredible."

I'm not quite sure what she means. I guess she doesn't do make-believe anymore because she's a grown-up. I can make up much stranger things than a grown-up version of myself in an apartment. Way more incredible, for example, would be imagining an evil flying octopus that paints moustaches on people while they sleep. The moustaches are made of a special sneaky squid ink and if you get moustached, you turn mean and want to tease kittens all day. Or maybe the Artist is thinking about the rain.

"The job at the clothing boutique?" the Artist asks.

I nod, grinning again.

"That's great," she says. Then she looks serious and crouches so our heads are the same height. "Listen, Ivy," she says, "it's not your fault."

I look at her confused.

She continues, "I mean, whatever happens isn't your responsibility."

I don't understand. She gives me a hug. It feels good, not like hugging myself. "It'll be okay," she tells me. Then I realize *she's* the one who doesn't understand. She's acting like something's wrong, but of course everything will be okay. Mom has a job. We won't be poor and everything will go back to normal.

Lunch on Repeat

I have a baloney sandwich for the fourth day in a row. I used to open my lunchbox and find roast beef on rye, Monterey Jack and tomato, or a peanut butter and banana sandwich. Mom would pack string cheese, a tiny box of raisins, or yogurt with M&Ms. There would be red wax cheese, grapes, or animal crackers. On tuna days, she always remembered a mint.

Now there's a new cook in the kitchen, and every day this week he has packed me the same exact lunch. The apple is always green and the potato chips are always plain old original. I feel like an animal, forced to eat the same food, like Mortimer and his kibble. Caterpillar Christa and Ladybug Melanie won't trade because they say baloney is gross and they only like barbecue-flavored chips. Cricket Sara licks her cookies so I can't have any. You can only share an apple if it's sliced, so I'm stuck with my own lame lunch. Today is Thursday, but you wouldn't know it from my sandwich. Dad has stopped time. I am stuck in a loop. Flip the tape over and press play. All living things eat, so I eat. Still, I wonder if it is possible to actually die of boredom, because these lunches are killing me.

In the afternoon we start a new unit on The Ocean. Seventy-one percent of the Earth is covered with water. Our ocean is the Pacific, which I love very much. One time at Drakes Beach, I came back to our blanket after shell hunting. My family had disappeared and a seagull was eating my lunch. I flapped my arms, screaming at it. I had a

139

turkey sandwich, which is kind of gross if you think about it because they're both birds. It would be like a person eating a gorilla sandwich. The seagull stared at me with its pale, beady eyes, waiting until the last possible moment before spreading its wings and taking off.

"Ivy, class is happening in here, not out the window," Ms. Kelley says. The kids snicker. The board is covered with lists of sea creatures. *Dolphin, starfish, crab, hammerhead shark, flounder …*

That day at the beach, I sat by myself on the blanket and tried to eat what was left of my sandwich, nibbling around the seagull bites. I couldn't see my family anywhere, and I worried they'd left without me. The beach is an hour's drive from my house, so it would take about a hundred years to walk. I would live my whole life walking back and by the time I got home I would be ready to die. I wouldn't be able to ask anyone for a ride, because hitchhiking is dangerous, and when they kidnapped me, it'd be my own fault. *Don't say I didn't warn you.* My sandwich had sand in it, so I tried not to chew too much. Finally, I spotted Dad in the water laughing with some lady in a bikini. I wondered if they were telling each other jokes and thought of a few myself.

> *What do you call a crab at Christmas?*
> *Sandy Claws!*

> *How can you tell if the ocean is friendly?*
> *From its waves!*

> *What does a mermaid eat for lunch?*
> *A peanut butter and jellyfish sandwich!*

I should have known my family wouldn't leave without the blanket and stripy umbrella. Just then, I saw Brice on his way back, dragging a big piece of driftwood.

"Ivy," Ms. Kelley says, cleaning her glasses. "Can you think of any other animals that live in the ocean?" Now there are even more sea creatures on the board.

"Jellyfish," I say. I felt relieved when Brice came back because then I wasn't alone anymore.

"We have jellyfish already." Ms. Kelley points.

"Um, octopus."

"Good job." She writes it under angelfish. I try hard to pay attention. Our Houses of the World drawings are coming off the bulletin board, with Animals of the Ocean taking their place. We each have to do a big research project using facts from books. We talk about the difference between facts and opinions. Ms. Kelley teaches us about the Food Chain and who eats who. Plankton get eaten by little fish, which get eaten by bigger fish, which get eaten by sharks! Plankton are so tiny it takes a lot of them to make a meal, even for a little fish. The higher up you go on the Food Chain, the fewer animals there are and the scarier their teeth. When you're at the top of the Food Chain, nobody eats you. At the very tippy-top is people. "We don't need super-sharp teeth," Ms. Kelley says, "because we have our clever brains instead."

We each choose an ocean animal for our projects. I figure everyone's forgotten about the sea fairy thing with Jenny, so I pick seahorses because they kind of look like horses (fact) and are pretty (opinion). If I was a seahorse, I would twist my tail around seaweed, holding on tight so I wouldn't get swept away.

After school, I go to Spider Erin's house for the first time.

"Beep beep beep. Come in, do you read me?" Erin touches her ear. Her dark hair is in a French braid. "Preparing for lift off." We're on our backs on two knocked-over lawn chairs, heads on the grass, legs dangling at the knees. I buckle an invisible seatbelt and give a sharp nod. Erin pushes more imaginary buttons. "Ten … nine … eight … " I squint at the bright sky as black birds fly overhead. Suddenly I see something out of the corner of my eye. Turning my head, I'm startled to see a little kid with pigtails towering over me. I scream.

"Abort! Abort!" Erin shouts. "Child on the launch pad!"

"Can I play?" asks the giant little girl.

"No!" Erin hisses. "Go away."

"Meany!" She runs off.

"Launch pad clear," Erin says. "Ready to resume lift-off. Three … two … one … blast off!"

I cup my hands around my mouth to make an explosion sound. Erin pulls on her cheeks. We shake, rattling in our seats as we zoom through space.

"Look down there," I say a few minutes later, pointing. "It's the Earth."

"Hello, everyone!" Erin waves.

We land roughly and climb on to Erin's trampoline. We bounce, flapping our arms. My stomach springs wonderfully. We jump high and for a moment there is nothing else. Just like when I'm spinning on the tire swing, I am filled with a feeling and no thoughts.

Then I look at Erin and yell, "We're on the moon!"

"On the mooooon!" Erin screams.

The pigtail girl skips back outside. From up here on the trampoline she seems little, not more than five.

"Can I play?"

"Ahhhh!" Erin yells, still jumping. "It's an alien!"

"Am not." The girl stomps her foot.

"Look at her weird antennas," Erin says to me.

The girl touches the top of her head. "Nuh-uh." She runs back inside.

Finally, we flop exhausted into a crater. Lying here feels

good. The trampoline would make an exciting bed. I wonder if Erin ever camps out here during the summer. How long do we have to be friends before I can pass the Sleepover Test?

I say we should do science experiments like astronauts.

Erin sits up and says, "Experiment number one: is there really a man in the moon?"

We walk in wobbly slow motion, calling out to him, "Ma-an. Moony man?"

"Nope. Okay, experiment number two. Is the moon made of green cheese?"

"Yum, cheese," I say. "Let's taste the ground and find out."

"Oooh, wait here." Erin disappears inside. I try jumping again, but my legs hurt and it's not much fun on my own. I wonder how much longer before Mom picks me up. I mean Dad. I keep forgetting. A plane flies overhead, drawing a white line behind it. There are hundreds of people up there, all on their way to somewhere. Maybe there's a boy my age, pressing his face against the oval window, looking down at the Marin hills, wondering who lives here. I'm thinking of him, so maybe he's thinking of me too.

"Hey there." I'm startled by a deep voice. "Who are you?"

I quickly sit up. It's a large man with a leather jacket, scraggly beard, and low ponytail. For a bizarre moment I wonder if he's the Man in the Moon.

"I'm Ivy."

"*Poison* Ivy?" The man laughs. My body tightens. "I'm Hank, Erin's stepdad. Whatcha doing there?"

"Waiting for Erin."

"Hm. Think I saw her messing around in the kitchen." He turns around and shouts, "Hey, Erin! Get your butt out here!"

"In a minute!"

Hank sighs. "Let's see you jump."

143

I shake my head. "Too tired."

"Bummer." Hank sits on the trampoline's edge. I scoot to the middle. If I'm still and quiet, like a possum playing dead, maybe he'll get bored and leave.

"Scared of me?" he asks.

"No."

He leans closer. "Boo!"

I jerk away.

"Just kidding," Hank says. "You know, you shouldn't judge a book by its cover."

Grandma says this too, but there isn't time to read everything, so you have to decide somehow. The cover tells you if a book's funny, or boring, or scary. That's a fact. Also, if you judge a cereal by its box, you know if it's tasty with marshmallows (Lucky Charms) or boring with no toys (Raisin Bran).

Finally Erin comes outside, holding something behind her back.

"You're a rude girl leaving your friend out here on her own," Hank says.

"I'm not rude," Erin says. "*You're* rude." My eyes widen. "You were fine, weren't you, Ivy?"

I nod.

"Just teasing, Erin," Hank says. "See you later, Poison."

Once he's left, Erin puts down a plate of crackers and green cubes.

"Moon cheese!" I gasp.

Erin holds up her stained fingers. "Look—I've got a green thumb."

We sit on the trampoline with our knees touching and hold the cheese in both hands, nibbling it like mice.

"What a deadbeat," Dad says pulling out of Erin's driveway.

After we explored the moon, Erin and I played a

different game, where we pretended to run away to join the circus. In the game, our families called us mean names, tied us up, and hit us. So we escaped! We did tricks on the circus trampoline, practicing every day for a year until we were the best acrobats West of the Mississippi. One time our horrible families came to the circus and we were so scared we almost fell off the trapeze. But we were all dressed up in sparkly costumes with face paint, so they didn't know it was us.

"What's a deadbeat?" I ask. I'm in the back seat because it's safer, but one day I'll get to ride up front like everyone else. The view will be better then, with the whole windshield in front of me like a movie screen.

"Who *was* that guy?" Dad asks.

"Who?"

"The ... big guy."

"Erin's stepdad."

"I can't wait to meet Erin's mom."

Working Woman

"The Boutique Ladies are hilarious," Mom says that evening at the kitchen table, smearing jam on her toast. Dad forgot about dinner until Mom got home from work. She went upstairs to get changed and he made scrambled eggs. Breakfast for dinner is kind of exciting and topsy-turvy, like wearing clothes in the bath, or eating noodle soup for breakfast. Mom continues, "Bev has been there forever and seems to have a story about everything. Gloria's on this huge health kick and always has yogurt and celery for lunch. Oh and there's this other lady ... I can't remember her name right now, but she's really funny too. Very glamorous, and she talks to the mannequins while she's redoing the window display."

"Does she know they're not alive?" I ask.

"Of course." Mom laughs. "She's just being silly. She'll say something like, "You're going to look so nice in this top. What? You don't like yellow? Okay, you can wear the blue one, then.""

"No wonder they're not doing so well financially if their staff is ... unhinged," Dad says.

Mom sighs. "They're fine. I'm sure I'm making them out to be stranger than they are. The issue seems to be that they've been stocking items *they* like instead of what will sell. And their jewelry really needs some help. They've got a whole display cabinet of charm bracelets."

"What's wrong with charm bracelets?" I ask.

"Well, they're fine if you're sixteen."

"What you need to do," Dad says, "is get rid of all that old merchandise and start fresh with commercially viable stuff."

"Maybe. But I have to be careful not to step on their toes."

"They hired you as the buyer, didn't they?"

"Sure, but I think I'd better keep observing before I make any radical changes. By the way, we're getting pretty low on food. Can you please go grocery shopping soon? Also Brice says his cleats are pinching his toes. It'd be great if you can take him to get a new pair this week before soccer practice."

"Jeez, Karen, you know I'm busy looking for work."

"This is your job for now."

Dad opens his mouth then closes it again. "Well, who sells kids' cleats, some department store?"

"My mother got him the first pair from Good Sport Mike's in Corte Madera, right off of 101."

Tuesday at ballet, one of the girls helps me put my hair in a bun and Miss Garville compliments me on my third position. Pointy Ear Girl hurts her ankle during a *sauté arabesque* and has to sit down for most of the lesson. I can't wait to tell Mom after class, and am surprised when Dad picks me up instead. I keep forgetting.

At home, I kick my shoes off in the hall and Dad makes me pick them up and put them in the closet. Meany. Mom never cared where I left my shoes.

When Mom gets home, she gives me a hug.

"This is to say thank you for finding my job," she says, handing me a little box. I pull off the ribbon. Inside are chocolates in the shape of a miniature paintbrush, crayon, and easel. I want to gobble them right this minute, but I also want to save them forever.

"I think I'm getting a sense of the boutique's clientele," Mom says when we're all at the kitchen table. Dad made chicken strips with oven fries for dinner. "They're mostly middle-aged ladies who are willing to spend a little money to look nice and aren't ready to dress like their mothers."

"I guess that makes sense," Dad says. "Pass the ketchup."

"So how was your day?" Mom asks.

Dad groans. "Painfully boring. I organized the medicine cabinet and threw out a lot of old junk. Then I started going kind of stir-crazy, so I took the newspaper to the library and looked for jobs there. It was funny seeing who's out in the middle of the day. There was this old guy who basically had a barricade of books all around him, as if he'd been researching in that exact spot for decades. I was surprised he wasn't covered in cobwebs. And these two women talked for ages about the best colleges while their little kids ran around the stacks. I kept waiting for one of the librarians to come over and shush them, but they didn't seem to mind."

After a minute Dad says, "You know, I think I'd like to meet up with the guys I used to work with soon. Have a drink, see how everyone's doing."

"That's sounds fun," Mom says. "Let me know when and I'll be home in time to watch the kids." After a few moments she says, "Thanks for taking care of the medicine cabinet. And while you're at it, the upstairs bathroom is looking kind of grimy. It'd be great if you can get to it tomorrow."

Dad makes a face. "I'll see."

"All the cleaning products are under the sink."

Wednesday after school, Dad takes us to Good Sport Mike's. A woman hands a football to her baby, who gums it hungrily like a dog with a chew toy. I look at the kids' bikes, like I might have when I'm ten and go everywhere fast. Two teenage girls shake pompoms; their chants are the more mature version of jump rope songs. I find a pair of white leather ice skates that are perfect and just my size, except the nearest ice rink is the Snoopy place, which is far away. Also I don't know how to ice skate. If Mom was here, she might buy them for me anyway, but Dad wouldn't understand.

"My mother-in-law just bought him a pair and they're too tight already," Dad tells the bald salesman, who kneels on the floor squeezing Brice's toes through a new soccer shoe. I take the other shoe out of the box. The bottom has rubber gumdrops like hippo teeth. Hippos are at the top of the Food Chain, even without sharp teeth, because they're huge and nobody eats them. Nobody would eat this shoe either.

"Growing fast, are we?" the salesman says.

"Apparently," Brice says.

In the car on the way home, I want to play that we're hippos in quicksand, but Brice just wants to look out the window. *Boring!*

"So what'd you do today?" Mom asks Dad over dinner.

"I got cleats for Brice," Dad says, dipping a chunk of long bread into his soup.

Mom turns to Brice. "Do they fit?"

"Yep," Brice says.

"Good. Thanks for taking care of that, Neil. What else?"

Dad shrugs. "I read the paper and went grocery shopping."

"Great," Mom says. "How did that go?"

"It was full of the same bad news and no jobs."

"No." Mom laughs. "I mean the food shopping."

"Oh, I don't know, it took a while. I spent about seventy dollars."

"You must have really stocked up."

"I wasn't really sure what we needed."

"Did you get milk?"

"Were we out?"

"Never mind, I'll pick some up tomorrow. How about bread, eggs, bananas, pasta, that sort of thing?"

"Jesus, Karen, write me a list if you want something specific."

"These are just normal staples. Well what *did* you get?"

"I got five baguettes besides this one. I thought they'd be good with cheese."

I nod in agreement. My favorite is brie, which is soft and white.

Mom shakes her head. "Next time you should just get one at a time. They go stale pretty fast. What else?"

"I don't know—crackers, soda, baloney."

"For seventy dollars?"

"I got some nice steaks I thought I could cook up on the barbecue. And I got this soup from the deli section," he says, pointing to his bowl. "It's good, isn't it? They normally serve it in these little containers so I got a whole bunch."

Mom runs her hand over her eyes. After a moment she says, "I'll write you a list next time." They're quiet for a minute, then Mom asks, "So, did you get around to fixing the sink?"

"Karen, I got groceries *and* shoes. Can't you just be happy with that?"

"Well, will you do it tomorrow?"

"Will you quit nagging me?"

"Sure," Mom says. "And if you can't figure it out, just call a plumber."

"I told you I'd do it."

We eat in silence.

"Well," Mom says, "I had a productive day too. I lined up appointments with new designers in Santa Rosa and Richmond. They'll show me their work and I'll decide if any pieces are worth stocking in the shop. One of them works with bold florals and the other one uses vintage buttons and lace."

"That doesn't sound like the kind of thing you usually go for," Dad says.

Mom chews her bread slowly before answering. "No, but I think I've got a sense of what our customers want. And innovative clothes might bring in new customers."

Thursday, Dad picks me, Ladybug Melanie, and Brice up from school. Just Melanie on her own without Caterpillar Christa is like a salt shaker without the pepper. You know it's salt, but you can't help feeling that something's missing. We drop Brice off at Memorial Park for soccer practice. Melanie and I play on my tire swing and she teaches me "Miss Susie" and "Miss Mary Mack." I'm not sure how the other girls know all this stuff.

"I have to use the bathroom," she says.

I go pale. I need to keep her out of the house so she won't see that the Beast is gone.

"Okay, but you have to use the upstairs one."

"Why?"

"Because the downstairs sink drips blood."

"Ew! That's disgusting."

She hurries back and we've just finished chalking the ground for hopscotch when Dad yells that it's time to get Brice.

In the back seat, Melanie and I do "Down by the Banks of the Hanky Panky," our hands brushing against each other's, while Brice's coach talks to the team. He has thick, muscly legs and a big belly.

"How was soccer?" Dad asks as Brice finally gets in.

Brice slams the car door. "Fine. What's for dinner? I'm hungry."

"Haven't thought about it yet," Dad says. "Any ideas?"

Dad makes macaroni and cheese, his best meal yet.

"I helped out on the shop floor today," Mom says. "They want me to familiarize myself with all aspects of the business."

Dad nods.

"It was hard being on my feet all day," Mom says. "But I feel like I learned a lot."

"Ivy had a friend over this afternoon," Dad says.

"That's nice—who was that?" Mom asks.

"Melanie," I say. "She taught me, *Hell … o operator, please give me number nine. And if you disconnect me, I'll kick you from behind … the 'frigerator … "*

"Brice had soccer practice," Dad says.

I keep singing. "*There was a piece of glass, Miss Susie sat upon it and broke her little … Ask me no more questions—"*

"Ivy," Mom says.

I sing faster. "*I'll tell you no more lies. The boys are in the bathroom zipping up their … Flies are in the meadow—"*

"Okay, Ivy, that's enough," Dad stops me. He turns to Mom. "You know, I feel like I spent the whole afternoon in the car. Pick 'em up, drop 'em off. Every time I sat down to try and work on something it was time to get back in the damn car again."

A slow smile slides across Mom's face. "Yes, I know exactly what you mean."

"Tell your mom about soccer."

"It was fine," Brice says.

"And your new shoes fit okay?" Mom asks.

"Like a glove."

"Thank God it's Friday," Mom says the next night when we're all around the kitchen table again. She pats her slice of pizza with a paper napkin.

"Tell me about it," Dad says, drinking a beer. Mom

got pepperoni and mushroom pizza on the way home to celebrate the end of her second week of work. She said Dad deserves a break from cooking and we all deserve a break from his cooking. Dad continues, "You know we're going to have to tell your mother."

"If we don't clean up around here," Mom says, "she'll *know* something's up as soon as she sees the house."

"Oh, come on. It's not even that bad."

Mom raises an eyebrow.

"I've been busy," Dad says. "Hey, I reorganized the shoe closet. Did you see?"

"Okay, tomorrow morning the four of us are going to blitz this place. Ivy, you're on dusting and mirror duty." I groan, even though I kind of like the smell of the blue window spray. "Brice," Mom continues, "I need you to vacuum."

"That *sucks*." Brice grins.

"Ha ha," Dad says.

Mom asks, "Neil, do you want to do the bathrooms or kitchen?"

"What a choice." Dad reaches for another slice of pizza. "Seriously, though, we will need to tell your mother."

"I know," Mom says.

"She's going to freak out!" Brice says.

"She might," Dad agrees. "But waiting longer isn't going to make it any easier."

"This is true," Mom says.

"Tell Grandma what?" I ask.

"About my job," Mom says.

I start picking the pepperoni pieces off my slice, notice Brice is eating his, and stick them back on. I look up at Mom and say, "You know, I bet she'll be really happy for you."

153

Freak Out

"You have a what?" Grandma asks, spilling her coffee across the dining room table. Mom takes a deep breath but doesn't yell. I try to touch the floor for luck, but my feet don't reach.

"Ivy, run and get something to clean that up," Mom says. She starts telling Grandma about the boutique, the designers she's meeting with, and the changes she's going to make. I race into the kitchen, grab paper towels, and hurry back so I don't miss the Freak Out. "The job's perfect for me, Mom," she is saying to Grandma. "Remember how I wanted to be a fashion designer when I was growing up? I used to sketch dresses and take notes during the Academy Awards."

I didn't know this. I picture Mom as a teenager, before me and Brice even existed and years before she met Dad. *The lines at the sides of her eyes disappear as her skin becomes soft and shiny. She sits on the floor in front of the TV, next to her big sister, Aunt Bea, who has braces. They watch glamorous movie stars walk down the red carpet. Young Mom chews her pencil and sketches in her notebook.*

"Sure," Grandma says. "I bought you that second-hand sewing machine for your sixteenth birthday."

"Exactly," Mom continues. "I've always been passionate about fashion. You know I have."

"But you were a lousy seamstress. Your Home Ec apron had a panel sewn in backwards and you always had me do the zippers."

Mom sighs. "You're right. I'm not a seamstress. I'm not even a designer. Ivy's more creative than I'll ever be. But I do know fashion. I know what's flattering on different people and I'm going to revitalize that little shop."

"Great. Good for you, Mrs. Career Woman," Grandma says, but she's not smiling. "And what about your children? Don't tell me they're home alone all afternoon. I saw a special about those so-called latchkey kids. I think their parents are so selfish."

"Well," Dad says, "actually, I'm taking care of them."

"Here we go," Brice mutters, dipping some pancake in his syrup puddle.

"But what about *your* job?" Grandma asks. I wonder if she's imagining me and Brice hiding under Dad's big desk at his old office. We'd play tic-tac-toe on Dad's knees, while he makes important phone calls. Or maybe Brice would just want to read a book and I'd have to play tic-tac-toe by myself. If we are quiet, Dad will give us a cookie after getting off the phone.

Dad folds his hands on the table. "My company unfortunately decided to downsize."

"You weren't fired, were you?" Grandma asks.

"No, definitely not," Dad says. "I was laid off. It's not personal; six of us were let go." He pauses, then adds, "These are difficult times." *The end, so good luck.*

"This is awful," Grandma says. "When did all this happen? Why didn't anyone tell me?"

"We didn't want to worry you," Mom says.

"I'm worried," Grandma says.

"We've been doing just fine," Dad says. "I'm looking for my next challenge, and in the meantime Karen has found something to keep us going."

"This clothes-buying job of yours can't pay as much as Neil was bringing in."

"We're fine," Mom says. "We're cutting back a little but we're managing just fine."

Grandma is quiet, her face pinched like she's stuck on a crossword clue.

"So is this why you went camping instead of going to Maui?" She asks. Mom nods. Grandma is quiet for a minute, then asks, "And the big TV? I guess it hasn't really been getting repaired this whole time."

Suddenly I picture Dad, Brice, and me, riding on top of the Beast, paddling our way to Hawaii. A school of little yellow fish swim beside us and dolphins leap out of the water. I scoop a seahorse into a jar so I can draw it later for my Animals of the Ocean project. Then we remember we need to be back before Mom comes home and misses us, so we turn the Beast around and paddle hard.

"I'm sorry." Mom touches Grandma's hand. Something inside of me unwinds a little. "Neil and I felt it would be easier this way. We didn't want to upset you."

"You should have told me sooner," Grandma says. "Maybe I could have helped. Does Bea know?"

Mom nods.

"So *that's* why she's been so strange on the phone lately," Grandma continues. "That girl never was good at keeping secrets." I vow to never tell Aunt Bea if I like a boy or she might accidentally tell everyone. After a minute Grandma asks, "What does it take to hear the truth in this family?"

Amphibian

The next week at lunch, Spider Erin and I swap crackers for cookies, three for three on the picnic table. Earlier, during Science Time, Ms. Kelley had us make-believe we were tadpoles, squirming across the floor, growing legs and transforming into frogs. Together we all changed into something new. I didn't think about my parents fighting. I didn't worry once about getting in trouble for taking the lip gloss or anything. Frogs don't worry.

"So, when can I come over?" Erin asks. She hasn't been back since the party and I got to play on her trampoline so it's only fair. I bet she wants to watch another movie on the Beast and make an ice cream sundae monster with gummy worms popping out of its nose. If I told Erin the bathroom sink dripped blood, she'd probably think it was cool and want to see it. But if she sees Grandma's old TV she will know I'm not really that lucky girl with lots of friends and her own movie theater.

"I don't know," I say, putting down my baloney sandwich. "I've had so many friends over lately, my mom says she can't hear herself think."

"Who? Christa and Melanie? Julie? Sara?"

"Yeah, Melanie. But also lots of girls you don't know."

"What, from other schools?"

"Yeah, they go to Wade Thomas. And some of them are even fourth graders."

"Really?"

"You bet." I finish my sandwich.

She is quiet, then asks, "Well, do you want to come play at my house again?"

"Okay, I'll ask my Dad. I mean Mom."

She tilts her head sideways, "You're not too busy playing with all your *other* friends?"

I wonder if that's the special kind of question I don't have to answer, or if she is waiting for me to say something. I think if I open my mouth, more lies will pour out like fish bubbles.

Finally, I jump on to the picnic bench and say, "I'm turning into a frog!"

Erin grins and darts out her tongue. *"Ribbit,"* she says. We hop around the picnic table on our powerful back legs.

Fatherhood

My big project is due tomorrow and I still know zero facts about seahorses. I find Dad in the downstairs bathroom, removing parts of the sink.

"Whatcha doing?"

"Fixing the drip." Dad sets the wrench on the counter, wiping an arm across his forehead. Chest hair bubbles up from the V neck of his undershirt. "While you were at school I went for my first run in weeks, and when I got back I decided it was time to deal with this." He shows me two small black rubber pieces called washers. They look like flattened Cheerios. I ask if I can have the old one. He responds with a shrug, which is sometimes better than words and if you aren't looking you'd miss it.

I tell him I have to do a report but don't know how.

"Why don't you get Brice to help you?"

"Brice is busy," I say.

"Busy with what?"

"I dunno. He just said, 'Don't come in, I'm busy!'"

A few minutes later, Dad drags my beanbag to my desk and flips through a book on Ocean Animals. I say we have to stick to the facts—no opinions. He shows me the long lists in the back of the book and says I should just read pages twenty-seven to thirty-four.

"But it won't make sense if I start in the middle!"

"It's okay to jump around in some books," Dad says, helping himself from my snack plate of Grandma's cookies. "Those are the pages on seahorses and this isn't a story."

I try to imagine my own life as small facts, like candies spilled across the floor. *One brother, two parents, no pets. Eight-year-old girl likes to draw. Lives in California: land of earthquakes and not much rain. Plays outside. Has a beanbag. Likes scrub jays. Loses her friend and makes a new one.* But who'd want to read that? Everything is better as a story. *One day a seahorse went for a swim in the big blue ocean. In the coral garden, she met a friendly oyster. He gave her a pearl that she wore around her neck on a piece of old fishing line.*

Dad tells me to pay attention.

"And don't just copy or it's *plagiarism*." He says that's pretending someone else's work is your own, and it can get you into a lot of trouble, especially when you're older. He looks out the window for a moment and then gets up to go.

"Wait!" I say. "I need more help." Dad sits down again and reads to me about seahorses holding each other's tails and changing colors when they're in love.

"'Incredibly,'" he reads, "'it's the *male* who carries the fertilized eggs inside his pouch. He gives birth to one hundred to two hundred tiny baby seahorses, which float away.'" He turns the book around so I can see the pictures.

"So, with seahorses," I say, "the dad is the mom."

He closes the book. "Get your shoes on, kiddo. I've got an idea."

A yellow seahorse wraps its tail around a plant while his orange friend hovers nearby. We're at the Red Hill Pet Store so we can see the actual real thing. Bells jingle as Cricket Sara and her mom come in. I hope she's getting a kitten and I can come over to play with it. But she's just here to look at angelfish.

"Yeah, same here." I nod to the fish tank. "Seahorses."

Dad introduces himself to Sara's mom. "Excuse my shirt," he adds. "I was fixing the sink earlier."

"Lovely to meet you, Neil," she says in a high voice. Her fingernails are fire engine red. She has straight hair like Sara, but cut short so you can see her neck, teased bangs fanning out from her forehead. "Olivia," she exhales, like it's the last word of a magic spell. A parrot squawks.

Dad says, "I was helping Ivy with her seahorse report and figured, why not come to the pet store to get a closer look?"

Olivia says it's refreshing to see an involved father. He smiles and rests a big hand on my shoulder.

"Look, hon," she says to Sara. "There's the angelfish."

Sara scribbles in a tiny notebook while I watch the seahorses twist in slow motion, changing direction. Tails hold and let go, curl tight and uncurl. The grown-ups talk about some people named Jesse Jackson and Michael Dukakis, which I think has to do with the election, and a stewardess who just got sucked out of an airplane near Hawaii, which doesn't. I tune them out, only pricking up my ears again when Olivia mentions my Movie Party.

"I guess you heard about the ice cream sundaes?" Dad asks.

"Oh, yes." Olivia laughs, touching a hand to her boobs. "Sara didn't have much of an appetite for dinner that night."

"Kids and ice cream." Dad chuckles. "It's funny, I don't remember seeing you when you picked her up."

"Actually my ex-husband has her on weekends."

"I'm sorry, I didn't realize you … "

"Don't be sorry," Olivia says. "I'm not."

I watch the yellow seahorse let go and drift. Olivia says they should arrange a playdate for us, and rips a page from Sara's notebook.

Outgrown

"Then they get too big and have to find a new shell," Matt the Ant says at school the next day, his dimple appearing. Ms. Kelley adjusts her glasses and asks the class how hermit crabs are like people. *They're not.* It must be a trick question because obviously we have nothing in common.

"We get bigger but our clothes stay the same." Ladybug Melanie plays with her gold †. "Then we have to get new ones."

"I like that," Ms. Kelley says. "What else do we outgrow besides clothes?"

Someone says that really little kids play with blocks and when you get older you play with Lego space stations. Someone else says that baby books are short with lots of pictures and our books are longer with fewer pictures. Grown-up books are, like, four hundred pages long and the only picture is on the cover.

"You can outgrow friends," I say. "People change, and the kid who used to be your friend maybe isn't anymore."

"Who else has experienced that?" Ms. Kelley asks. I am surprised to see a lot of people raise their hands. I think maybe Brice is changing too. Even if he is too grown-up for make-believe, he should still want to do things together.

"Babies cry a lot and grown-ups never cry," Melanie says.

"Almost never," Cricket Sara corrects her.

"Yeah, it's okay for a woman to cry if she's really really sad," Caterpillar Christa agrees. "But men only cry if someone kicks them in the balls or they've got something stuck in their eye."

Dad had a job and now he doesn't. Mom didn't and now she does. Grandma didn't know and now she does. Facts make the story. My favorite clothes and books change, but I don't. I am always me except maybe when I'm pretending. I shape my hands into crab claws and pinch the air.

That night my throat hurts, my nose is stuffed up, and I can't sleep. So I get out of bed and sit in my beanbag with my afghan wrapped around me. I breathe slowly until I'm back in the apartment in the faraway place and time. It's night time here too, so the air isn't as hot as usual. The tall lamp in the corner is on. I hear a man's voice on the radio in the other room saying something about "subprime mortgages" and "credit crunch." I think a subprime is probably a kind of submarine. Maybe credit crunch is a kind of Chex Mix for grown-up parties, with pretzels and cut-up credit cards. I call for Marmalade, quietly and then a little louder.

"Did you hear that?" asks the man on the radio. I freeze and hold my hands over my mouth. It's not the radio. There's a stranger here. Maybe it's a bad idea to be here at night.

"Shhh, I'm listening," a woman says. I think it's the Artist, but I'm not sure. I hear my family whistle and, without thinking, whistle it back.

"Jesus!" the man says. "She's actually physically here?"

"I *knew* you didn't believe me!"

"I thought you ... meant it metaphorically."

"Metaphors don't whistle."

"I've got to see her."

"Wait—"

I hide under a little table in case he's a kidnapper and she's trying to protect me. There's never been anyone else here before. I hug my knees to my chest.

"First of all," the woman says, "I don't know if anyone else can see her."

"Let's find out."

"Secondly, she's probably scared. Stay here."

I scrunch up even smaller, squeezing myself into the darkness. I breathe hard. I hear footsteps coming closer as she calls my name.

I whistle again so she'll find me. She looks under the little table. She smiles and I smile back. She's wearing flowy pants that fold over themselves at the waist.

"Come on out of there and I'll give you some juice or something." She disappears into the kitchen and comes back after a few minutes with a glass of thick orange liquid. I crawl out and have a sip. "Have you had mango juice before?" she asks. I shake my head. It tastes like creamsicles.

"Can you come visit me in California some time?" I ask.

"I don't know," she says. "I can try. Stay right here." I think that means don't go home and also don't go anywhere else in the apartment.

She goes back into the room with the man.

"Don't I get some juice too?" he asks.

She snorts like this is a good joke. They're both quiet then she says, "Okay, seriously, what if this messes up the future? Our future."

"Do you remember coming here as a kid?"

"No. Maybe. I used to daydream about being an artist. It's hard to remember."

"And do you remember ever seeing me?"

"I don't … Wait, I've got an idea."

The Artist comes out holding a cloth headband. I hand her the empty glass.

She bends down to my level and says, "Ivy, there's someone here who wants to see you, but you can't see him."

"Is he invisible?"

I hear a laugh from the other room. The Artist smiles. "Guess again."

I think for a minute then whisper, "Is he your boyfriend?"

"Bingo."

"You've got a boyfriend?!"

"Sure I do. Don't look so surprised. But you aren't allowed to see him yet." She hands me the headband. "Put this over your eyes. Now, no peeking, okay?" I nod, blindfolded. "Okay, honey, come here, but make it quick." I hear footsteps.

"Wow," the man says. "She looks just like you."

"You think?" the Artist asks.

"Definitely." I peek through the gap at the bottom of the blindfold. I can see the man's big bare feet. They're mostly tan with matching pale bands of skin. He says, "Amazing." I'm trying to figure out how he got stripes on his feet when I hear coughing far away. I open my eyes and I'm back in my room on my beanbag. The person coughing was me.

Sick

My throat is raw and I can breathe only through my mouth. Last night I kept waking up having to blow my nose, honking like a goose, throwing endless, heavy tissues into the dark. This morning my floor looks like a field after an egg toss. My eyes are watery and my neck is stiff. I think I am going to die.

"I don't feel good," I tell Mom and Dad in the morning. My voice is scratchy and doesn't sound right, like a piano that needs tuning. If it's my turn to go to the hospital, maybe Brice will try and take over my room. He might want *two* rooms, spreading out like in Monopoly.

"What's wrong?" Mom asks. "Does your tummy hurt?"

"No, I feel sick." Mom wants symptoms and I describe my snot in a lot of detail. I hope they let me stay home from school so I can snuggle with Mom on the couch and watch cartoons. Mom tucks me back into bed, straightening my afghan. I ask her to make me chicken noodle soup.

"Sorry, baby." She picks dirty tissues off the carpet. "I've got to go to work. Dad'll take care of you."

"But I want *you!*"

"I'll call at lunchtime to see how you're doing."

I shake my head and start crying, snot dripping from my nose. She says if I'm good I can earn back another dress.

"I don't care."

She sighs and hands me the box of tissues. "I need to go." She kisses me on the forehead. "You'll be okay."

I shake my head.

"I'll get Dad to bring you some breakfast."

"I don't want any breakfast!" I wail. She leaves and I throw the box of tissues hard against the wall. I scream, crying my pillow wet. Snot runs down my lip, into my mouth. "Come back!" I croak. I do the family whistle, but no one comes. Finally, I get out of bed to pick up the dented tissue box. I wipe my face and flip over my pillow. My eyes become heavy, then I've been kidnapped by robots and am running away from hot lava.

When I wake up again, there's orange juice and toast triangles next to my bed. I won't have a single bite, to teach Mom a lesson. Then I'll grow a pot belly like the kids in Ethiopia. I picture flies eating my eye crust, because I'm too weak to swat them away. Tonight, Mom will come home and find my orange juice has gone moldy, with ants crawling all over my stale toast. She'll gasp, dropping her purse to the floor, the flies buzzing away.

"My poor little darling." She holds me, rocking my fevered body in her arms. "Jesus, I'm a terrible mother. Ivy, I had no idea you were so sick. Can you ever forgive me?"

I cough up blood, watching her frightened face. Then I die, which serves her right for leaving.

"Hey there." Dad comes in, jolting me from my daydream. "Wasn't sure if you'd be awake. Feeling any better?"

I shrug and blow my nose.

"You should eat. Keep your strength up." I scowl and nibble the toast, but it tastes so good I eat the whole triangle. "Good girl." I drink some juice. He says Grandma is bringing soup over this afternoon. He gives me sticky grape medicine from the tube spoon.

"I wish Mom was here." I sigh.

Dad frowns. "Do you want me to read you a story or something?"

"I know how to read."

"I know you do. But if you're not feeling good, sometimes it's nice to hear a story."

"Okay." I fluff up my pillow. He pulls my beanbag over and starts reading *The BFG*, which is about an orphan girl and a giant who catches dreams. He's the only giant who doesn't eat people. Mom used to read to me when I was little, and now I read to myself. Dad turns the book around to show me the pictures. He has a nice voice.

Later, when I'm feeling a little better, we build a fort together out of couch cushions. Dad crawls inside with me, but he's so big we pretend he's a friendly giant I found in the woods. We eat popsicles, which feel good on my throat.

"It tastes like berries," I tell him. "Do you like berries?"

He nods and takes a careful lick. "Cold!" he says in a slow, deep voice.

I laugh. "Yes it is cold. And I bet you get cold in the woods sometimes."

"Brrrrrr." He shakes himself.

"Maybe my grandma will make you a jacket out of one hundred blankets and then you won't be cold anymore."

"Big jacket," he says.

I didn't know Dad knew how to do make-believe.

Next, Dad and I move to the kitchen table, drawing together and drinking ginger ale. He sketches houses and I draw myself ice skating with my family, using a few photos to make it look good.

"That's really good, Ivy," he says, leaning over to look at my picture. "When did you become such a talented artist?"

Under the Table

The stable was a gift to Cricket Sara from her dad. It has four narrow rooms with a wooden bar that comes down like a railroad crossing. Part house, part prison. Grandma says it's too late to close the barn door after the horse runs away. But I think you should anyway, just to teach him a lesson in case he decides to come back. *"Let me in!" the horse whinnies, scraping the barn door with his hoof. "I'm hungry and it's cold out here."*

Sara says her dad still needs to get her little saddles and bridles and other things. She's lucky because when she wants, he gives, and when she wants more he keeps giving. We're playing in her room at her mom's house. Her horses have realistic muscly legs and swirling manes, not at all like My Little Ponies. I make my horse tap-dance on the stable roof and Sara rolls her eyes.

"That wouldn't really happen."

"Neigh!" I say in a funny voice. I bounce my horse over to the trough of Triscuits and make munching sounds. "This is good hay!"

Sara giggles. "I want some too!" she says as her horse, trotting it over.

The doorbell rings. We each grab a cracker and tiptoe downstairs to the kitchen where the air smells heavy and sweet.

"They're probably playing upstairs. Come on in," Olivia says from the hallway. "I-vy!" she yells in a high voice. "Your dad's here."

"Let's hide!" Sara whispers. I see a gap between the kitchen cabinets and the trash. It looks perfect except it smells like onions and it's only big enough for one person. The footsteps are getting closer. Sara lifts the tablecloth and we crawl under the kitchen table just in time.

"It smells amazing in here," Dad says. I see his shoes under the tablecloth. Olivia says it's cream of asparagus soup and she's about to make a cheese soufflé. Dad asks if she's having a dinner party.

Olivia laughs. "No, I just felt like cooking. A soufflé isn't that hard. You beat a lot of air into it and serve it immediately so it doesn't fall."

"I'm such a lousy cook," Dad says. "I wish I knew how to make things like that. I don't even know how to make soup, let alone a soufflé."

"You've just got to know when to follow the recipe and when to do your own thing." I hear metal clanking, then she says, "Here, have a taste."

"Mmmm, really creamy. How'd you get it so smooth?"

"I used the blender."

"Of course, dumb question."

"Not at all," Olivia says. They're both quiet.

"Come on, Ivy!" Dad yells. Inside the table cave, Sara and I clamp our hands over our mouths to trap the giggles. Sara pinches me. I pinch back.

After a moment, Olivia says, "You know, if you don't have to run off straight away, I can show you how to do a soufflé. I mean, if you're interested." He is, so we get comfortable against the table leg. Olivia talks to Dad about egg whites. He asks lots of questions and she answers.

Blah-blah cheese, question mark?
Blah-blah blah cheese, answer.

I play with the old rubber washer from my pocket. Sara finds some string and we play cat's cradle, pinching the x's.

Olivia talks about oven temperature, Iran-Contra, Swedish massage, and high-sided dishes. Being a spy is boring. I wish they'd talk about something besides cooking. We play thumb war then ro-sham-bo. Sara threads string through the washer like it's a bead.

"It feels good talking to another grown-up," Dad says.

"I know just what you mean," Olivia says.

Once the food's in the oven, they head upstairs, calling our names. We burst into the living room, rolling and giggling on the couch.

"Down here, Mom!" Sara shouts and we are found.

"See you both in a few days," Olivia says as we're leaving.

"Quiche!" Dad has flour on his collar. "Looking forward to it."

Driving past the fire station, Dad says I get to play with Sara again later this week while her mom gives him a cooking lesson.

"What's quiche?" I ask.

"It's a kind of fancy pie with egg."

"Egg pie? Gross."

"No, it's good." He catches my eye in the rearview mirror. "Is that a washer around your neck?"

Dirt for Sale

I crunch along the gravel path at Sunnyside Nursery, carrying a tray of pansies. Turning at the bird baths, I pass shovels and big sacks of dirt. It's funny that anyone would actually buy dirt when you can just dig it out of the ground for free. It's like selling air. A hummingbird hovers, tasting the honeysuckles.

I spot Brice's shoe sticking out from a little potted forest of bamboo. My brother is sitting on the ground, reading. I put down the tray of pansies.

"Hey," I say.

He doesn't look up. I nudge his shoe.

"Hey, Ivy," he says.

I squint at him and try to decide if he might want to play or just wants to read. "Look what I picked out for the garden," I say, pointing to the pansies.

"Nice," Brice says and starts to go back to his book.

"I've got an idea," I say. "Let's pretend we're explorers in the jungle!"

Brice makes a face.

"And," I continue, trying to find a way to get him interested, "I've got a broken leg because I tripped and fell off a cliff. And it really really hurts and I need your help getting back to civilization because otherwise I'll die."

Brice looks at me for a moment like he might say yes.

"I've got an idea," he says. "How about *you're* a jungle explorer, and I'm a professor."

I grin at him. "Okay!" I say. "How do we play?"

"Well, you go off ... exploring. And I stay right here at the college, teaching about jungle theory."

"Wait a minute," I say. "You don't want to come exploring with me?"

Brice looks around nervously, but no one's around. "I'm afraid that would be impossible," he says in an English accent. "I must stay here at Bamboo University and study my books."

"But wouldn't you learn more about jungle theory in the jungle?" I ask.

"Quite possibly. But my books would also get damp. And my spectacles might get swallowed by a boa constrictor."

I groan. This isn't really a game at all if Brice is just going to stay here.

He continues, "It would be a great benefit to the university if you, my explorer friend, went into the darkest jungle on your own. Then come back and tell me what you found."

"I'll go into the jungle," I growl, picking up the tray of pansies. "But I might not come back."

I continue down the gravel path and find Mom chatting with a lady with a long sweater covering her curvy butt. I can't see the lady's face and I stay near the bottle brush plants, hoping they won't see me.

"He's started running again," Mom says. "And the other day he went out for drinks with his old coworkers. But it sounds like they didn't have that much to talk about anymore."

Mom says something about Grandma and the boutique, and then they're talking about some woman who's "on the prowl" now that she's single again. I think this is what cats do when they're looking for mice. I wonder what the woman would do if she caught a mouse, and then they're on to something else.

Sweater Lady says, "He must have been able to make something." I don't recognize her voice.

"You're right," Mom says. "He microwaved soup." They both laugh.

"Barbecues?"

"Barbecues," Mom agrees. "Eggs, toast. But seriously, that was it. I don't have the energy to cook these days. My job's fantastic but I come home completely drained. Besides, it's getting late by then and the kids are used to eating early."

"And now?"

"Now he's making real food from scratch. Cream of carrot soup, lasagna … cheese soufflé!"

"Soufflé?"

"I kid you not. And it's all good too. He's checked out some cookbooks from the library. It's really cute."

"Why the sudden interest?"

Mom shrugs. "Necessity, I guess. Looks like he didn't want to keep eating mac and cheese anymore than we did. Well, than *I* did. The kids will eat anything if it's covered in cheese."

"Not *anything*!" I come out from my hiding place. "I wouldn't eat glass or rubber bands that were covered in cheese."

"Not even if it was brie?" Mom teases, putting the pansies on her cart. Sweater Lady turns and I see it's Maxine Ludlow.

"You must be so proud of your Working Mother," Maxine tells me. The clown on her sweater is juggling pompoms.

"I found her the job!" I brag. Mom smiles and says it's true. Maxine asks me how everything's going at home. *I love spending time with Dad, but Brice is too busy to play with me and I miss Mom so much that sometimes I want to hide her car keys.*

"It's fine," I say.

"You know … " Mom turns to Maxine and I'm invisible again. " … the other day Neil complained about feeling like a chauffeur, having to drive the kids everywhere."

"Uh-huh. Did he think you just stayed home and baked cookies?"

"God, my *mother's* started with the cookies. She made us three dozen snickerdoodles and then two dozen oatmeal raisin a few days later. What are we supposed to do with that many cookies? It's a bit over the top. We froze most of them."

"She's just trying to be nice."

Right—so let her bake cookies if she wants. But the other day she actually dropped by while I was at work and insisted on cleaning our house."

"What?" Maxine says. "You're kidding."

"She said, 'I'm here to clean. Where do you keep the vacuum?'"

Maxine snorts. "Did he let her in?"

"He told her he had everything under control and offered her a cookie. But, after she left, he decided cleaning wasn't a bad idea." Mom holds up a finger. "Turns out *he* didn't know where we keep our vacuum either."

"Ha!"

"So," Mom can barely get the words out, "he called me up at work to ask!"

Maxine hoots. She asks if I know where our vacuum is. It's in the closet under the stairs, but I feel like they're making fun of Dad, so I shake my head. If you don't say the words it's not so much of a lie.

Later, Mom and I are on our hands and knees, digging in the backyard by the stone wall. Brice is inside the house because he didn't want to help. Mom says we haven't seen much of each other lately and that she thinks about me and Brice when she's at work. I squeeze the roots like Mom showed me, helping another pansy out of the tray. Gardening earns me one more piece of clothing. So far I've gotten back two shirts, three skirts, one pair of jeans, and two dresses. Grandma sewed up the holes so they're almost as good as new. I press dirt around the flower, hoping it will be happy here and grow into a big pansy tree. I water the plants and wonder if, in between his Asshole Boss and Idiot Coworker, Dad ever thought about us at work.

Under Fire

I like the way they squish in my mouth. Mom passes me another deviled egg. Brice helps himself to a scoop of Dad's pasta salad. It's the middle of May, and my family's having a picnic in the shade of a plum tree at Robson Harrington Park. Nearby, a girl runs to her mom with a rooster kite bouncing along the grass. Two boys catch bugs in a jar. I think that's mean because those bugs are used to hopping around the whole park and now they only have a little jar to hop in. I hope the boys let them go.

"The sixth-grade Science Fair is coming up soon, isn't it?" Mom asks, lifting the flap of the picnic basket for a soda.

"Yeah," Brice says. "Trevor and I were going to brainstorm ideas together. But now we have to wait."

"How come?" Dad pops an olive in his mouth.

"Because he's grounded."

"Trevor? Grounded?" Mom snorts, settling back on the blanket. I'm surprised too. Trevor with the stinky feet and braces is annoying, but I can't picture him ever getting bad grades or cutting holes in his clothes or shoplifting.

"Well," Brice says, "Trevor got in trouble because his mom made Rice Krispie Treats for something, but she didn't say 'don't eat them' and he thought they were up for grabs and he ate some and then she got really angry. So now he's grounded. Plus he has to help his mom make another batch."

"She didn't put a sign on them or anything?" I ask.

"Nothing," Brice says. "How was he supposed to know?"

I sigh. I don't even like Trevor but it's not fair.

Mom says, "I guess Margery should have told him, but Trevor should have asked before digging in."

"It's not fair because grown-ups *can't* get in trouble," I say. "Except for jail if you kill someone, but not just normal trouble."

"Grown-ups can get in trouble for all sorts of things," Dad says handing me a strawberry. "You don't have to go to jail to be in trouble."

"Like what?" I ask.

"Like if you break an agreement with someone you care about," Dad says. "I agree to pick you and Brice up from ballet and soccer practice. I can't just leave you there. If I did, I'd be in trouble with you and Mom and your instructors."

I picture all the other girls getting picked up after ballet. I'd keep expecting Dad to arrive but he wouldn't come and then it'd just be me and Miss Garville left. She'd glance at the big clock near the door until finally she'd shrug and leave me there alone. I'd do a sad dance in the big empty studio and sleep in a nest of tutus.

"Married couples have an agreement not to love anyone else," Mom says, touching Dad's knee.

"Do you get arrested if you do?" I ask.

"No, baby," Mom says. "It's not illegal. But the other person would be very upset and hurt."

"Then you get a divorce, which is big trouble," Brice says. "Also, if you do something really really awful at work you can get fired."

"Like lighting the office on fire!" I say.

Mom laughs. "Are you sure you aren't just saying that because 'fired' sounds like 'fire'?"

"It doesn't even have to be that bad," Dad says. "Sometimes people lose their jobs because they have a difference of opinion with their boss."

"Okay, but usually you have to be really lazy or bad," Brice says. "Like not doing your work, or always showing up three hours late."

"It's more complicated than that," Dad says.

"Mom, what would happen if you got fired?" I ask. If Mom lost her job then maybe we really would be poor and would have to sell all our stuff except for two books and one change of clothes each. I'd also get to keep two crayons and five blank pieces of paper, even though that wouldn't last me very long. Then we'd move to a dirty apartment in the City with hungry rats. I'm not sure which two colors of crayons I would keep. Maybe blue and red. Hopefully they'd let me keep more than that. If I could keep five colors I'd go with red, yellow, green, blue, and black. But then there'd be no pink or purple, which are pretty, or brown, which is kind of a yucky color but is really useful for drawing shoes, hair, and trees. Also dogs. And poo.

"I'm not going to get fired," Mom says. "I care about the boutique and respect my colleagues. And you guys are all counting on me to bring home the bacon. Getting fired is a pretty big deal. If someone has a problem with your work, they talk with you about it first. They don't just get rid of you."

"Well, it really depends," Dad says.

"Neil, why are you being so contrary?" Mom asks. "You're scaring the kids."

"I'm not scared," Brice says. "I know only stupid or lazy people get fired."

"That's really not true," Dad says.

Mom looks confused. "It's not like that's what happened at your old firm," she says. "You were laid off. Nothing personal. A bunch of people were let go." A funny look comes over Dad's face. Mom stares at him like she was just stung by a bee. "Neil?"

Dad sighs and drops his head in his big hands. "They accused me of plagiarism."

Mom looks stunned. "Well, that's ridiculous! Didn't you tell them they were wrong?"

Dad rubs his forehead and stares at the picnic blanket. "Not exactly. It's complicated." Mom picks up a strawberry, looks at it and puts it back in the bowl. Dad continues, "Remember I told you about that guy Randall who was always making an ass of himself, forgetting projects, and telling our boss they'd slipped his mind?"

Mom nods, lips tight.

Dad says, "We were on a project together, except the jerk kept forgetting to do his part of the work. So I had to cut a few corners to make up for lost time. I figured no one would have to know."

I picture Dad's Asshole Boss, fat and bald, sitting behind his huge desk.

"Here you go," he says. He hands Dad and his Idiot Coworker Randall a big project designing a new San Francisco skyscraper. "That should keep you both busy a while." He laughs.

"Thank you so much, sir," Randall says, running his fingers through his greasy hair. "We won't let you down."

Two weeks later, Dad goes over to Randall, who's playing with a snow globe. I bet Randall has a whole collection of them in a long row between his pencil mug and dead plant. He has snow globes of the Eiffel Tower, the Taj Mahal, and Sleeping Beauty's Castle at Disneyland.

"Hey, buddy," Dad says. "You still on track to get your half of the big project to me today?"

"Today?" Randall leaps out of his chair, spilling his pencils. "I'm sure it's here somewhere." He paws through the candy bar wrappers and Post-it notes on his desk. Then he stops and asks, "Wait, what project?"

"Jesus Christ," Dad says. "Remember the skyscraper project? I was going to design the bottom forty storys and you said you'd do the top forty?"

"Oh, yeah! I remember now!"

"Great, well, it's due today. You almost finished?"

"Not exactly ... "

"Okay, how much more time do you need?"

"Kind of a lot ... The thing is, I haven't even started yet."

Dad panics and jogs straight out of the office without telling anyone where he's going (which is bad because they could worry). He runs up city roads so steep they have stairs on the sidewalks, and zigzags down Lombard Street, the crookedest street in the world. Then he stops suddenly, his tie blowing in the breeze. He screams into the fog, "Nooooo!" Then, head down, he walks back to work.

With the clock above his desk ticking down to the end of the world, Dad copies the top of some other skyscraper.

"Hey, buddy," Dad interrupts Randall, who's busy shaking a snow globe of the Statue of Liberty. Dad unrolls the scroll from under his arm. "I figured it out on my own. Just don't tell the boss, okay?"

He hands his Asshole Boss his stack of blueprints.

"Here's the building we designed. Hope you like it."

"I'd better like it." His boss smirks, rubbing his big belly. "Hmm ... looks kind of familiar. Wait a minute—the top looks a hell of a lot like the Empire State Building."

"That's because it is!" Randall bursts into the office, holding a snow globe. "Neil copied!"

"Copied?" Dad's Asshole Boss shouts. He looks at the miniature Empire State Building in the snow globe and back to the blueprints. "No one plagiarizes in my office! Neil, you're fired!"

Mom looks pale and small on the picnic blanket. "I don't even know what to say."

"It was time for me to move on anyway." Dad stretches his long legs. "You know how miserable I was there. The hours, my Asshole Boss."

"Excuse me? What about your family? I can't even comprehend that you pretended you were laid off all this time." Mom bites her lip. "You lied to me."

Dad looks away. "I just couldn't tell you the truth."

After our picnic, Brice and I put the leftovers away while Mom and Dad go upstairs to yell at each other.

"I can't fucking believe you got fired!" Mom screams from their room.

"What difference does it make now?" Dad shouts.

I empty the pasta salad into Tupperware and picture Mom and Dad riding a see-saw. Up is going to work and down is staying home. Up-down, up-down. As long as someone is up and someone is down, they can pay the bills and Brice and I aren't latchkey kids. Brice gives me a sad smile and finds a place in the fridge for the pasta next to the last of the strawberries and deviled eggs. When Dad lost his job but before Mom got hers, they were both down, which meant the see-saw was broken. I think about how Mom likes working with the funny mannequin lady, Yogurt Gloria, and Bev the Storyteller from the boutique. But Dad couldn't stand his Idiot Coworker and Asshole Boss. Maybe it's better this way.

"So honesty doesn't matter anymore?" Mom yells from upstairs. "What else are you keeping from me?"

A few minutes later Dad comes downstairs in his short shorts and sweatbands. His face is red even though he hasn't started running yet.

"Hey, kids, I'll be back in a bit. Be good."

On my way upstairs I see Mom and Dad's door is closed. I hear Mom crying, which must mean she's really really sad.

I go to my room, keeping my door open so I don't miss anything. Getting out my deluxe box of sixty-four crayons with the built-in sharpener, I feel grateful at least to have so many colors to choose from. Brice goes into his room, closing the door behind him. I draw a picture of my family sinking into quicksand. We're all wearing explorer hats, and because some of us have been sinking longer than others we're all the exact same height. Brice would have preferred to stay back with his books, but I say we're *all* explorers so we *all* have to go into the jungle together. Now we're in this mess and no one can save us. There's a crocodile next to the quicksand licking his lips. He'd like to eat us, but he knows he can't get us without sinking in himself.

How could Dad have gotten caught? I've done all sorts of bad things that no one's ever found out about. Like when I was grounded and snuck over to Jenny's house and got my hair crimped. Or when I shoplifted that lip gloss with Erin. And there's the embarrassing things that no one knows about either, like when I got lost in the woods and Lucy rescued me. Or last year when I got sick at school and missed the toilet and some of the throw-up got on the floor. But I just left the bathroom real fast and no one knew it was me so it was okay. Dad is so smart, but he got caught all the same. He knows how to stretch the truth and how to say the right things, but it wasn't enough, or maybe he stretched the truth too much and it broke. He still hasn't found a new job, so if I hadn't found Mom's job, then we'd probably all have starved to death by now. With a chill I realize I really have saved my family.

Table for Three

Mom is very busy at the boutique these days and keeps having to work later than usual. And then after work she needs to meet up with Maxine Ludlow or some other friend. This means Dad, Brice, and I have dinner without her. Mom's chair is across from me like normal, but it's empty.

"Fine," Brice says, pressing the back of his fork into his mashed potatoes.

"Fine," I say.

"Come on, kids," Dad says. "Work with me here. Let's all tell something interesting from our days."

"I just went to school," Brice says, eating a broccoli tree. "Nothing interesting happened."

"Well, someone needs to say something," Dad says. "Otherwise we're just going to sit here chewing in silence."

"Fine with me," Brice says.

"Me too," I say. I pick up a chicken drumstick and chew loudly. The barbecue sauce is sweet and tangy and gets all over my mouth. There's something wrong about eating the food Dad made when we're angry at him. But what else can we do? We're hungry.

Dad sighs.

"Look, if I could go back in time I would have done things differently. But you guys giving me the silent treatment isn't going to get me my job back or change anything. We need to move past this as a family."

"I thought you were supposed to be our role model," Brice says, scrunching up his face. "Oh, yeah, when I grow up I want to be just like my dad. I want to get a really good job and then lose it and pretend it wasn't my fault."

"That's enough, Brice," Dad says. "I never said I was perfect. I'm doing the best I can. I'm going to make it up to all of you. I just need a little support."

"Can we go watch TV?" Brice asks.

"Not till you've finished your dinner." It's the sort of thing Mom would say and it sounds funny coming out of Dad's mouth, like a duck mooing.

"Come on, Dad," Brice says. "What does it matter anyway?"

Dad looks out the window for a long moment. "Fine," he says. "Just don't make a mess on the couch."

Brice and I carry our plates to the family room. Watching TV in black-and-white is better than having to sit at the same table as Dad the Big Fat Liar. In the hallway, Brice asks, "By the way, Ivy, can I have some of your old baby teeth? It's for a good cause."

I'm in bed asleep by the time Mom comes home. She sits on the edge of my bed and fixes my blankets, tucking me in tight. I want to ask her something but I'm too sleepy and I can't get the words out. She just sits with me, stroking my hair in the dark. I think she looks sad or maybe just tired, but in this light I can't tell.

Part V

Deception

Take Two

"It's not true," says the teenager the next day, refilling the saltwater taffy bin. "It's just a rumor."

"Are you sure?" I ask. "I heard if you eat too many they can explode in your stomach and kill you dead."

"Honestly, they're perfectly safe." He coughs. He's wearing a plaid shirt and his nose looks too big for his face. "They're just fizzy candies." He glances across at Erin, the only other person in Sweet Stuff. She studies the candy like she's counting every jellybean.

"What's in them?" I ask. "I'm not buying any if they're made with dynamite."

The boy stretches like a seagull about to take off, flashing the damp patches under his arms. His back is to Erin as he reads me the ingredients. I keep interrupting to ask what the words mean. Erin keeps out of sight, silently stuffing her sweatshirt pocket, like a hamster filling its cheeks with sunflower seeds.

"And ... dynamite!" I say when he reaches the end.

"That's not what I'm saying. There's no explosives in Pop Rocks!"

I put my hand on my hip, "But you said they were made with dynamite."

Erin slips outside and I exhale deeply. I am doing this for her. Whenever I am a criminal it is because I love her.

"No," he growls. "I totally never said that. These things are seriously safe. It's just rumors." I nod like he's finally convinced me and give him the quarter from my shoe.

I find Erin at the sailor boy fountain.

"Hellooo!" I grin, shaking the packet of Pop Rocks.

"Ho ho ho!" She pats her bulging sweatshirt. We sit on the bench and divvy everything up. Then we start munching our loot. Erin says, "We make a good team."

"You were so fast in there."

"I just said to distract him, but that was great. You sounded pretty worried."

"Boom!" I yell. A crow flies overhead. I swing my feet, kicking the air. "Hey, do you want these?" I offer her the Pop Rocks.

"What, you scared?"

"No." I roll my eyes. "I just don't like them is all." I eat a saltwater taffy, which sticks my teeth together. The sailor boy is getting on my nerves. He always looks so happy in his stupid barrel boat, like Hawaii is just around the corner. But of course he never gets there. He never goes anywhere, and neither do I. Without wanting to, I'm thinking again about Dad getting fired. I work my teeth free and wonder if I should tell Erin. She's sucking a lollipop. Maybe she can help somehow, but I'm not sure how anyone can make it okay.

"I've got an idea!" she shouts suddenly. For a strange moment I wonder if she can hear my thoughts and knows what to do about Dad. But then she says, "Let's go to Various and Sundries." The store has *piñatas* and stickers and metal wind-up toys which probably don't cure lying dads, so I figure she probably can't read my mind after all. Just to be sure, I think about boogers and poo but she doesn't make a face, which proves she's not psychic. She says she needs to go to the store to spell out her name with the plastic monsters shaped like letters. But Various and Sundries is in town, on San Anselmo Avenue, near Bubba's and the little store with the crystals that smells like incense, which makes it too far to walk. I point this out to Erin … as if she didn't know.

A mysterious smile crawls across her face. "We can hitchhike."

I gasp. That's as crazy as playing with fireworks blindfolded or brushing an alligator's teeth. The TV says kids are getting kidnapped every day and there's nothing worse than getting into a stranger's car. *"Come with me, little girl."* The Bad Men trick you with candy and kittens, or candy kittens. They tie you up and throw you in the back with your mouth duct-taped so you can't scream. I saw it all in a movie. They keep you trapped in a dark room and your picture shows up on milk cartons. Then you probably die. This is Erin's worst idea ever.

But Mom says sometimes it's good to do what scares you, like reading out loud in class or holding your breath underwater. If I hitchhiked with Erin, she might want to be my best friend. I need one now more than ever.

"Come on." Erin leans in. "It'll be fun."

I picture myself in the apartment in that faraway time and place. I imagine breathing in the hot, wet air, which makes me more calm. I see a painter's palette shaped like a lily pad, a jar of smelly liquid, and a tube of red glitter. Now the big painting on the easel is of a small girl in a red dress, surrounded by blue ovals. Taped to the Artist's wall are pictures of girls my age ripped out of magazines. Marmalade is asleep, stretched out on the floor like he's leaping. The Artist stands at the window, looking out. What does she see? I wonder if she's looking at traffic or maybe she is lost in thought as well. I notice a world map on the wall. Like the astronauts' flag on the moon, there are pins sprinkled across Europe and Asia and America. I search the Pacific Ocean and smile when I find a pin sticking out of Hawaii. So maybe I will get there one day.

Looking back at the Artist, I'm about to ask her about hitchhiking, but she's a grown-up so she'd probably say it's too dangerous. And she'd probably be right.

I come back to Red Hill and Erin. I ask, "Your mom and stepdad *let* you hitchhike?"

"Aw, they don't care what I do," Erin says. "Come on. You scared?"

I shake my head. "I'm not hitchhiking."

"Pretty please?"

"No way, José."

"I thought we were friends." Erin folds her arms. "Friends do things together."

I picture myself at the side of the road, sticking out my thumb. I'm standing between Erin and the punk ostrich I drew for Brice. His feathers are puffed out to show he's tough and not afraid of anything. I've already lost Jenny and I can't lose Erin too. If I don't do this, it might be over between us. But if I do …

"Not going to do it," I sing, surprising myself. "I'm going home."

Later on, I find Dad on the couch, taking notes. The woman on our little TV cooks gray food in a black-and-white kitchen. She stirs a pot that she tells us is coming along nicely. Dad says he's learning how to make a béchamel sauce.

"What's that?" I ask.

"A kind of white sauce."

"How can you tell what color it is?"

"It's called a white sauce. It's made with flour, butter, and milk."

"Oh. Can you make me a snack plate?"

"Just get yourself an apple or something. I'm making eggplant parmesan for dinner."

The kitchen smells like hot tomatoes. I find a stack of library books by the phone. I flip through *Italian Cuisine in a Flash* while I eat a banana. Then I look up "Jell-O" in the back of a dessert cookbook. I can only find jelly rolls, which sound pretty good too. The next time Erin and I play on her trampoline, we can pretend we're mice, ice-skating on a giant bowl of Jell-O. A huge imaginary cat could chase us and we'd bounce like crazy trying to get away. *"Aaargh! A cat's trying to eat us!"* Unless of course she got kidnapped today.

I pick up the phone to call Erin, but there's no dial tone. I'm about to hang up when a lady says, "I miss you." I hold my hand over the receiver. "I can't stop thinking about you," she whispers.

"Yeah," Dad whispers back.

This isn't Mom calling from work, so who is she?

"It's silly, isn't it?" the lady asks. "You're so cute. I like your hair. I liked you instantly, as soon as I saw you. I thought you might like me too, but I wasn't sure."

My stomach feels bubbly. I'm eavesdropping, which is like being a Peeping Tom. The lady talks quietly about them making dinner and looking at each other across the table. She says she couldn't wait for them to be alone. "And then that kiss … " she says. "You make me feel like I'm … sixteen."

I've got a winter storm in me. My lungs are full of cold wind and there's muddy run-off in my arms. I should definitely, absolutely hang up—but I can't. How can Dad listen to this strange lady? He needs to tell her that he doesn't like her back. He can't; he loves Mom.

"I want to kiss you again like against that tree," she says. "Would you like that?"

"Yeah," he says. My eyes widen.

"I want it more than anything."

"Me too."

"Omigod," she hisses. "I think someone's coming. I need to go."

I wait for the line to go dead before hanging up.

Outside on the tire swing, I stare at poison oak wrapping around a tree. Don't touch it or your skin goes red and itchy. Looking is okay, but sometimes even that feels dangerous. There's no point spinning because I am dizzy already.

Guilt

"Whatcha reading?" I ask Brice, sitting at the foot of his bed. It's the end of the weekend. We've cleaned our rooms, watched *The Disney Sunday Movie,* and now it's almost time for sleep. I half expect him to say he's too busy to talk.

Instead he says, "*Hatchet,*" which apparently is a kind of axe. He tells me the book is about a kid who crash-lands a plane in a lake in the middle of nowhere, after the pilot drops dead from a heart attack. "The kid almost drowns and is stranded in the wilderness all by himself."

I shudder, remembering my night lost with the raccoons. Brice says the kid has to figure out how to survive. "It's a good book because he really suffers. It feels real. Lucy liked it too."

I wonder if pain makes a story better. If someone was reading the story of my life, would they like it when bad things happen to my family? Brice got sick, Jenny stopped being my friend, Dad lost his job, we lost our TV, and now Dad's cheating on Mom. Plus I've probably lost Erin too, either kidnapped and chopped into little pieces or else she just won't want to be friends anymore. Would our hurt make the readers smile? Also I wonder if there's a moral to all of this or if it's the kind of story that's just a story.

"Brice?" I scoot closer. "Have you ever heard something you shouldn't have?"

"What do you mean?" His face tightens.

"What would you do if you were ... " The word gets caught under my tongue. "eavesdropping and heard something bad? But you didn't want to tell anyone because then they'd know you were eavesdropping which is also bad."

Brice relaxes and lays the book on the bed. "You know no one likes a tattletale."

"I know, but it's not like that. What if it was something important?"

"Like what?"

"I dunno."

"What did you hear?"

I sigh. Maybe it was a bad idea to ask Brice. "I don't know if I should say."

Brice stares at me with raised eyebrows.

"I think Dad might be having an affair."

"What?" Brice spits. "How do you even know that word?"

I roll my eyes. "I watch TV."

"Okay, Ivy, this is important. What makes you think that Dad … " He trails off like it's a swear word he can't say.

I explain what I overheard on the phone. "They've already kissed and they want to do it again!"

"Well, who was she?"

"I don't know. Honest. I didn't recognize her voice, but she talked lots and definitely wasn't Mom. What should we do? I don't want them to get a divorce but … but … " I sniff, wiping my eyes on my pajama sleeve.

"Shit," Brice says. "I need to think. Let's talk in the morning."

"Okay." I touch his foot through the blanket. He tells me it'll be okay but I think he might be lying.

Tucked into bed in the dark, I pull my afghan around me and imagine Dad and Phone Lady kissing against a tree in Memorial Park. I don't know what she looks like so I picture her as a life-sized Barbie with big, stiff boobs and long blonde hair.

"Mmmmm," he says. "I missed you so much."

Then I realize Mom is sitting on the grass nearby, behind an olive tree. I pray Dad and Barbie will hurry up and stop kissing before she sees. All that separates Mom from not knowing and knowing is this single tree. Horrified, I watch as Mom stretches, looks around and sees them! She screams and throws olives.

"Hey, cut it out!" Barbie shouts, covering her face. "Relax, we were only kissing."

"Only kissing?" Mom hisses. "Only kissing ... my husband!"

Barbie looks shocked and Dad holds his head.

"You know, Phone Lady's right," Dad tells Mom after a moment. "You should relax, Karen. It's not like you're home much these days anyway and I've been lonely. So just chill out."

Then Mom stomps over and pulls off Barbie's plastic arm with a loud "pop."

"My arm!" Barbie screams, holding her shoulder stump.

"Just chill out? Just chill out?" Mom yells, hitting Dad with the arm.

"Ow!" Dad cries out. "My head!"

I rewind my imagination, until Mom's safely behind the tree again. Dad and two-armed Barbie go back to kissing and Mom sits, sadly poking the grass. She senses something's wrong, but as long as she doesn't know, we can all pretend it's not happening.

"Oh, Barbie, I want you," Dad says.

"I want you too, Neil." She touches his face.

Mom looks up suddenly, alert and panicked. My heart stops. But Dad and Barbie keep kissing and Mom doesn't turn around.

In the morning, Brice and I are alone in the kitchen. I'm

fixing myself a bowl of Dino Pebbles, which have more marshmallows per box than any other cereal. Brice doesn't like milk anymore and is eating toast with globs of strawberry jam, the best kind.

"I mean, did they actually say they'd kissed?" he whispers.

"The lady did, a hundred percent positive."

Brice sighs. "Okay, here's the plan. Neither of us should say anything to anyone." I nod, glad I haven't already told Erin. "We have to pay careful attention to everything."

"Like detectives?" I ask.

"Yeah, sure. But we need more information. We can't jump to conclusions."

That afternoon after school, we're in the backyard, lying on the lawn near the stone wall and the new pansies.

"Does she have good legs?" Brice asks.

"I don't *know*," I moan.

"She must if she's a ballet teacher. What'd you say her name was again? Mrs. Landfill?"

"Miss Garville."

He writes her name in a notebook. I wanted to call it the Detective Notebook, and get Sherlock Holmes hats and magnifying glasses to look for clues, but Brice said that's stupid because this isn't a game.

Ms. Kelley is young and pretty, but Brice's teacher, Mrs. Stanton, is too old and besides she smokes, which is gross. We discuss our neighbors and I ask about Alice Miller.

"With the baby and the rose bushes?"

"Mom always says how beautiful her roses are. And they had a stone wall before we did. Maybe Mom's jealous."

"Interesting." Brice adds her name to the list. "Didn't Dad used to have a secretary at his office?" He writes something and chews the pen cap. "Do any of your friends have sexy moms?"

"I don't know!"

"Whoa, easy there. Let's just go through the ones Dad's met."

"Ooh! Write down Erin's mom," I say. "Dad called her stepdad a deadbeat."

"Perfect. That sounds like jealous talk too. How about Jenny's mom?"

My eyes squeeze shut. Honeybee Girl across the street, cat-trainer, dirty blonde peanut-hater, bad pretender, ex-best friend. "Jenny's not my friend anymore."

"Whatever—she still has a mom, doesn't she? Does she work?"

I nod. "Both her parents do."

Brice writes something down. I ask about Stinky Feet Trevor's mom.

"Hello—have you *seen* Margery Cunningham?"

I have—she has a nice smile and makes really good Rice Krispie Treats. But Brice says, "No way would Dad like her."

"Why? Because she wears glasses?"

"More like her giant butt and hairy chin wart."

We're both silent. I pick at my cuticles and Brice draws boobs in the margin.

"Sara's mom's divorced and Dad's been going over for cooking lessons."

"Say what?"

"Cooking lessons. She's teaching him how to cook."

"Jesus Christ."

"What?"

"Never mind. I'll give her a great big star. What's her name?"

"*Oliviah*," I exhale in that breathy way of hers. I catch a ladybug and let it crawl across my hand. "Melanie's mom used to be a musician." She and Dad talked for ages the other day after soccer practice. Brice says he almost died of boredom. I brush my fingers across the lawn. He teaches me how to whistle through a blade of grass. Together, we make the sort of loud, squeaky music that grown-ups find annoying.

"By the way," Brice says, "can you draw me a smiling cow some time?"

"Okay."

After a minute he asks, "What about Maxine?"

"Maxine *Ludlow*?"

"Why do you always call her that? Do you know any other Maxines? Whatever. She's got those really big … eyes. And they've known each other for years. Dad might even like those silly sweaters because they're so different from anything Mom would wear. And they're both home during the day, so lots of time to *do it*."

My skin prickles. "Give her a star."

"How'd my girl do today?" Dad asks when he picks me up from ballet the next day. It's Tuesday, and we've been practicing our *pirouettes*. We learned about "spotting," which is looking at something that's not moving while you spin so you don't lose your balance. I don't want to fall over, but the thing is, I *like* getting dizzy. Without dizzy, the tire swing would be no fun. I'd outgrow it like a hermit crab and its shell.

"Good," I say.

"Really good," Miss Garville says, organizing her tapes for the next class.

"Great," Dad says.

"Dad, look what I can do." I *sauté arabesque* and *pirouette* to the mirrors.

"I thought so," Miss Garville is saying to Dad when I skip back. "My boyfriend actually thinks the Stapleton School should interview each girl during registration."

"No kidding. What do you think?" Dad asks.

"He's probably overthinking the whole thing, which is pretty much par for the course for him. Honestly, the girls who don't want to be here never stick it out for very long.

He's pretty cute with his theories, though. Anyway, I'm glad Ivy's enjoying herself more now."

I go home and cross Miss Garville's name off the list. No one would cheat on a "pretty cute" boyfriend.

Wednesday after school, Sara teaches me the difference between a trot and canter and Dad learns how to make sweet and sour beef. I'm hunting for clues because Olivia's got a star. Sara and I gallop up and down the hall, popping into the kitchen. She wants to peek into the big pan Olivia calls a wok and I want to see if they're kissing. Olivia's wearing stonewashed jeans with a sparkly top under her apron. Her lips are bright red, short hair teased into soft strands. Dad's got an apron on over slacks and a polo shirt. They laugh, chopping vegetables. While passing a spoon, his hand brushes against hers. I imagine pointing a finger at them.

"Aha! I caught you. I saw your hands touch and I know what that means."

Dad looks at Olivia and clears his throat. "It means Olivia needs a spoon?"

"Wrong! It means you're in love and are having an affair."

Olivia's mouth drops open, the spoon falling from her hand to the floor.

"How do you even know that word?" Dad asks.

"Ivy … " Olivia kneels on the floor and touches my shoulders. "Please don't tell anyone. That would ruin everything. I'll get you your very own artist's easel if you're a big girl and keep this a secret."

"No." I pull away. "I need to tell my mom. She deserves to know the truth."

But instead I just say I'm hungry. Olivia smiles and gives me a cookie.

In the car on the way home, we bounce over a speed bump and I realize this is my fault. Okay, Dad losing his job was a hundred percent his fault. But the affair is mine. Mom would still be home if I hadn't found her the job. Sure, they'd still be fighting about money and Dad wouldn't know how to cook, but at least he'd still love her. And isn't that the most important thing? I wish I could rewind time and leave Mom's job ad in the recycling where it belongs. Or maybe I'd rip it up into little pieces and flush them down the toilet.

"You know," I say from the back seat, "Mom sure loves your cooking."

"She seems to like it okay," Dad agrees.

"No," I say. "She seriously loves it. She told Maxine Ludlow that you're the best cook in the world and she loves you so much."

"She said that?" He glances at me in the rearview mirror.

I tell him that Mom knows he'll do something really good to make it up to us for losing his job. I say Mom is so glad he's taking such good care of me and Brice. I say Mom misses him when she's at work and thinks about him all the time.

"She really said that?" Dad asks.

"Is this sweet and sour beef?" Mom pours herself a glass of wine. My fingers stiffly work the chopsticks. "Smells delicious," she adds. It's the first time in several days that Mom's joined us for dinner.

"Thanks, I hope you like it," Dad says quietly, watching her across the table. "Ivy, do you want a fork?"

I shake my head because I need to practice.

"Mmm, this is really tender," Mom says. "What's in the sauce?"

"Dad probably bought the sauce, right, Dad?" Brice asks.

"Actually I made it myself," Dad says. "Let's see: it's got ketchup, white wine vinegar, soy sauce, sugar, and a little cornstarch to thicken it up."

"I'm impressed, Neil. Is this from one of those library cookbooks?"

Brice and I look at each other. Dad nods.

"Great, which one? I'd love to photocopy it so we can make it again some time."

"Oh, actually, it's not one of those," Dad says.

"No?"

"No. I remember now, it's not from a cookbook ... but I know what goes into it."

"But where'd the recipe come from? You didn't just make it up. Was it from a cooking show?"

"Um ... yes. *Yan Can Cook.*"

Mom looks at Dad. Brice looks at me. I look at Mom.

"Mom?" I ask. "Can you tell us about the time when you were little and got lost at the beach?"

"Not right now, honey," she says.

"Dad," Brice says. "Trevor's volcano's not working. Can you help?"

"Sure." A line appears between Dad's eyebrows. "What seems to be the problem?"

Surprise Visitor

When I come home from school, there's a little boy in the backyard.

"Vroom! Vroom!" Stink Beetle Tommy Ludlow in muddy overalls is pushing a toy dump truck over the little stone bridge. Maxine Ludlow is Mom's best friend, but Mom should still be at work.

"What are you doing here?" I ask. I am a detective in a trench coat and Sherlock Holmes hat.

"Playing," he says.

I look at him close up with my invisible magnifying glass.

"But *why* are you here?"

"Beep beep!"

I tiptoe inside the house. I was supposed to play with Ladybug Melanie today but her mom has a headache, so I'm not allowed over. I'll have to wait to see if all her clothes are really lavender. Brice is at Stinky Feet Trevor's, working on their science projects. Brice won't say what he's doing and refuses to even give me a clue. I don't know why it has to be such a secret. I hear laughter in the kitchen. I freeze in the hall, listening.

"I'd feel strange lying to her," a woman's voice says.

"Of course, Maxine," Dad says. "Me too. But it's just for a few weeks."

"Does she suspect anything?"

"I don't think so. She's so focused on her job right now, she's hardly come up for air."

I think they're talking about Mom. I lean in closer. *Could*

Maxine Ludlow really be Phone Lady?

"Poor thing," Maxine says. After a minute she continues, "So how about we pretend we're just having a quiet dinner at my house? Then she won't ask too many questions." I scribble on a new page of the Detective Notebook. If it's not really a quiet dinner, what is it? A noisy breakfast? They talk about making it dark and everyone hiding. Then it hits me. They're planning their Big Sex Night when they *do it* for the first time. I'm dizzy and my stomach does cartwheels. I practice my spotting, staring at the pictures on the wall, but it doesn't work. Then it starts to make sense. Everyone knows people have sex in the dark and if anyone else finds out they'll *hide* the truth from Mom.

"Are you sure you don't mind hosting?" Dad asks.

"Not at all," Maxine says. "And this way I can decorate." I picture her lighting candles everywhere and throwing some of Alice Miller's rose petals on the bed, sexy-style. "I'm thinking nibbles rather than anything too heavy." My mouth drops open. *They're going to nibble each other?* I imagine Dad working his way along Maxine's bare arm with his lips.

"Sure," Dad agrees. "Something you can eat while standing." Like an arm, I guess.

"With a drink in one hand," she laughs.

Maybe "drink" actually means boob.

"How about miniquiches, shrimp cocktails, pretzels, nuts?" Maxine asks.

"Exactly. Finger food." It sounds like Dad and Maxine are planning ahead in case they get hungry from having sex all night.

"Should we say 'no gifts'?" Maxine asks. Gifts say *I love you*, like Mom got me the miniature chocolate art supplies when I found her the job. I've eaten the paintbrush but am saving the rest.

"I think gifts are nice," Dad says. "And most people

won't anyway." He probably means other people won't suspect anything when Dad starts getting Maxine jewelry.

"*What a lovely charm bracelet,*" *Mom will say (even though she hates charm bracelets) when she sees it jangling on Maxine's wrist.*

"*Oh, thanks,*" *Maxine will say, trying to cover it with her other hand. "I ... decided to treat myself.*"

"*Wait, does that gold heart say 'I love you'?*"

"*Um, yes. Because I think I'm grrrrreat!*"

"How big should this be?" Maxine asks Dad, bringing me back to reality.

"Let's really go for it. I want this to be a night people talk about for a long time." This is surprising because you'd think they wouldn't want anyone to know.

"Should we try and get some entertainment? A tarot card reader or something? Or maybe a pianist? We had our piano tuned last fall. Or even a small local band?" A penis is what boys have and sex is naked with private parts. I thought that meant the whole thing is supposed to be private.

"Nah, I think just schmoozing and eating will be enough," Dad says. "Good point about needing music, though. I've been thinking sixties rock—something fun to dance to." I'm pretty sure *schmoozing* is another word for kissing. Maybe dance music also makes good sex music.

"Balloons and streamers?" Maxine asks. I raise my eyebrows, writing this down. I realize there might be a lot I don't know about sex.

I creep upstairs, put on my tutu, and burrow into my beanbag to review the facts. Dad and Maxine are in love and are going to get each other gifts and listen to dance music in the dark during their Big Sex Night. They'll tell Mom they're just having dinner together, but really they'll have sex and eat finger food.

I put the notebook away and pick nubby balls off my

sweater. I don't want Dad to love Maxine Ludlow. I don't want Mom and Dad to get a divorce. Like being smacked in the chest with a dodge ball, I remember that this is my fault too.

"Veronica's Boutique," a woman answers the phone. I wonder if it's the lady who likes celery or the one who talks to the mannequins. I stand in second position while she gets Mom.

"Everything okay?" Mom asks.

"Yeah," I sigh, wrapping the phone cord around my finger. "When can you stop working?"

"I'll be home for dinner."

"No, I mean when can you quit your job and stay home again?" I stick my fingers into Brice's baby shoe and make it hop along the windowsill.

"Oh, sweetie, if I stay home how will we pay the bills?"

"Dad can get a job." *Come home come home.*

"You know your dad's looking. Do you miss me? Is that what this is about?"

I want to warn her that her best friend is no friend at all. She needs to stop work right now or they'll have to get a divorce. But I remember my promise to Brice and take a deep breath. My voice cracks. "I just wish you could be home."

"I'd like that too, baby. But the job's good for me. It's good for all of us. Got to go! See you tonight."

All in the Crust

"I'm impressed, Neil." Mom takes a bite of Dad's latest concoction, ham and zucchini skillet. "This is really good."

"Thanks." Dad smiles. "Glad you like it."

"So is this one from a cookbook or the TV or what?"

I told Brice about Maxine Ludlow and Dad's Sex Night. He said it's disgusting what grown-ups talk about when they think no one's listening. I said we need to do something fast. He agreed this is bad, but said we need to wait until the time's right. I just hope we don't wait too long.

"Actually," Dad says, "Olivia Hutchinson's been giving me a few pointers." Brice and I glance at each other.

"Sara's mom?" Mom asks.

"Nice lady," Dad says. "Good cook."

"I'm not sure I understand." Mom puts her fork down.

"Well, one day Ivy was playing at her friend's house and I told Olivia what a terrible cook I was." He chuckles. "She was making dinner and showed me a few things."

"Like what?" Mom asks.

"Like smashing garlic with the flat of a knife to peel it faster."

"And she taught you how to make this?"

"Well, I went back a few days later and she showed me how to make a quiche. She's good at explaining things. You know, how to cut butter into flour to make the crust and what goes in the egg mixture. The lesson went so well that she invited me back again. I'm learning all sorts of things. Olivia says I'm making real progress."

"I didn't even know you liked quiche."

"Sure, a good quiche is all in the crust."

"How come you never showed any interest in cooking before?" Mom asks. "I could have taught you some of those things."

"I'm sure you could have." He touches her arm. "We all know you're a good cook. But before, I was busy with other things and you had it covered. And now you're busy with work and it's my turn for a while."

Mom sips her water, studying the spider plant in the corner. "Is that all that's going on?" She crosses her arms. "Just cooking?"

"What?" Dad asks. "God, yeah. It's not like that at all. And Ivy's there with her friend, what's-her-name."

"Sara," I say.

"Right," Dad says. "Ivy plays with Sara, and Olivia teaches me how to put together a few meals for you guys."

I poke a zucchini with my fork.

"Why didn't you mention this before?" Mom asks.

I picture Dad and Olivia letting their hands touch with the spoon and running outside to kiss under a tree. Brice and I kick each other under the table.

Finally, Dad shrugs and takes a big bite of his food. "I was afraid you might freak out. And after you found out about my job … I didn't want you to worry."

"Oh, great," Mom says. "So what else aren't you telling me because you think I might freak out?"

"Take it easy, Karen," Dad says. "There's nothing else. There's nothing to tell."

"Sure, as long as you've got your little chaperone there."

Dad looks hurt. "Don't you trust me?"

Mom sighs. "I trust *you*. Not so sure about Olivia."

Science Is Always Fair

At the Sixth-Grade Science Fair, I walk past an ant farm and papier-mâché solar system. An earthquake display shows that we live on the San Andreas Fault. We're overdue for "The Big One," which basically means we're all doomed and are going to die. Brice has kept his project a total secret, and today I finally get to see what he's been working on. Nearby, someone makes Stinky Feet Trevor's baking soda volcano erupt and ooze toward the plastic dinosaurs at its base. The next display has owl pellets with tiny mouse bones put back together like a skeleton puzzle. They swallow them whole but can't digest the bones and fur, which they spit up in a little bundle. I wish I could spit out my worry about Dad's affair and the taste of saltwater taffy with Erin begging me to hitchhike. I can't digest them and I can't get rid of them either, so they're stuck inside, making me sick.

I look at a diagram on how helium makes your voice squeaky. Mice have naturally squeaky voices, especially when owls catch them. I walk past a display about magnets and almost bump into Honeybee Jenny. I wonder if I should ignore her.

"Seen anything good yet?" I ask, ready to gallop away if she says anything mean. She likes the one about Koko the Gorilla who's learned sign language. I'm surprised there's such a thing as a deaf gorilla. I ask if she's taught Mortimer any new tricks. She says she's trained him to stand on his hind legs and hit a bell with his paw. "No way," I say. Jenny smiles and fingers her new friendship bracelets. I wonder who they're from.

"Well," she says, "maybe I'll see you around."

I move on to a display about microscopic pond life. It's called "A World in a Drop of Water." It's got to be Brice's. There's a *Far Side* cartoon about amoebas, and a drawing of a *paramecium*. So this is what he's been working on. I bet Lucy's dad would be pleased. But then I see the name and actually some girl did it.

"Gross!" Tony the Earwig walks past. "I'm never drinking milk again."

"Me neither," Matt the Ant says. "Vomit city."

I find a display with grass growing out of an egg carton. I run my hand over the delicate blades of grass. The sign says, "Did you know, bird seed is grass!" I didn't know. Apparently if you water the little seeds from a bird feeder, they can turn into a lawn. I'm thinking about how our food doesn't work this way when Cricket Sara finds me.

"Hey," she says. "My mom wants to know when your dad can come over for another cooking lesson."

Every time Dad and I go over, he learns more about food, I learn more about horses, and Mom gets more annoyed. But it's not the horses or the food that makes Mom angry.

"Tell your mom my dad doesn't want to come over anymore."

"How come?" Sara asks, scratching her elbow.

"Because he's already learned everything about cooking."

"Really? Everything?"

"Yeah, he took the cooking test the other day and he scored a hundred percent."

"Oh." Sara looks at her shoes. I look at them too in case there's something interesting going on down there. There's not. "You know," she continues, "I thought maybe we could have been sisters."

"You mean we could pretend to be horse sisters?"

"No, like real sisters. If, um … if your dad and my mom got married."

"No way! My dad's already married! And anyway, I don't want your mom to be my mom."

"What's wrong with my mom?"

I think about all the things that are wrong with Olivia. Her nails are too red. She's too good at cooking. She's trying to get Dad to fall in love with her. Then I realize this is one of those special questions that you're not supposed to answer.

"Nothing," I say. "My dad just isn't going to come over anymore. Tell your mom not to call him or anything."

Sara thinks for a minute. "But, can *we* still play some time?"

Our parents would see each other during pickup, but it wouldn't be for a long time like when they're cooking. Besides I still have Maxine Ludlow to worry about.

I nod. "We can still play."

Moving on, I see Erin in front of a tornado display and my heart leaps a little. I've seen her around at school, so I know she didn't get kidnapped and chopped up. But we haven't talked since Red Hill and she's probably still mad at me for abandoning her. My throat tightens because it's very possible she doesn't want to be friends anymore.

"Look out, Dorothy! It's a twister!" I say.

Erin turns and grins. "Auntie Em! Auntie Em!"

"Can I try?"

"Sure." She hands me an hourglass made from soda bottles. I turn it upside down, liquid spiralling to the other end.

"Did you have fun at Various and Sundries?"

"Didn't go," Erin says. "I just went home. I'll hitchhike some other time."

I blink, putting the tornado back on the table. I'd really

thought she was going to do it.

"Want to come over to play this week?" I ask.

"Okay. I'll have my mom talk to your mom."

"Dad," I say. "My mom has a job now and my dad takes care of us."

"Whatever—your dad, then."

"Ew!" Caterpillar Christa walks past. "That's disgusting."

"I thought milk was *good* for you!" Ladybug Melanie says, touching her †. "No way am I drinking it now."

"Not ever ever ever," Christa agrees.

I look at Erin, who shrugs. Then I see what everyone's talking about. The posterboard asks, "Does milk rot your teeth?" Underneath is my drawing of a grinning cow, her teeth colored brown. Dishes of milk are lined up on the table. In the dish labeled "Day 1," there's a baby tooth the same bright white as the milk it's soaking in. The tooth in the "Day 4" dish has brown spots. In the dish marked "1 Week," the tooth is completely brown and half melted away. "2 Weeks" is just milk with no tooth at all. I feel a warm glow in my belly.

"Hey," Erin says. "Your brother did this one." I smile. *Everyone's looking at my teeth.*

More Bang For Your Buck

I want Dad to push me fast in the shopping cart again. Right now I am holding my family together because, as long as Dad's safe with me, Maxine Ludlow and Olivia can't kiss him. Brice is at soccer, so it's all up to me.

Dad puts a carton of milk in the cart. Most of the kids at school have stopped drinking milk. If they catch anyone drinking it at lunch, they say they're gross and all their teeth are going to turn brown and fall out.

In aisle three, Dad and I talk about fancy jam versus regular jam versus the supermarket's jam, which he calls *generic*. That's what old people are. He asks if I like strawberry. I do. I show him a giant jar, which he says is actually cheaper per ounce because the supermarket gives you a deal if you buy a lot of something.

"You get more for your money," he says.

"Yummers. Let's get the big one."

Dad smiles. "We don't need that much jam." I hop on the cart and he wheels me down the aisle, tossing in a loaf of bread. I beg him to push me faster, faster. He does, and I howl with delight. Mom never does this. She slowly crisscrosses the store, grabbing one last thing. Peanut butter, then olive oil. Zigzagging for lemons then raisins then tuna fish. Dad goes up and down every aisle like he's mowing a lawn made from bird seed.

"Olivia says you can make a great pesto with these," Dad says, throwing a packet of walnuts in the cart. I hop down to examine the bags of almonds and pecans. Protein food group.

"That reminds me," I say calmly before I change my mind. "Sara says Olivia doesn't want you to come over for cooking lessons anymore."

"What?" Dad freezes. "Why not?"

"Her mom said you've learned everything she can teach you, so you're all done."

"What?"

"Yeah, you graduated! Congratulations, Dad."

Dad gets lines between his eyebrows. I smile and walk ahead, swinging my arms. He starts pushing the cart, then stops again.

"I don't believe you," he says. "I think *you* don't want me to go over to Olivia and Sara's house anymore."

I skip back to him and hop on the cart, "Dad, Dad! Can you push me again?"

"Ivy, I'm serious. Is this because of what Mom said at dinner the other night?"

I nod.

"Shit," Dad says. "Tell me the truth. Did Mom tell you to say something to me?"

I shake my head.

He puts his arm around me. "Aw, kiddo ... Mom's just a little stressed with her job. But we're fine. You have nothing to worry about. Now show me that happy face."

I try to bend my mouth into a smile but it comes out wobbly. Dad tickles me and I laugh even though I'm trying to be serious. I force a frown but, snorting, start to smile.

"That's my girl."

We roll through the pet food aisle, pausing so I can squeeze a squeaky toy. Then we're in an aisle I've never been in before.

"What a rip-off." Dad hands me a tiny jar. "Seriously, how hard is it to mash a banana?" He says that, spoon for spoon, this stuff is twice as expensive as our *generic* jam.

"How come?"

"Supply and demand. That means if people really want something, they'll pay more for it."

"And people want baby food?" I guess babies do, and they cry if they don't get what they want. I look at the shelves of tiny jars. "Why are they all so little?"

"Babies have little stomachs. The apple sauce would go bad in a larger jar."

"What if it was in the giant jar?"

"Then it would definitely go bad." I ask what kinds they used to get for me and Brice. He says money was tight then too, so they made their own, mashing simple foods with a hand blender. Chicken and rice, sweet potato and spinach. I like to think of Mom and Dad way back when I was a baby and Brice was only four. I bet they sang to us, back before our family had any problems.

Dad holds a little jar in his big hand, studying the ingredients.

"Lost your dentures, Neil?" a woman asks. I spin around to see Maxine Ludlow, her boys trailing behind her like a double shadow. She's in a flowery sundress which makes me notice her round boobs and hips. I give her a dirty look. "Or do you and Karen have some important news to tell me?"

Dad turns red and, laughing, says, "Oh, no, we were just … I was just teaching Ivy about … "

Caleb and Tommy knock over boxes on a low shelf, squealing as they topple.

"So are we ready for our big night?" Maxine lifts Stink Beetle Tommy into her cart's toddler seat.

"Getting there," Dad says. "I went for a run today and picked up some confetti."

"Fun," Maxine says. "We're up to seventeen already." Even though I don't want to, I picture Dad and Maxine dancing to sixties rock in their underwear, throwing seventeen colors of confetti in the air. They laugh as it sticks to their sweaty skin.

"Great," Dad says. "How many 'nos'?"

"Maybe four."

"Not bad."

Maxine points to me and mouths something to Dad. He clears his throat and shakes his head. Maxine's lips form an "O," like a surprised mime.

"Ivy, I think you must *live* at Red Hill," she says. "Aren't we always bumping into each other here?"

Part VI

Rebirth

Cardboarding

"Whoa," Erin says a couple of days later. "Your mom's having a baby?"

"No way," I say. We're in the kitchen, eating Grandma's cookies and blowing milk bubbles through curly straws. For a while, the teachers couldn't figure out why the kids weren't drinking their milk anymore. Finally they realized it was because of Brice's Science Fair experiment and were really annoyed about the whole thing. Well, it turns out Brice was just *pretending* about the milk and used soda and maybe some other stuff to make the teeth dissolve. It was a joke, but the grown-ups didn't think it was funny. So now Brice is grounded again. But a lot of the kids still won't drink their milk.

Erin drums a stack of new library books. I hadn't noticed that Dad's cookbooks were gone. The cover of *Infant Nutrition* has a happy baby with food smeared across his face. I read the other titles:

Past Puréed Peas: Innovative Baby Food You Can Cook Yourself

Bonfire of the Vanities, by Tom Wolfe

Can It! How to Make Jam and Other Preserves

"Can't you just *buy* baby food?" Erin asks, brushing her dark hair out of her face.

"Yeah, but it's a rip-off." I didn't know babies were allowed to eat jam, but I guess you can't get cavities if you don't have teeth. "Anyways, I think I'd know if my mom was having a baby."

"Are you *sure*?" Erin asks, taking a slow sip of milk. "Why else would all these books be here?"

She's right. It's the only logical reason. Now that Dad likes cooking so much, if he and Mom had a baby, he'd make it all sorts of special things to eat. I don't know what "vanities" are, but a bonfire is a giant fire on the beach. I picture Dad with a baby on his shoulders, wearing matching chefs' hats and aprons, each roasting miniature hotdogs over a huge fire.

With a little thrill, I realize this is good news. Everyone knows that parents only make babies when they love each other very much. This calls for cardboard.

Erin and I go into the garage, stepping around bags of recycling, and past bikes lined up like horses in a stable. I see our stripy umbrella, beach blanket, and picnic basket. There's a bookcase full of everyone's extra books that won't fit in the house. The bottom shelf has Mom's fashion magazines, some of which are even older than she is. Now the skirts are short, now long, now short again. I lead Erin deeper into the garage, past folders of my old artwork: *Ivy 1984, ages 4–5, Ivy 1985, ages 5–6.* Mom saves the best ones because one day I'll be a famous artist and they'll each be worth one million dollars and ninety-nine cents. Erin and I pass my family's earthquake supplies: gallon jugs of water and canned food, for just in case. Finally I spot the cardboard against the wall. We each grab a big piece and take them outside into the powerful sunlight.

Erin and I follow deer trails past the tire swing and up the steep hill behind my house. The wild grass is mostly golden again, like it's supposed to be. Erin drops her piece of cardboard, but she's too slow getting on and it takes off down the hill without her. "Wait!" she yells, running after it. I hang on tight to mine, sitting with my feet planted into the ground. I exhale and lift my feet. Slipping down the hill on the dry grass, I quickly pick up speed. I throw my head back, feeling the wind in my hair.

"Woo-hoo!" I yell, grinning wildly. *Mom and Dad love each other again.* Erin slides past me, laughing. We slam our feet into the garden fence at the bottom.

"You know," she says as we carry our cardboard back up the hill, "if your mom's pregnant, you'd better watch out."

"How come?" Surely anything is better than divorce. Erin moans about her annoying stepsister messing up her room and breaking her toys. I shrug. It'd be fun having someone to give drawing lessons to and play with when Brice is busy. I imagine a new artwork folder appearing in the garage, a jar of mashed bananas in the picnic basket, and a baby seat on the back of Mom's bike.

"Also," Erin says, "if there was a baby, you wouldn't be the youngest anymore."

A chill runs through my body. I have always been the youngest. I thought I would always be the youngest. If it's another boy, then at least I'd still be special. But a baby girl would replace me.

We slide down the hill again. This time I'm not shouting.

"By the way," Erin asks at the bottom, "where'd your giant TV go?"

I could tell her it broke or was stolen. Instead, I stretch my arms and say, "We had to return it."

She nods as though this happens all the time and we walk back up the hill.

Secret Admirer

I am dancing around my room, not ballet with straight legs and rules but my old style, bendy and fun. Suddenly I notice flowers on my windowsill. There's a glass with ivy, pansies, and daisies. Where'd they come from? Of course they're from Mom, saying she misses me and is sorry she has to work. Or maybe she's trying to tell me that she'll still love me after the baby is born.

"Mom gave me flowers!" I shout, bouncing into Brice's room. He looks up from his book and grins. He's proud of his milk experiment and doesn't care that he was grounded. I *chassé* into Mom and Dad's room and press speed-dial.

"Veronica's Boutique," answers a gravely voice. I hear music in the background and picture customers dancing around the store as they try on dresses. I bet Gloria is handing out celery sticks with every purchase. I imagine Bev chatting with a customer about the history of the puffed sleeve, while the other lady has an argument with a mannequin who doesn't want to get changed. I squirm waiting for Mom to come on the line.

"Did you give me … um … " I clear my throat. "Do you feel sick?"

"No," Mom says. "I'm fine. What's wrong?"

"Have you been puking lately?" Erin said ladies throw up when they're pregnant, which is how they know even before their bellies get fat and round.

"What? Is everything okay? Do *you* feel yuck?" The gravelly voice says something. "Sure thing, Bev, be right there. Ivy, honey, it's pretty busy here. Go tell your dad if you're not feeling well. He's supposed to be taking care of you."

I study my little bouquet. If Mom's not barfing, then I guess she's not pregnant. Erin was positive about that. But why else would there be baby books downstairs? I wiggle in my beanbag, soaking up ideas. Then it hits me. Is it possible that *Dad* is having a baby? I picture his belly, swollen like a hairy beach ball. I shake my head. People are not seahorses and this is impossible. Unless ... Dad is having a baby with *someone else*. Maybe Phone Lady is pregnant!

Obviously, the flowers were from him. They must be his way of saying that he'll still take care of me when he and Maxine Ludow or Olivia have their baby. I pop back into Brice's room with an update.

"I got it wrong," I tell him. "The flowers are actually from Dad." Brice's grin gets wider.

I find Dad in the kitchen, sprinkling green powder into a bowl of mush. There are piles of ingredients on the chopping board and a big pot steaming on the stove. I jump up on the counter to look inside. But it's not food, just little jars in boiling water.

"We're eating *glass*?" I ask.

"I'm sterilizing them." Dad swats me off the counter. "We're having chicken with wild rice."

I wonder if Olivia showed him how to make that one, her hand on his back as he chopped parsley. Maxine Ludow was acting weird at the supermarket the other day, but I'm not supposed to know about the affair, whoever it's with, so I can't ask about the baby. Instead I ask if he gave me flowers.

"Sure. Remember I got you those flowers for your eighth birthday."

"Yeah, I know, but what about today?"

"Can't today, I'm busy." Dad tastes the mush, nods

thoughtfully and adds more green powder.

I find Brice working at his desk.

"It was you, wasn't it?" I ask. He looks at me blankly. "You know, in my room?" Still nothing. "The flowers?"

A slow smile travels across his face. "It *might* have been."

"I was sure it was Mom and then it had to be Dad, but it was you all along. Why didn't you say?"

"Sometimes," Brice puts his book down, "it's nice to do something just because you feel like it, not because you want everyone to know it was you."

"Ivy for Ivy," I whisper, hugging him. "Brice?" I ask after a minute. "I think Dad and Phone Lady are going to have a baby."

I think he'll yell, freaking out, but instead he says, "You found the books in the kitchen?"

I nod.

"Dad's working on something, alright, but it's not a baby."

Market Research

We have to be quiet because of the baby sleeping in the next room. Babies sleep a lot even though they don't do anything. They get all tired out just from eating and crying. Our neighbor Alice Miller smells like vanilla and her hair is in a loose bun with wisps escaping along her long neck. Part of her shirt is unbuttoned, so I can see the freckles on her chest and the smooth skin on the tops of her boobs. I'm next to Dad on the Millers' scratchy plaid couch.

"Natural," Alice Miller tells Dad, arranging fat roses in a vase.

"And what do you mean by 'natural'?" Dad looks up from his notes. I try to follow where he's looking.

"No sh ... " Alice Miller catches my eye. "No preservatives or artificial colors. That stuff's not good for anyone, especially not babies." She talks about junk food and busy schedules and quality ingredients.

At school, I talked with Moth Caleb and Cricket Sara, just to be a hundred percent sure, and they say their moms aren't barfing either. So it turns out Brice is right and no one's having a baby. I pretended to be interested in Dad's "market research" so he'd let me come along. I'm actually here on official detective business. Brice says, just because Dad wants to do gross things with Maxine and maybe even Olivia, that doesn't mean we can let our guard down with the rest of the ladies on our list. The more we can learn about what's going on, the better we'll know what we should do next.

Alice Miller pulls leaves off the roses and asks, "Did you hear about the mercury in the yogurt and peaches baby food last fall?"

"Mercury?" Dad scribbles on his paper.

"Lord knows what's going on in those factories. Huge product recall. And then there were the glass shards in Gerber's baby food two years ago."

Dad smiles like this is good news, then becomes serious again, shaking his head. "Scary stuff," he says. I squint, trying to decide if they're flirting. Are they talking in that special joking I-like-you way or just talking?

"Anyway, besides all that," she says, rotating the vase so the heaviest flowers are looking into the room, "I think people would like those fun flavors like you were saying." I pray to God that she will give me a rose. I wonder if she uses a magic potion to grow them so big. She says if you give babies lots of different foods to try, then they're less likely to become picky eaters. Dad makes little noises of interest. She asks if I like broccoli.

"It's okay."

"You liked it in that cheese pilaf casserole I made the other night," Dad says.

I nod. In a back room, the baby starts crying.

Alice Miller sighs and looks at her watch. "Here we go."

"We'll get out of your hair." Dad stands, thanking her.

"Neil, just let me know when you're ready for guinea pigs. I can round up some babies from Gymboree for a taste test." Dad thanks her again. I think a Taste Test is a kind of Like Test. I don't think they're flirting. The baby stops crying. It probably got tired again and decided to go back to sleep.

"Excuse me," I say. "My mom wants to know how you get your roses so big."

Alice Miller bends down. "You like my rosie-posies?"

"They're pretty." I tilt my head, hoping to look adorable.

"My secret is to be mean to them."

"Do you call them names and stuff?" I picture Alice Miller spitting on the rose bushes and telling them they're disgusting, worthless plants. Sad roses swell up bigger like your eyes go puffy after you cry.

Alice laughs. "Not quite, but I do give them a hard time. If you let rose bushes do what they want, they go wild, which means they grow lots of little skinny branches and little flowers. But we don't want that, do we?"

I shake my head. "We want big flowers."

"Right," she says. "So every winter I clip them back. It's called pruning. Tell your mom to keep cutting and not be afraid of hurting the plants. They're tough; they can take it."

"And then what?"

"Then the plants put their energy into growing nice fat, heavy roses instead of lots of little branches."

I nod. *If you love them, you have to hurt them.* I cross my fingers for her to give me a rose. But instead, Dad thanks her for the five-hundredth time and she walks us to the door.

Taste Test

Dad's been busy inventing different kinds of baby food and packing them into little jars. He's like a mad scientist with potions. He stirs in a pinch of this and a spoonful of that. Before babies can eat the mush, their parents will have to buy it. So Dad is trying to make something that parents will think is a good idea, and babies will like. He's got a bunch of flavors in his "Green Baby" line, where every flavor from apple sauce to chicken and wild rice is bright, kelp green. Kelp is a kind of extra-tall seaweed. Dad hopes babies who connect the color green with "yummy food" will eat their vegetables when they're bigger. Grown-ups are apparently pretty concerned about this, but I don't care at all what they eat.

Every time I go into the kitchen, Dad's there with some new kind of mush for me to taste. I'm not a baby but I've got kid tastebuds so he wants to know what I think. I like Strawberry Oat Medley even though it has wheatgerm in it, which is some weird health dust. There's another bunch of flavors he calls "Big Baby—Adult Meals Pulverized'" *Pulverized* is a fancy way to say mashed-up-in-the-blender. These are flavors like Banana Garbanzo Bonanza and Citrus Spinach Sunrise. They sound weird but they actually taste really good. Sometimes it's better if you don't know all the stuff that Dad puts in them.

Today is Saturday, and Alice Miller's coming over with a whole bunch of other moms and their babies for a Taste Test. Brice and I will help keep track of everything on clipboards.

Mom is off running errands because she's got things to do and doesn't want to be in the way. Suddenly there are eight babies and their moms in our living room. The ladies balance their babies on their hips and chat proudly about who can lift themselves up on their own and who can say Dadda. Big deal. I can climb trees by myself and know really difficult words like *generic* and *pulverize*.

Everyone gets settled and Dad talks the ladies through what he calls the different "product lines" and how everything will work today.

"If something doesn't taste good to you or your baby, I want to know. Being nice isn't going to do me any good," Dad says. "This is a brand new business venture and I really need all of you to be brutally honest. If something tastes like slime, tell me it tastes like slime." The ladies laugh nervously. Dad continues, "And of course, if something tastes amazing I want to know that too. Brice and Ivy here will help me keep score."

Dad introduces Creamed Carrot Cobbler, one of the Big Baby flavors.

"I roasted the carrots instead of boiling them, which brings out a richer flavor," Dad says. "Also, no sugar added. That goes for all of these, by the way." The ladies nod with interest. They have a taste from the little jars, which Dad said they can take home afterwards like a party favor if they want.

"Ooh, I like this," says the woman in my group with frizzy red hair, waggling her spoon.

"Very hearty flavor," says the woman next to her with big glasses. I take notes and ask their scores on a scale of one to five, for flavor, texture, and color. Then it's time for the babies to have a taste. They vote by smacking their lips or squirming. "She definitely likes this one," the woman with the glasses tells me as her baby reaches for the spoon.

We go through several more flavors. I look over at Brice,

surrounded by three ladies and three babies. He's nodding and writing everything down. He looks up at me and smiles. I really want this baby food thing to work. If Dad makes lots of money selling all-natural, healthy baby food, then that can be his new job and Mom won't have to work anymore. If Mom was back at home then Dad wouldn't like Phone Lady anymore. Also you can't get fired if you own your own business so we would be safe forever.

Dad introduces the next flavor, Baltic Beef Bulgur. The woman with the glasses scores the texture a 2 for being "too gritty" but the frizzy-haired woman likes it better, giving it a 3.5. Just then one of the babies in Dad's group squirms and knocks several jars to the floor. The glass breaks, startling a few other babies who start crying. Then they *all* start howling like dogs.

Later on, my family goes for a walk in the neighborhood. We pass by Alice Miller's house, with the stone wall and the big roses out front. I picture her cruelly chopping them back with her clippers.

"Ah!" the rosebush wails. "Please stop! I need that branch!"

"Toughen up," she says. "You'll be fine without it. You were getting too wild anyway."

"I'll be good! I beg you! Noooo!"

"So how was the big Taste Test?" Mom asks. Brice and I give each other a look.

"Went well," Dad says. "The ladies were all enthusiastic."

"I hope they weren't just being nice," Mom says.

"I told them not to pull any punches," Dad says.

"Well, what about the babies?" Mom asks.

"They were messy!" I say.

"Babies are messy eaters. That's why they wear bibs."

"We had to wrap things up early after a few got a little cranky," Dad explains.

"But they really liked the food," Brice jumps in. We don't mention the broken glass, spilled mush, or horrible screaming. I think Erin's right about them being bad news. I'm so glad we're not getting one.

"I got such a kick watching everyone enjoy the food," Dad says. "I wish you could have seen them. I think there's a definite market for this stuff."

Mom asks about Chicken Cherry Chickadee.

"The babies couldn't get enough of that one," Dad says. "I really think I'm on to something here."

"Time will tell." Mom shrugs.

We pass the new house at the end of the road, which is still empty, with its For Sale sign out front. We turn the corner and head up the hill.

I ask Mom if she can stop working now that Dad's going to make lots of money selling his baby food. Dad chuckles and says it can take years to build a successful business. *Why does everything have to take so long?*

"Besides," Mom tells me, "I really like my job, so you may as well get used to it." I groan.

"Looks like you're stuck with me." Dad squeezes my shoulder. The hill makes my calves burn. I pick a leaf off a bay tree so I can smell it. Maybe Dad *wants* Mom to keep working so he can keep having secret kissy time with Phone Lady. The whole thing makes me want to throw up (and I'm not even pregnant). I don't know if Dad likes just Maxine Ludlow or Olivia too. Or maybe it's someone else we haven't even thought of yet. Brice says we shouldn't do anything until we're a hundred percent sure, but what if we're never a hundred percent sure? What if we just keep waiting forever, slowly collecting clues, and meanwhile Dad and Phone Lady keep kissing and like each other more and more? And at the same time Dad will love Mom a little bit less and less and Mom won't even know and will just keep working and then … divorce!

"I didn't tell you guys," Mom says, "but the other day I got to meet with this incredibly talented designer in Mill Valley. She's been working out of her spare room, but she hopes to start renting a space soon."

"Oh, yeah?" Dad asks. "Her business is growing?"

"Exactly," Mom continues. "She's having a lot of fun with black-and-white stripes. Very elegant. She showed me her original sketches and fabric swatches. I loved learning about her creative process from conception to finish. Then, back at the boutique, I got the ladies together and talked them through the samples. Gloria put down her yogurt drink and got really excited about one of the skirts."

"Can you imagine when *my* business gets so big that I need to rent an industrial kitchen?" Dad asks.

"Mmm … That would be exciting," Mom agrees. "There you are, directing your team to put just the right amount of kelp powder in the Green Baby Apple Sauce. You'd have some special machine to sterilize several dozen jars at a time and have professionally printed labels."

"I like that," Dad says. "It all feels like a long way off, but it sure sounds good."

Raise the Alarm

I'm in my room, drawing babies for Dad. He wants happy babies eating mush and wearing T-shirts with pictures of vegetables. There's a different baby for each flavor. I'm working from baby photos of me and Brice so my drawings will look more real. This is how you make a baby: big head and eyes. Chubby arms and legs. No teeth. Dad says to make my drawings fill the whole page and he'll have the printers shrink them down (like magic). I asked if he wants me to write "Banana Garbanzo Bonanza" and the other names, but he says he'll type them with a word processor.

Outside, I hear someone clapping and yelling, "Mortimer!" I put down my marker and run to the window. Maybe he's finally become a famous circus cat and crowds are cheering him on. I can't see anything, so I run outside to investigate.

"Is Mortimer hiding under there?" I ask Jenny, who's crouching under a bush. She's been calling his name and her eyes are red, dirty blonde hair messy with leaves.

She shakes her head and whispers, "Mortimer is missing."

"Really?" He is Lost. Lost like my red glitter. Lost like the kids on milk cartons.

"No one's seen him since before school yesterday," she sniffs. I tell her I'm sorry and put my hand on her shoulder like you touch the stove to see if it's hot. She doesn't pull away, and I ask what she's going to do. She doesn't know. She's been looking for hours and he's nowhere.

I race back into the house and find Dad at his post in the kitchen, whistling as he fills little jars with orange porridge.

I say I'm going for a walk with Jenny. He says have fun and come home before dark.

All over the neighborhood, Jenny and I look in the high branches of trees and under parked cars, calling Mortimer's name. I wonder what makes a cat run away. Maybe he was tired of doing tricks, or maybe he thought there'd be more tuna cans to lick somewhere else.

"I haven't seen your kitty-cat," Alice Miller says at the door. She meows to her baby, bouncing him on her hip so her boobs jiggle. "Kitty-witty says 'meow'!" Jenny and I look at each other. It's hard to believe she's mean to her rosebushes, which just goes to show you can't tell about people sometimes. Alice suggests we make "missing" posters.

Jenny and I sit cross-legged on her floor, looking through a photo album and drinking Hawaiian punch through curly straws. Jenny apparently hasn't had milk since the Science Fair.

"Look how small he was." She points to a picture of herself as a little kid holding Mortimer as a kitten.

"Hey, Vine Girl," Natasha says, walking by. She smiles and heads downstairs, like she hasn't seen me for a few of days instead of months.

Jenny turns the pages, flipping past birthday parties and picnics, the Marin County Fair, and days at the beach. Page by page, Jenny and Natasha grow up. Then I see one of me. Jenny and I are selling lemonade. Then more: me and Jenny on my tire swing, playing dress-up, making sugar cookies.

"So who are you playing with these days?" I ask.

"Nicole and some girls from gymnastics," Jenny says. I nod, remembering the Roly-Poly's messy hot fudge sundae at my party. I wonder if Nicole has seen Mortimer's tricks or if Natasha has crimped her hair. If they go to Red Hill together, does Nicole bring enough money for jawbreakers? "What about you?"

"Mostly Erin," I say. "Also Sara and Melanie. I didn't

know you did gymnastics."

"Yeah, I started in March. We get to do cartwheels and the balance beam."

"I'm taking ballet," I say, and suck hard at my fruit punch.

"Here's a good one," she says, peeling a picture of Mortimer from the album. I look into his clever yellow eyes, at the dark markings along his back and the white tuft of fur on his chest. Even though I haven't seen him for ages, I feel a wave of sadness that he's gone. I hope he's gone on an adventure, but I know from TV that sometimes, when cats are missing, they've actually been hit by cars.

"He's probably fine," I say. "But if something bad happened to Mortimer, would you want to know? Or would you rather *not* know so part of you could always hope he was okay?"

Jenny tapes the photo to a piece of paper and writes, "Lost Cat" in her most careful handwriting. "I think it's better to know the truth even if it hurts," she says. "The worst is when you don't know and everyone else does." She says she saw a made-for-TV movie about a girl whose dad went away to Alaska. The other kids were mean to her, which made her super-lonely. Every day she waited by the window, but her dad never came home. Years later, she learned that the Alaska story was a lie and her dad was actually in jail. "Everyone knew except for her."

Jenny will photocopy the signs tomorrow and then we'll stick them to trees and telephone poles after school. Maybe we'll stick some real low down, so if Mortimer sees them he'll know we miss him. Walking home, I say a little prayer to Baby Jesus and Mother Nature that, if Mortimer comes back, I'll stop asking for so many wishes.

I dig through our recycling for an envelope addressed to Mom. Brice is in his room listening to the radio. I can't let him catch me. I won't let him stop me. It's better to know the truth even if it hurts—a moral from Jenny. I cut letters out of a newspaper, kidnapper-note-style, and glue down my warning.

Déjà Vu

In my picture, Mom stands grinning on the roof of the boutique. I draw a long line of customers, wrapping around the whole world, waiting to go inside. I study a map while drawing, to make it more real.

I was six when Brice turned ten. That's one decade. He had a Lego Party and joined the Double Digits Club. I'm still single digits. Soon it'll be the start of a new decade for Mom. Dad will frame this drawing for Mom's fortieth birthday, because that makes it a better gift.

I'm sitting in my beanbag, eyes closed, deciding what to draw next. I imagine the bumps under me are ideas, flowing through my skin and into my brain.

Suddenly I'm walking barefoot across hot sand. I think it's a desert until I see the water. Rocky cliffs on one side, the ocean on the other. I recognize this place as Drakes Beach. I hear yelling; a little girl chases a seagull.

"Get lost!" she shrieks. "Bad bird. My lunch!" She throws herself down on a picnic blanket. She brushes off her sandwich, making a face. I feel a chill.

I go over to her. I think about Lucy and the raccoons and smile so she'll know I'm friendly. "Are you okay?"

She shakes her head.

"What's wrong?" I ask.

"Sand in my sandwich."

I open my bag and, imagining the best lunch in the whole world, pull out a turkey sandwich on a big sourdough roll from Belly Deli.

She hesitates. She doesn't know who I am.

'It's okay,' I say. "I'm ... a friend."

She eats the sandwich with hungry bites. I get up to go.

"Wait." She holds the edge of my T-shirt. "I think they left without me."

"Your family?"

"Uh-huh." Why on earth does she think that? I wonder.

"Don't worry, they're still here. Isn't that your dad in the water?" I notice he's laughing with some lady in a bikini and I flush with anger. The girl shields her eyes with her small hand.

"Oh, yeah!" Her face lights up.

I spot a boy way down the beach, dragging a piece of driftwood. "And your brother'll be back soon. They wouldn't leave without you. I promise."

"Wanna build a sandcastle?" We play in the sand and I make her laugh, telling jokes about the ocean. Before I know it, a younger Brice is just a few yards away.

"Gotta go," I tell her, and hurry off.

"Who was that?" Brice asks her.

The phone rings, breaking me out of my daydream. I run into Mom and Dad's room. Maybe it's Jenny saying someone found Mortimer. "Hello?"

"Hi, Ivy," says a girl with a deep voice. "How's it going?"

"Good." I don't think it's Jenny but I don't want to ask.

"Do you know who this is?"

"Um, no."

"It's *Lucy*!" She laughs. I picture her, tall with slinky curls, in her house in Oakland I've never seen. I imagine a room with a microscope and a hundred history books. I ask if she's read *The BFG*. "Sure," she says. "You reading it for school?"

"No, just for fun." I untie the laces of Brice's baby shoe on the windowsill.

"If you like that, try *James and the Giant Peach*. It's got giant insects and it's even better. Hey, is Brice around?"

I run downstairs to the family room where Brice is watching *Transformers*, clipping his toenails.

"Lucy's on the phone," I sing.

He gasps, jumping off the couch, and wipes his hands on his jeans. He twists down the volume, gray trucks silently changing into gray robots. Cartoons just aren't the same without color.

"Hello?" He tilts his chin, lowering his voice. I giggle and he shoots me a look.

Back in my room, I'm drawing a picture of the beach when I remember I left the phone off the hook. I sashay down the hall to Mom and Dad's room, but before I hang up I can't resist lifting the receiver to my ear, just for one quick listen.

"I miss you," Lucy whispers, making me shiver. "You know I've been thinking about you lots. I want to see you again."

"Yeah," Brice says in that funny deep voice.

Something feels familiar.

"That was the best, when we kissed in the forest against that tree."

Like a week of baloney sandwiches, somehow history is repeating itself.

"Hey," she continues, "maybe we can get our families to meet up for dinner. Do you think that would work? Oh my God, I want you so bad."

"Me too," he says.

Then it hits me. I am falling, somersaulting off a cliff. Wide-eyed, I set the receiver on the table and back away like it's an angry dog.

"Really bad," I tell Brice, twisting the corner of my shirt.

"Spit it out." Brice narrows his eyes. I hand him the

Detective Notebook, opened to "Phone Call Facts."

1. They miss each other
2. Lady thinks Dad is cute
3. Kissed against a tree
4. Cooked together

I stare at him with a sad smile, hoping he'll put the pieces together.

"Right," Brice says. "And Phone Lady is ... drum roll please ... Maxine!"

My throat is full of marbles. I shake my head. "I made the most horrible mistake."

"What?"

"It isn't Dad and Maxine Ludlow."

"Wow, so it really is Olivia? You know those cooking lessons ... "

"No, it's worse than that."

"Then who?" Brice asks. "Alice Miller? Your ballet teacher?"

"It's not Dad at all." I squeeze my eyes shut. "It's you and Lucy."

"*What*?" Brice studies the list. "You eavesdropped on me talking to Lucy?"

"I'm really sorry. I didn't know it was you. You were both whispering and I thought ... I thought."

"That's really bad, Ivy!"

"I know."

"Hang on." He flips through the notebook. "Even if you got the phone call wrong, you were right there when Dad and Maxine planned their Big Sex Night. Remember, he's going to get her jewelry and she'll have candles and rose petals?"

I nod.

"We just need to keep looking for clues," Brice continues. "We shouldn't do anything stupid like tell Mom until we're absolutely sure."

"That's the other thing," I say.

"Jesus, what now?"

Brice and I practically trip over each other running down the stairs. Dad's in the kitchen stirring a pot, clinking an accidental rhythm like an acorn woodpecker.

"Has the mail come yet?" Brice shouts. Dad nods and points toward the dining room. We skid into the other room, socks on wood floor, and frantically paw through the huge stack of letters. No one's gone through the mail in days.

"I didn't write the address myself," I whisper. "I used an old envelope and I got a stamp out of the telephone drawer."

"What'd the envelope look like?" Brice asks.

"White?"

"Dammit, we're going to have to take all of these."

We carry the mail up to Brice's room and close the door. There are about two dozen letters just for Mom. Brice holds one against the window and then up to his desk lamp. I squint hard for X-ray vision.

"Nothing," he says. He carefully slides the letter opener under the flap. The paper tears. "Christ!" He tries again. "Shit dammit!" He rips it open, the envelope already ruined. But it's not my letter.

"Hey, kids," Dad yells from the stairs. "Stop whatever you're doing and come down here."

We freeze. Opening other people's mail is like being a Peeping Tom. Also, I think it's illegal.

"Be down later," Brice shouts, stuffing the ripped letter in his desk.

"I've got something fun to show you."

"Um—we're busy!" Brice works on another envelope, tearing it badly. "Aaargh!" He rips it open but this one's not my letter either.

"I made chocolate pudding," Dad sings. We look at each

240

other, then at the unopened pile of envelopes.

Brice and I sit on the stools, hunched over the kitchen counter. I can tell he's angry at me from the way he slurps his pudding and also his death stares. I take tiny spoonfuls to show how bad I feel. Dad checks on the stuffed peppers in the oven. It's dinner, not baby food, though he may grind up some leftovers. He may as well grind me up too, because when Mom finds out I'll be dead meat.

"I got something back from the printers today," Dad says, making me perk up. "But you can't tell Mom."

Afterwards, Brice and I go back upstairs and open more envelopes, but they just have bills and other junk. I want so bad for my note to be there, but sometimes wanting isn't enough. My note with the cut-out letters isn't there. So we do what any detective would do. We hide the evidence. We stuff everything into Brice's desk and go watch TV.

Stable

Dad glances at me in the rearview mirror. I make a face and he makes his eyes wide like he's being chased by a monster and we both laugh. I'm sharing the back seat with a box of little jars that clink against each other like wind chimes. It's a Cooking Lesson Day, and Sara and I are going to play horses. We drive past the fire station. Dad wants to show Olivia our special printed labels. He's curious what she'll think about his new baby food flavor, Lentil Peach. Too much lentil? Not enough peach? Or is it the other way around? Olivia will tell him. We go over a speed bump, making the jars rattle.

"Wanna know something funny?" I ask.

"Is it a joke?" Dad asks, his big hands on the wheel.

"Not that kind of funny."

"Okay, let's hear it."

"I used to think that you liked Sara's mom."

"I do like her. Olivia's a nice lady and a good teacher."

"Noooooo," I groan. "I mean, I thought you *like*-liked her."

In the rearview mirror Dad's eyes tighten. "Why would you think that, Ivy?"

"I dunno."

"Well, that's not true. I love your mother."

When we get to Sara's house, the grown-ups disappear to get something from the garage. Sara and I pretend that I'm a horse and she's a mean farmer. She makes me crawl up and down the stairs. If I'm still strong enough to pull a cart to market then I can live, otherwise she'll have me turned into glue.

"Giddy-up!" she shouts. "Hurry, you stupid, lazy horse."

I go as fast as I can and get rug burn on my knees. But I'm not fast enough. As punishment, I get sent to my stable with no dinner. The stable is the small gap between the kitchen cabinets and the trash. It smells like rotting oranges and fish, but I try to pretend it smells like fresh hay. Sara says if I'm a good horse then she'll let me out and I can have a sugar cube. I think she's still angry from the Science Fair when I said I didn't want her mom to be my mom. It's like when Roly-Poly Nicole wants me to try her peanut butter and cream cheese sandwich or jam and pickle pita pocket, saying it's the best thing ever. I take a bite and tell her it tastes disgusting, which makes her mad even though it means more for her.

Sara leaves the kitchen, and I hear Dad and Olivia come in. Something heavy scrapes the floor. I keep quiet. From my hiding place I can see only a small section of the kitchen—the sink and part of the counter with the chopping board. The cabinets are like those blinders they put on horses so they can only see straight ahead.

"That's the one." Olivia walks into view, pointing at the ceiling. "It blew last night when I was making dinner."

The lights blink on and off. "You sure it's only sixty watts? They look pretty bright," Dad says. "I'm guessing one hundred."

"You think?"

Dad sets up a ladder, climbing up until I can see only his feet. He hands her a light bulb and says, "Seventy-five. We're both wrong."

She passes another one up to him. Then the lights blink on. "My hero," Olivia says.

Dad clears his throat. "No big deal, I'm happy to help."

He leaves with the ladder, and she stays in the kitchen, putting dishes away.

After a few minutes, I hear footsteps and clinking.

"Check it out." Dad carries his box past the sink and out of view again, like offstage in a play. "I got labels printed!"

"Oh, those are adorable," Olivia says. "Did Ivy do the artwork?"

"Yeah, and look: they're all different. These are the twelve launch flavors."

"You must be so proud of her. And you ... you've got a real product here." They're both so quiet I stop breathing in case they can sense me with their parent radar. "So what do you think?" Olivia asks, "Am I too big to taste the new one?"

"Actually that'd be great. It's called Lentil Peach. I made it last week," Dad says. "Where are the girls?"

"Upstairs," Olivia says. "Why do you ask?"

"I thought Sara might like to try some too."

"Trust me, my daughter won't touch it."

"Because it's a weird flavor or because it's baby food?"

"Both." She laughs.

"Her loss."

I hear the lid pop and metal against glass.

"Mmmmm!" Olivia moans. "Oh, wow. It's kind of nutty and fruity. And is that basil I'm tasting? This is really good."

"Thanks. Yep, just a touch of basil. I was hoping my teacher would approve."

"Your teacher's very impressed. Great consistency. Really interesting flavors." From my hiding spot, I see Olivia's arm and hear the spoon scraping the glass. The rest of her and Dad are still out of view. After a minute she says, "You know, I've really enjoyed getting to know you since you stopped working."

"But I am working," Dad says.

"Oh! Did you get a new job?"

"No," he says, "I mean taking care of my kids and the baby food business."

"Right, but I mean since you left your real job."

"I don't know, this all feels pretty real to me."

"Whatever. Sorry." She softens her voice, "So, what'd you say this was again? Lentils and apricots?" She steps aside so I can see the whole sink again.

Dad steps into view to wash his hands. "Peaches," he says.

She lowers her voice and says, "Hey, Neil, how'd you like to cream on my peaches?"

"Excuse me?" He turns the water off.

Olivia laughs. "Just kidding." Her hand gives him a dish towel, "Jeez, can't I joke with you anymore?"

Dad's back is to me, shoulders up near his ears. He puts the damp towel on the counter, not saying anything.

"But that does excite you, doesn't it?" Olivia asks. She puts her hand on his arm. "No one would have to know."

Finally Dad says, "I have a family."

"Good for you. I'm not asking you to run away with me."

They're both silent for what feels like a long time. Olivia's hand stays on Dad's arm like it's stuck there with glue made from old horses. I breathe in the fish stink, wishing it was warm hay. My legs are getting pins and needles, but I don't move.

"I have to go," he tells Olivia, stepping back and out of view. "Ivy!" he calls upstairs. I stay still and silent like a good horse.

"Fine," Olivia says. "Pretend I never said anything. I'm just in a funny mood. I was thinking next time we can make cannelloni."

"I'm sorry, Olivia. Thank you, but ... Sorry." They're both quiet. "Ivy!" he yells, "Time to go!" I hold my hands over my mouth and stay put. They don't say anything else. Finally I hear footsteps leaving the kitchen. It's quiet now, so I squeeze out of my stable. I freeze. Olivia's still here! She's at the counter, her back to me and a hand on her forehead. I try to sneak past but she turns and looks at me with big, wet eyes. I give her a super-nasty glare and go find Dad.

Surprise

Grandma has new cow-shaped salt and pepper shakers. Today Dad surprised Mom with a bouquet of roses. It was the big kind, but I could tell they were from a store and not Alice Miller because they were wrapped in tissue paper. Now they're having a special grown-ups-only meal at a French place they like and Brice and I are at Grandma's house for dinner. Brice is doing his homework in the other room. I want to play farm with the cow and chicken shakers, but Grandma says they're not toys. Instead, she shows me how she makes her yarn pictures, which she calls needlepoint. She pokes a stubby needle through the mesh. There's a picture printed on like a coloring book, which is also cheating and not real art. She shows me one she's started of a cat playing with a ball of yarn. I think it's funny using yarn to make a picture of yarn. It'd be like drawing a picture of a crayon.

"Mortimer came back," I tell Grandma while she works the needle.

"Is that a boy in your class?"

"No, Jenny's cat."

"That's nice," she says. "I bet she was worried."

I nod. Mortimer had been missing for three days when the big man arrived. There were no dead cats on the side of the road, and no news of a performing cat showing up at the circus either. Our posters were everywhere, but no one called. I imagine how it must have been that afternoon, with Jenny pacing and looking out the window. Three days is a long time to worry and it's even longer in cat years. I picture Jenny home alone, making herself a tuna fish sandwich.

She tosses the empty can into the recycling, thinking how Mortimer always came running for lickies. Then the doorbell rings.

"Hey, there," says the large man on the doorstep. He's a Deadbeat like Hank, Erin's stepdad, with a beard and low ponytail, wearing a bulging trench coat. "I've got something to show you."

He slowly smiles and she backs away. He opens his coat and … it's Mortimer!

Mortimer was stuck in the neighbor's garage for three days. I thought he'd have made it all the way to Lake Tahoe by then. The man saw a Lost Cat poster and brought him home, wrapped in a towel and frightened.

At Grandma's kitchen table, she passes me a plate of meatloaf, broccoli, and mashed potatoes. Brice says it's okay to eat the meat because it's probably been sitting in Grandma's deep freeze forever and we don't want it to go to waste. Also it smells good, and I think he's hungry.

"Your hair looks pretty, Ivy," Grandma says.

"It's crimped," I tell her. This was Jenny's "thank you" for my help with the posters. Not just a single strand this time, but the whole everything in soft waves. Mortimer is back, but he doesn't want to do tricks anymore. At least not for now.

Grandma asks, "Do you miss your mother now that she's working?"

"Sometimes," I say. I drink my milk and think about the work see-saw. *Don't tell Grandma about Dad's baby food.* "But before, I missed Dad, so it's the same."

"It's cool having Dad around," Brice says. "And Mom likes her job and all that."

Grandma frowns and pats the ketchup bottle over her plate. Ketchup is a stubborn sauce.

The next afternoon, I'm in my room drawing a mashed potato farm with playful salt and pepper shaker animals. The phone rings, and I run into Mom and Dad's room. It's Aunt Bea calling all the way from Chicago.

"I don't like any boys right now," I tell her when she asks.

"Do you like any girls?"

"No-o." *What a weird question.*

"Your Uncle Ronald and I are looking forward to seeing you soon."

"When?"

"Oh … Well, it would be nice to see you soon."

I go looking for Mom and find her in the family room reading a book. She smiles, picking up the phone. I wait in the hall to listen. It's automatic, like the way your leg jerks when the doctor hits you with the knee hammer. Maybe, once you start being a detective, you can't stop.

"Well, we were both right," Mom tells Aunt Bea. "The bitch *was* bad news but Neil's golden." She's quiet for a moment then half-laughs. "Well, he finally gets why I felt so funny about the cooking lessons. He kept insisting I was just being jealous and there was nothing to worry about. But it turned out that Olivia did have feelings for him." Mom pauses then says, "You know, I'm not sure if she actually made a pass. Maybe he just finally realized she was after more than just playing teacher. To be honest, I don't even want to know. The thought of it makes me sick." Mom is quiet for a moment and then says, "Ugh. Exactly. I wish you could see her. Like Mom would say, this woman is a total vamp. Plenty of men wouldn't have had the willpower." She's quiet again, then continues. "Sure. And I

248

want to trust him. But after he lied to me about getting fired ... " She waits a moment and says, "I know," and is quiet again. "He's trying to make it up to me. But it takes time. Maybe I'm not ready to totally forgive him yet."

The following night, I'm in a red dress and patent leather shoes because we're going to Maxine Ludlow's for dinner. Dad's running errands and will meet us there. I'm in my room, wrapping Mom's birthday present in Sunday comics. Dad helped me frame the drawing of Mom with her customers looping around the world. I don't understand why Mom said Olivia was a vampire. Vampires have fangs for sucking blood and have black hair, not blonde. But Mom seems happier now that Dad's not having anymore cooking lessons. I'm pretty sure she still hasn't seen my note. I think it's horrible how her supposed best friend is having us over for dinner all innocent like nothing's going on. Brice and I kept searching for the right envelope, until Dad caught us and told us to quit messing with the mail. He couldn't find a bill and was pretty sure we'd been playing around and lost it.

I bounce downstairs, carrying Mom's gift and card. If Maxine tries to poison Mom so she can have Dad to herself, I'll bite her. Yeah, I'll bite her arm like Dad wants to nibble her, only much harder. I find Mom at the kitchen counter in a black-and-white striped dress. She's holding a piece of paper and looks like she just found a beetle in her sparkling water. She looks at me then back down at the paper. She takes a deep breath.

"Ivy, have a seat."

I shrug and climb onto the stool opposite her.

"That dress looks very pretty on you," she says.

"Thanks."

"Red suits you."

"I like it."

"Did you make this?" She smoothes the paper on the counter. I feel an awful twist in my stomach and my shoulders jump to my ears. It's my note with the cutout letters.

Dear kaᴙen, nᴇɪl iꜱ hᴀᴠinɢ ᴀN affair!
sᴛOᴘ woRKiɴg or no lᴏᴠe!

I take a deep breath and let it out slowly, thinking through my options.

Lie.

Run away.

Tell her.

I picture myself throwing my arms up and yelling as I run into the night, my dress blowing in the wind. *"Ivy! Come back!"* Mom would shout into the darkness. *"What does it mean? I need to know!"* But I wouldn't come back, not for months, and when I did, maybe Mom would be gone and Maxine Ludlow would be living with Dad instead, with Moth Caleb and Stink Beetle Tommy sleeping in my room. Except I can't run very fast in these shoes because they have smooth bottoms, not hippo teeth. I'd probably slip and fall before I even made it past Jenny's house.

I look Mom in the eye and nod.

"Okay, so what's it all about?" she asks in a calm voice.

"I think something's going on with Dad and ... *someone.*"

"And who is that someone?" She might be testing me.

I shake my head.

"Is it Olivia?" Mom asks. "Look, I know I acted jealous before, but Dad promised me he's not going over for anymore cooking lessons and I trust him."

I look at my lap. "It's not Olivia."

"What?"

"There's someone else but I don't want to say."

Mom looks angry, sad, and confused all at once, like the Beast when Brice flipped through the channels too fast.

"Tell me," she says.

Sometimes it's best to know the truth even if it hurts.

"Dad is ... planning something with Maxine Ludlow."

"Go on."

I take a deep breath. "They're going to have a Big Sex Night with miniquiches and balloons and confetti!"

"A big what?"

"A Big Sex Night! They're going to have sex and pretzels and streamers. There's going to be sixties music. And balloons. They're going to *schmooze* each other, and they want people to talk about the whole thing for a long time."

But instead of Mom screaming and dumping Dad's baby food down the drain, a funny smile spreads over her face. She shakes her head and, smirking, rips my note into little pieces.

"Okay, honey, thanks for telling me the truth."

"Happy birthday!" Maxine Ludlow answers the door in a wide-shouldered dress with square buttons and wraps Mom in a big hug. Mom gives her a bottle of wine and I give her a dirty look. "Aw, thank you," Maxine tells her. "You didn't need to bring anything."

Mom waves her hand. "No trouble at all."

"Love your dress," Maxine says. "Come on in!" I want Brice to punch her in the stomach. Then I'd step on her foot, hard and we'd both run screaming into the night.

"Thanks!" Mom says. "It's actually from a local designer. And you look very sharp."

My mouth drops open. I don't know how Mom can even pretend to be friendly to her best enemy. I look at Brice and he shakes his head.

Mom says, "Thanks again for having us over for dinner."

"Are you kidding?" Maxine says. "It's my pleasure." She leads us down the hall. My stomach flutters as we reach the dark living room. Then I think I see something move.

The lights switch on.

Suddenly everyone in the world pops out from behind the couches.

"Surprise!" shouts the crowd throwing confetti. I scream like I'm being kidnapped or a pet lion is biting off my leg.

"Oh, Jesus!" Mom says, hand on her chest. Brice laughs. People cheer and clap. The room is decorated with balloons and streamers. There's music, and people break off into little groups and start chatting. Someone hands Mom a glass of champagne and someone else asks me if I'm okay. I can only nod, still too startled to speak. I see the Millers and lots of Mom's friends. Grandma is talking with Aunt Bea and stinky Uncle Ronald, here all the way from Chicago. By the time I've counted thirty-five people, I'm breathing normally again. Mom bends down to point out her coworkers from the boutique: Gloria who likes yogurt, Bev who tells stories, and the woman who talks to mannequins. Caleb and Tommy run across the room with pretzel sticks up their noses. Lucy steps away from her parents and skips over to Brice. He looks around and they hug. I see a family I don't recognize, a tall man with a moustache and a small, lively woman. Their kids are a girl my age and a little boy with glasses. Mom knows so many people. The girl moves her hands through the air as she tells a story, making them all laugh. Then I notice a young woman, chin-length hair hiding her face and wearing a silky dragon dress that could be Chinese or something, but she's not Asian. She stands a little apart, watching the crowd. I notice paint smudges on her hands. She turns to face me and I gasp. It's the Artist! I start to walk over, but she winks at me. I wink back and pretend not to know her.

Dad gives Mom a kiss and says, "Happy birthday, beautiful."

"You sure looked surprised," Maxine says, taking Mom's hand. "And poor Ivy here looked scared out of her wits." I blush, and Maxine continues, "This is your big night, Karen. Neil and I planned the whole thing while you were at work. We kept it quiet from the kids so they wouldn't spoil the surprise."

Mom's eyes sparkle.

"You didn't suspect anything, did you?" Dad asks.

"I had no idea." Mom smiles at him. "You are so sweet to do this for me." They kiss, a long, on-the-lips kiss, and I have to look away because it's so disgusting. Of course I'm glad they're in love again, but I don't want to see it.

Later, I taste the shrimp cocktails and see Brice and Lucy dancing. I eat miniquiches and someone turns off the stereo so the small, lively woman can play the piano for us. I stand near Mom and wait until she's finished talking with Alice Miller. There are no lies left inside of me. When we're alone I wrap my arms around Mom's waist.

"I'm really sorry." I try to feel for the right words. Not the words to get out of trouble, or the words I think Mom wants to hear, just the truth. I tell her, "I was wrong. I made a big mistake."

Mom rubs my back and says we'll talk about it later. From across the room, the Artist tilts her head to me and turns to leave. Mom says she wants me to enjoy her party. I look up at my Working Mother, forty-years-old today. She has a strong face.

Never Tell

Disguised in my curly blonde wig, I sneak outside before anyone else is up. My supplies rattle in my backpack as I gallop down the hill. I pass Jenny's, then Alice Miller's, and stop in front of the new house at the end of the road. There are toys on the lawn and the For Sale sign is gone. I draw a chalk balloon on the sidewalk and write, "Welcome!"

I pass through the school gates and cross the empty blacktop. Locked-up classrooms to my left; to my right is the giant sandpit with the slide and swings. Here are the monkey bars where the blood rushes to my head when everything's upside down. But today there's not a single girl practicing tetherball or boy shooting hoops. No one is playing hopscotch or foursquare or kiss tag. I stand in the absolute center of the blacktop and close my eyes. I strain to pick out the sing-song of jump rope, or teasing, or laughter, or Red Rover. I open my eyes. The entire playground is still. With a chill, I decide this is how it would be if everyone was taken away by the Pied Piper, or got AIDS and died. But it's just Sunday and early-early morning.

I pull a dustpan brush out of my backpack. Singing to myself, I sweep a patch of blacktop, clearing away rocks and bottle caps. I straighten my wig. I get out a photo and chalk and begin to draw.

Over waffles yesterday, Grandma told us about her friend's architect son who might have a job for Dad.

"This is exactly what I've been praying for," she said. "Isn't that good news?" A new job would push Dad out of the house, back in an office, back in a tie, with Mom home with the kids. Meaning us. Meaning everything back to normal, same as it always used to be.

Mom and Dad looked at each other. The answer to our problems, but the question has changed.

Then Dad told Grandma about his baby food project. Mom mentioned his small business loan. I said Strawberry Oat Medley is my favorite flavor. Dad said how good Mom is at her job and Brice agreed. Then Dad said how good Mom's job is for all of us. Mom and Dad looked at each other and smiled.

Grandma sipped her coffee and said *she* was always happy to just be a mother. "Isn't that important anymore?" she asked.

"We're okay, Grandma," I said, touching her hand like grown-ups do. Startled, she looked at me with watery eyes.

"Ivy's right," Mom said. "She and Brice are growing up and they don't need me so much anymore." I tried to touch my feet to the floor for luck and, for the first time ever, they reached.

I get out my poster paints, working quickly on the school blacktop. I splash color inside my chalk lines and wonder if it's true. Are Brice and I really getting older?

I picture myself back in the faraway apartment. Today there are spices and coconut in the air. On the table, there's a bowl of fruits that look like pink Koosh balls. Nearly finished now, the big painting on the easel is of a little girl with paint splatters on her red dress. She's surrounded by perfectly drawn scrub jays and is smiling wildly. I notice photos and sketches of scrub jays stuck to the wall. Marmalade is curled up at the window and stretches, meowing when he sees me. Looking out, I watch a motorbike weave through the street, carrying two grown-ups and two kids. It's a lot of people on something with two wheels. It looks like fun.

I shake my head to pull myself out of my daydream. On the blacktop, I paint the tail and paws. It's a giant cat with zigzags and polka-dot fur. It is a little bit realistic because of the photo, but it is also imaginary because cats don't really look like this. I am making something where there was nothing. I am creating something new.

I imagine diving back into the wet heat of the apartment. The Artist stands in the kitchen doorway, holding a spoon. She looks at me then her painting, then back at me. We are the same.

"What are those?" I point to the pink fruits. She picks one up and carefully peels away the furry skin, revealing white fruit underneath.

"Rambutan," she says, handing it to me to try.

At the playground, I step back to get a good look at my work. I've painted a giant cat as big as a horse, with clever eyes and a twisty tail. I am an artist. I am Ivy. This is a secret, so I'm not signing it and I'm never telling anyone it was me. I put everything in my backpack and head home. I have been eight-years-old for just about forever, but next week school lets out for summer. Then I will turn nine, and in the fall I start the fourth grade. I stretch my fingertips to the sky. I have arrived.

The End
(So good luck.)